BLUE GOWANUS

MICHAEL HARTNETT

Black Rose Writing | Texas

First printing

This is a work of fiction. Names, characters, businesses, places, events, and incidents are either the products of the author's imagination or used in a fictitious manner. Any resemblance to actual persons, living or dead, or actual events is purely coincidental.

ISBN: 978-1-68433-539-8
PUBLISHED BY BLACK ROSE WRITING
www.blackrosewriting.com

Printed in the United States of America
Suggested Retail Price (SRP) $18.95

Blue Gowanus is printed in Calluna

*As a planet-friendly publisher, Black Rose Writing does its best to eliminate unnecessary waste to reduce paper usage and energy costs, while never compromising the reading experience. As a result, the final word count vs. page count may not meet common expectations.

Cover art by Sean Mahoney

Praise for
BLUE GOWANUS

"Let me say it plainly: this book is work of genius."
– Len Boswell, author of the *Simon Grave* mysteries

"Imaginative, Intriguing, Prophetic. Hartnett at his best!"
– Joe Edd Morris, author of *The Prison* and *Torched!*

"An entertaining, witty, and thought-provoking companion to *The Blue Rat* from one of the best novelists around. Michael Hartnett's *Blue Gowanus* is a literary feast – something for everyone."
– John Vance, author of *Touched Back* and *Secret of the Chimes*

*To my parents Jerry and Bridget, my wife Amy,
and my children Brittany, Patrick, and John.*

BLUE GOWANUS

CHAPTER 1
LIGHTING OUT FOR THE TERRITORY

He noted only the briefest of flashes, but El Buscador knew he had a problem. He could run back out the hidden door and onto the street, though he was pretty sure if they were waiting down in his room, others would grab him as he stepped into the open air. He had expected that Tolland's men would eventually track him to the abandoned city hall subway station. He'd lived there for a dozen years and had been careful never to be followed. But he'd taken too many chances lately, let too many people into his life. He was so certain that Tolland's men would come that he had planned his exit, an exit he couldn't convince himself to take until necessary.

He stood still for the next minute quieting his breath. Let them question whether they actually heard the door open or were alerted by a random street noise – the banging chassis of a delivery truck or the intrusive judder of the jackhammer. Painstakingly, El Buscador took one silent step at a time. About three minutes passed before he arrived at the stairwell and the foot of the curved subway platform. The murky darkness was his friend, more so for him than even Tolland's men, who were well acquainted with the night. Tucking himself behind a vent pipe, El Buscador sucked in his breath and waited for the inevitable beam of the flashlight. The leader cast the ray down the empty curved subway platform, its elegant lines shrouding the deeper recesses where El Buscador hid. The flashlight even peered into the ribbed, vaulted ceiling that looked more like it belonged in an abbey than in a station. Did Tolland's men fear El Buscador could climb the walls?

As he waited for his only hope to arrive, El Buscador contemplated why they took action after refraining for so long. Did he put too many blue rats in the wrong basement? Did he deliver the right evidence for the wrong indictment? Did he finally apply enough financial pressure that Tolland was not able to move forward on at least one of his major projects? Did Tolland simply have enough? He could believe that final question might be at the core, since even El Buscador was starting to feel he too had had enough. The fight had been knocking the hell out of him. He could use a change in scenery.

Well, he would get one, whether it was entering a metaphysical underworld or forming a new life in an outer borough.

Then he heard the rumbling and he knew his train was arriving. No, it wouldn't be stopping. Hell, the subway hadn't stopped here since 1945. He thought of all the ways he could screw up his next move. He had only one factor in his favor: the 6 train gliding on the tracks moved slower than most. The express lines could zip along at 55 miles per hour while the locals, like the 6, generally chugged by at 30. But since the 6 would turn around in a few hundred yards to head back north, it plodded along at closer to 20. Still, that meant El Buscador would have to time this leap perfectly. He could not leave his spot behind the air vent until the absolute last moment. He had to calculate how long it took to sprint (hey, could he even sprint anymore? he damn well better be able to sprint) from across the platform onto the back of the 6 train. He also had to allow for the number of subway cars and the speed of the train. It was the type of math problem that made his head hurt. Fortunately, he'd watched the 6 train chug by for the last portion of his life, so many thousands of times that it was synchronized into his daily rhythms.

The train took an excruciatingly long time to arrive. Its light, noise, and presence only made Tolland's men more alert; El Buscador fed off their vigilance, springing back on his hush puppies waiting for just the right moment. He counted cars. The 6 train had 11. At five, he took off. Initially, Tolland's men couldn't believe what they were seeing. What was that shadow in a hat and trench coat flying across the platform? It looked ghostly. By the time they started shooting, he'd made the leap onto the back of train, grabbing the caboose door handle and using it to swing to the far side. Bullets ricocheted off the station walls and the tracks. One shattered a 6 train window and another sunk into the metal door next to his contracting waist.

At this moment, with the train moving past Tolland's men, they had the cleanest shot at their target. Aware of his vulnerability, El Buscador quivered before he swung his body around to the far side of the train, toward the dark end of the tracks, where the subway car separated Tolland's men from their target. The doleful clatter of the metal wheels along the metal tracks filled up his ears even as he gasped. Last week, he had been much more willing to die, a concept eminently less attractive when serving as the prey to his enemy. Now, he smiled with the possibility of death arriving at someone else's subway stop today.

As the train chugged out of the abandoned station and hurtled toward blackness, El Buscador couldn't resist raising his free hand and waving to his antagonists. They answered with bullets. El Buscador withdrew his greeting and checked his palm for holes.

Returning to the back of the car and clutching onto the caboose, he swayed as the 6 train rounded back north and stopped at the Brooklyn Bridge station. Rather than slipping inside of a subway car and taking the train uptown, he hopped off at the station, glided into the transfer passageway, and picked up the J-Z line out to Brooklyn. Then he knew the real journey would begin. He'd have to get off next at the G train stop, find his way along that slow bending line until he wended all the way to the most contaminated place on earth.

Then, and only then, upon slouching into Gowanus, could he pronounce to all who would listen, "Honey, I'm home."

CHAPTER 2
PYGMALION OF GOWANUS

El Buscador was dreaming of Jeanne. She was just about ready to fall out of her wheelchair and amorously into his arms when he felt a kick to the ribs. He curled into a ball.

"Hey," said the homeless man looming over him. "This is my home. No squatters."

"Then what are you?"

"I got here first."

"I didn't notice."

"Now you know."

Almost 20 years in the abandoned city hall station, nobody bothered him. One night in Brooklyn and he had to look for another place. El Buscador murmured to himself that his displacement came from not knowing the territory. He wasn't the type to ensconce his carcass into a cozy home. He could never be accused of, heaven forbid, nesting, but he did need a hovel of his own. Bidding farewell to his slumbers in the middle of the night, he'd worry about finding a hidden nook in an abandoned building much later, in the shadows of the next evening. Good thing he hadn't invested yet in a cot. Since he was up and had nowhere to sleep, he walked the Gowanus Canal – the gastric digestive track of his new neighborhood.

Distant lights reflected on the green water's oil and other matter. He probed out further along the canal banks and deeper into the night, praying that it wouldn't rain. The delivery trucks were still picking up piles of anything and everything – scrap metal and Snapple cases, sheet rock, flatbread, plumbing supplies, and space dust. In the hurly burly of this stream of deliveries shone a single flashlight along the canal side of a brick building, tight up against the water. A rope hung off the peak. It was tied to a coed with spray cans hooked to her pants, her beaming ray creating an aura around her even as the light shone directly onto the figure she was painting. El Buscador first studied the drawing, since the flashlight so nicely projected a shimmering sphere. What the hell was it? It looked a bit like a seal but had its share of dolphin qualities with a long beak and a dorsal fin. The artist was more easily defined, given her brown, sinewy arms, her dreadlocks, and her intense concentration.

El Buscador would wait until she was done, even it took all night.

It took all night.

The creature consumed three quarters of the twenty-foot wall and looked like it could swallow a block's worth of canal water and not only survive, but nourish her children with it as mother's milk. The exotic, toxic beast looked so comfortable on the brick wall that El Buscador could be easily convinced that it had always been here. The work joined the other creatures hovering on the factory edges of the canal. Many of them seemed quite alien, with their green tints, hints of anime, and pocky tentacles.

The graffiti artist untied the knot in the rope, slowly sliding her way to the ground; then with a deft jerk, she loosened the fastening from the roof's eave and watched the rope drop next to her. Gathering the spray cans and twine into her backpack, she could've been any college sophomore heading off with the rising sun to meet the challenges of campus life. Her radiant skin was dark, only in the awakening light could he see how dark. El Buscador almost let her leave without comment, but he couldn't resist offering praise.

"That is absolutely magnificent."

"Thanks," she said, turning away back toward DeGraw Street, picking up her pace.

"Hey wait. Don't worry, your secret's safe with me."

"Not if you keep talking to me."

He caught the slightest lilt of an accent, definitely Caribbean – he'd bet Dominican. Now he could fully take in her delicate features and her espresso brown skin. "C'mon, I won't let anything happen to you."

She looked at the aging man in the trench coat and the fedora. "No offense, but you don't look like you're in much of a position to protect me."

"Perhaps not. But can I ask you about your work at the exhibit?"

"What exhibit?" she said.

El Buscador rolled his eyes, opening his arms toward the Gowanus Canal. She laughed. "Oh, I get it."

"At your exhibit, I noticed this strange creature looks like a mythological beast, like something that doesn't exist. Why the seal/porpoise thing?"

"I stare at the canal and I imagine what would like to live in there. I paint what I think swims under the surface."

"Mmmm. You just made the canal much more intriguing."

"Yeah," she said, walking away, "the more time you spend here, the more you'll know that there are many things in that canal, and some of them are living."

He caught up with her. "You signed it Pygmalion. Is that your name?"

She just smirked and kept moving.

El Buscador felt like he was talking to the niece he never had. He persisted. "I think I'll call you Pygmalion."

She arched her eyebrows. "You can call me anything you like. Just don't expect me to answer."

As she picked up her pace, El Buscador drew close enough to tell her. "I won't. But I do hope to see more of your work."

"If you are by the canals, you will."

As he parted ways with her, El Buscador knew he didn't praise Pygmalion to make her feel good. Her creature nudged him to peer into the water in search of movement and possibility.

With only his backpack and his cash to his name, he'd need to once again abandon his past. The raid by Tolland's men of his home in the abandoned city hall station had been inevitable. He'd done too much damage to Tolland for the real estate mogul to resist hunting him down. Between his efforts, those of his buddy Pratt's, and *The Herald's* investigations, they exposed Tolland's money laundering, his building violations, and even his rat breeding program. In the process, Tolland lost tens of millions in investments and more importantly lost the approval of his massive Manhattan construction project on Canal Street. That building was to be Tolland's crowning achievement, where he would brand the city with a massive T structure to follow in line with his other three rectangular skyscrapers that ran down Manhattan's spine. Tolland may have even suspected El Buscador's role in other attacks, including a physical one at the old Trinity Church graveyard. No, after many years of discretion and secrecy, El Buscador had taken too many risks with Tolland. Little wonder his men arrived with guns at the city hall station.

He had been prepared. The $10,000 El Buscador had left in the world remained at all times in his pockets instead of the usual place under his mattress. He kept flashlights, flasks, clean underwear, dry socks, and various sundries all in plastic bags inside his backpack. Yet now that he had made his escape, he remained stunned by the reality of leaving his home of almost twenty years.

He continued to walk and wander as the sun rose over the Gowanus, the pumping station and the flushing tunnel at the canal's head caught the light, giving the brownish foam just enough highlights of khaki green to convince the optimist that he wasn't staring into a cauldron of cavalierly treated sewage.

To get out of his funk, he tried to think the way he had for many years as the city's most exclusive tour guide. The wealthy in-crowd of celebrities, stockbrokers, and cognoscenti would line up at 5:37 a.m. on ancient Stone Street deep in the financial district, willing to pay anything for El Buscador to show them something no one else in the city had seen before. He'd take them to hidden historic wells, underground streams, and forgotten ruins. He trespassed as if he owned the city and they would follow and pay. Now, his time as the Tour Guide would have to end. He tried to figure out if his time as El Buscador, the city's legendary searcher, also would terminate.

He spent the morning in Gowanus looking and learning and absorbing, gamely trying to figure this place out. As he walked the perimeter of the canal, scrambling past random piles of debris back in and out of dead-end streets where the business signs were light and the machinery heavy, El Buscador learned that many questions had the same answer.

Where do all the boxes on boxes of cardboard go after serving as vessels for delivery? Gowanus.

Where do all the old chairs go, chairs that were salvaged from broken dining rooms? Gowanus.

The rubble from construction sites? Gowanus.

The poop from portapotties? Gowanus.

Where are the billions of flickering Christmas lights, the plastic Santas, the wicker reindeers, and the blinking neurosis that illumine Yuletide in Dyker Heights housed for the other eleven months? Gowanus.

Where do the food trucks go when they're not serving a line of grimly determined customers in the cold winds? Gowanus.

Where do the orange cones go when they take a break from diverting traffic? Gowanus.

Where do the dignified remnants of old buildings go – their stained glass and cupolas and weathervanes and balustrades – relics that even the heartless contractor doesn't have the heart to toss? Gowanus.

Indeed, in Gowanus the poop is purified, the cardboard boxes are crushed and compressed into the biggest boxes of them all, and the traffic cones mark the end of the line because there is nowhere else for them to go if they've arrived at the dead end of Gowanus.

And El Buscador planted himself here in Gowanus because he had to escape and what better place to be than where Tolland would build next. Yes, his friends would say El Buscador was foolhardy to reside in the very spot where his deadly enemy would soon prowl. But he could only fight the real estate mogul if he knew the territory and remained one step ahead. That meant finding out where to hide and what he would need to penetrate.

Over the ensuing days, El Buscador trespassed often, always wearing thick gloves to negotiate the barriers. He learned the answer to yet another question? What is the razor ribbon fencing capital of the world? Gowanus.

Even with the gloves and the work boots, he bled and bruised. He was used to going around, over, and through obstacles, but everything in Gowanus was a little coarser.

Walking along the canal by Bond Street, opposite of Whole Foods, he came across a crane with a claw, pulling debris from the water. A couple of dozen onlookers gathered to see what surfaced. He listened to a local who managed to sport a herringbone newsboy cap yet still show his man-bun. "They're pulling up the body now."

"Do they know who it is?" El Buscador asked.

The man-bun rubbed his tattooed arms and answered with authority. "It's a Gambino crime family associate. Typical mob hit. They tied him to a cinder block. In the old days, it'd take years to find them, but with the canal getting cleaner, the cops saw the fish gathering."

"The canal's getting cleaner?" asked El Buscador, this nugget the most extraordinary revelation of the last 24 hours.

Man-bun took a hit on his e-cig, "Yeah, can't you tell?"

El Buscador decided it was best not to argue. "How do they know it's the mafia guy?"

"He's been missing." With that information, man-bun walked away, heading northward, apparently toward Williamsburg.

Much of the crowd waited ten minutes. But the crane was moving slowly. The locals didn't have all day to stand around, so they took off. El Buscador did have all day. At first, he was going to ask the crane operator what he was looking for, but then he wanted it to be a surprise. If it were the mafia guy, it might be an awful mess of a carcass, but worth a look (albeit he knew it'd be more likely that some guys in scuba gear and hazmat suits would be recovering the body).

A half hour later, with El Buscador the last onlooker, the crane finally lifted its prized booty. The hulking industrial equipment was covered with black muck. Through the ooze, he could recognize a big scoop-shaped hunk of heavy metal. It was caked with rust and sludge. The crane operator pivoted his massive cargo, dark, viscous water continuing to drip from its edges and belly. Slowly, methodically, he positioned the metal carcass onto the pebbled bank. Adjusting his hardhat, the crane operator dropped down from his perch, his ample gut shuddering as he landed, moving closer to inspect his treasure.

El Buscador spoke to hardhat. "Do you know what it is?"

"I think I know."

"Yeah?" asked El Buscador encouragingly. He instinctively trusted hardhat more than man-bun. Hardhat wouldn't be giving him some line about a mafia stiff.

"It looks like a dredging bucket." Hardhat laughed.

"A dredging bucket?" El Buscador needed a moment for that to register before he chuckled too. "Let me get this straight. You found the equipment used to dig out the canal abandoned in the canal. That's crazy."

"You're telling me," said hardhat. "That's like after I pulled the dredger bucket out, I dumped my crane in the canal."

"This place doesn't make sense."

"Welcome to Gowanus."

CHAPTER 3
MEATDAD IN PRAISE OF TOLLAND

Melville delivered a special passenger on his evening ferry to greet El Buscador. About a year ago, the notorious celebrity MeatDad Catharsis was granted an unforgettable outing with the Tour Guide. They bounded from one touchstone of power to the next, as El Buscador gave the rapper/actor/comedian an earful about banking systems, money laundering, and famous shady deals in New York. To offer MeatDad an insider's perspective, he broke into two boardrooms under renovation. Over the years "special arrangements and accommodations" were fashioned across these mahogany tables among such luminaries as Edison, Rockefeller, Vanderbilt, and Roosevelt. MeatDad was even more impressed by the subversive access El Buscador delivered than the Cristal and *foie gras*, than the Courvoisier and macaroons. MeatDad may well have been El Buscador's biggest fan and proponent, which is why El Buscador agreed to break with tradition, providing the one-man entertainment industry with another tour.

True to his saturnine mood, El Buscador regaled MeatDad Catharsis with lurid tales of the Brooklyn waterfront, cut throats and smugglers of booty, broken bones and busted souls; he spoke of turf wars, gang initiations, floggings, lynchings, burnings, and drownings, every crime delineated in detail to show how far the cries rang out and how distant the blood splattered. MeatDad was sufficiently impressed, but even as El Buscador felt he was gaining his footing as a tour guide in his new borough, the rapper/actor/comedian was more interested in telling the Tour Guide an important conversation he had with one Timothy Terrance Tolland.

"I got your back, Buscador," MeatDad said, tapping his right fist on his heart, which confused things a bit anatomically.

"Yeah?" El Buscador answered, trying to mask his concern. He knew that when most people said they had his back, they were meddling where they didn't belong.

"I told Tolland that Buscador loves you and respects you."

"But I don't," El Buscador pointed out, trying to mask his anger.

"That doesn't matter," MeatDad reasoned. "You don't want to be dead, am I right?"

"I'd prefer not to be dead," El Buscador conceded.

"So what do you care what I tell him?"

"It makes me look like I have no principles."

"To Tolland?" MeatDad asked, his voice betraying a measure of exasperation (he added a sad cluck to leave no doubt). "What do you care what he thinks? You should only care if he wants you dead."

"Hey, I don't care," lied El Buscador, "but I can't have other people thinking Tolland's right, that he's been right all along."

"That's easier to fix if you're not dead." Funny how MeatDad Catharsis never seemed so damn rational in his rap songs. "Anyway, I gave him my word that you respect him, and that you know he's done a lot of good things and you've been whispering your appreciation of him to many of your clientele like me. I've even convinced some bros who've taken your tour to tell Tolland how solid you've been about him." The Tour Guide did his best to mask his horror. "Hey, I'm in it all the way with you, Busc. I've even told Tolland that I'd perform a song at his niece's sweet sixteen."

"Jesus," said El Buscador. MeatDad's interpretation that El Buscador had been moved by the media star's magnanimous gestures may have been slightly off.

Oblivious to El Buscador's mortification, MeatDad prattled on. He asked whether El Buscador had tried the Ganja Ganache. When El Buscador just looked confused, MeatDad explained, "It's the newest thing in gourmet weed. It looks like a chocolate bar, and there's no denying its velvety texture. The finish is really forward and the kick is unbelievable." Damn, thought El Buscador, now even the rappers indulge in pretentious winespeak. MeatDad would not be denied. "The Ganja Ganache must be made by one of those genius celebrity chefs. It's all the rage in Brooklyn. Only the freakiest cats get their hands on it. I'm surprised someone like you doesn't know about it.

I surprised someone like you doesn't have it." Boy was this tour heading downhill fast.

After thanking MeatDad with all of the grace he could summon and bidding him farewell, El Buscador wandered about, searching for a place to rest his head – a head simmering and stewing about what MeatDad told Tolland. But he wasn't looking for a place to sleep because sleeping at this point was unimaginable. He walked east until he ran into Flatbush and followed the avenue south through Grand Army Plaza and Prospect Park. Then he kept going and going, past South Midwood and the Flatlands. He gazed at Mill Basin to his left and Marine Park to his right until he pressed onward to the tall grasses and Dead Horse Bay. He crossed the bridge into the Rockaways and walked straight ahead toward the mighty Atlantic. He thought about swimming, but the waves were crashing angrily and even the spray told of water that would chill him clear through to the bone. He could die in such water, and he understood better than ever that he did not want to die. Nobody walks this far to die.

He could've wandered down toward Rockaway Beach and picked up the A train, but he liked the metaphor of having to hike all the way back. It was the price of the journey.

El Buscador took most of the night to shake off the dread resulting from MeatDad's incorrigible support. While he preferred not to appear as a craven traitor, El Buscador gradually came to realize the lifeline MeatDad had tossed to him. The last words MeatDad Catharsis said to him before he hopped back onto Melville's boat were, "You must know better than anyone, Busc, that this is all theater."

Acts of loyalty always moved El Buscador. Just as he thought he reached a new low, he grasped at a straw of inspiration. In the "theater" MeatDad described, he recognized an opening. The whispering would begin with how El Buscador had opposed *The Herald's* continual attacks on Tolland, and that the three skyscrapers erected at 72nd, 42nd, and 14th streets had immensely grown on him, that the skyline was now framed in three distinct segments that he ultimately realized gave the city layers it heretofore had been denied in the jumble of rag-tag styles. Hearing those reports, Thackeray would at first be skeptical, but El Buscador would let them accumulate and appear from so many quarters that confirmations of El

Buscador's appreciation would become simultaneously widespread and undeniable. And if Thackeray believed, Tolland would soon follow.

El Buscador wondered if the toxicity of Gowanus had seeped into his thyroid and gizzard. Was he merely playing the final, trickiest hands, ones of low cards and lots of bluffing? Or had he already folded in the most humiliating fashion possible. The second possibility would be too awful to bear. And yet, he would embark on his least satisfying battle with Tolland, one where he'd equate descriptions of his enemy with ones of himself.

Later that night (or was it morning?), he sat on the bank of the Gowanus by Sackett – two blocks down from the pump stations. On the brick ledge of the building next door, Pygmalion painted an egret. This time she didn't have any spray cans. Instead, she held an artist palette in her right hand and dabbed with the tiniest of brushes with her left. She had already been at the painting for many hours and still had much feather work to complete. As opposed to her frantic swirls of spray the other night, Pygmalion embraced precision and discipline. In her painstakingly tedious effort, she rendered an egret that would have been photographic if not for subtle brushstroke flourishes. That El Buscador looked at her endeavor rather than the mesmerizing water spoke of the allure of the egret's shimmering white feathers, its probing, hooked beak, and its rooting, clawed feet.

"So," said El Buscador as he edged closer to Pygmalion, "when the live egret flies off and you go home –"

Pygmalion finished the sentence – "this one stays."

They smiled at each other. El Buscador walked to an all-night bodega on Bond and grabbed two cups of coffee, putting in enough chocolate caramel creamer to hide the fact that the pot had been sitting on the burner since sundown. Returning to the canal, he offered a cup to Pygmalion, who put down a tiny brush and took a sip.

She nodded in appreciation, the soft lines of her dark skin glistening in the dying moonlight. The coffee wasn't exactly robust, but it was warm, and hey, what can you expect at this time in the morning. "Now, I won't be able to get to sleep," she said mischievously.

"Like that was going to happen," said El Buscador.

She painted and he watched, each enjoying the best early morning in many months.

CHAPTER 4
THE INCURSION

El Buscador knew it was unwise to return to downtown Manhattan. But he had to see Jeanne, his old love, and she certainly couldn't come to him. The planning involved in achieving the dual goals of seeing her and not getting killed were akin to a minor military operation. First, he had to walk a couple of miles to the very end of Van Brunt Street in Red Hook, then far out on the pier at the mouth of the Erie Basin to hail Melville, who sailed close to the docks every afternoon in case El Buscador needed to pass a note or have a chat. Today, El Buscador wanted both.

He asked his old explorer friend, "When are you coming into the canal?"

"When I feel like taking down the sail and the tide is right," said Melville. "Those bridges are awfully low. They're the ducking, folding-yourself-in-half kind, and I don't see anybody opening drawbridges for me. My visit won't make anybody money."

"Plan on it soon. I've got a few things to show you . . . a few things you'll want to see." From Melville's furrowed eyebrows, El Buscador knew he baited the hook well. He wouldn't be surprised if Melville were paddling under the BQE tomorrow. El Buscador leaned his hand against the tiny mast to steady himself and passed a note. "Give this to Pratt."

"Anything you want me to say to him?"

"Tell him, it's a priority," said El Buscador. As his protégé and his best underground ally in his war on Tolland, Pratt would certainly deliver. "Tell him, he can empty his traps later. Tell him, he must have it all ready when I see him."

Melville eyed his friend with concern. "You're not going over to the other side, are you?"

El Buscador was grim. "I don't have a choice."

Melville shook his head. "You do have a death wish, don't you?"

"I used to."

"Yeah? What happened to it?"

"People started trying to kill me."

Melville laughed. "That'll cure you. But if you're crossing the river, it sure doesn't sound like you're watching out for yourself."

"This one can't be helped," El Buscador said. "But I'm taking precautions. That's why it's so important for Pratt to follow my instructions explicitly. You know how he can be. Will you do that for me?"

"Got it," said Melville. "Funny," he paused ruefully. "When I first took on this adventure, I never thought I'd spend a good portion of my time as a courier service."

El Buscador knew Melville wasn't complaining, even though his initial plan was to circle Manhattan in his small sailboat day after day for a year. Alas, to be friends with El Buscador meant to take detours. And once he threw in his lot with a man who'd been ripped up by a pit bull, beaten down by a homeless man, and shot at by Tolland's Russians, Melville knew his sailing itinerary would entail diversions.

"Isn't it nice to know that if you give up your strange obsessions with exploration, you could land a job at Amazon?" El Buscador's playful tone belied the gratitude in his eyes.

Melville nodded. "I better get going before Pratt moves onto his dumpster traps." Those dumpster traps were not along the waterfront. As it was, Melville would have to hope for a good wind to catch Pratt at his regular spots below the FDR Drive. As he pushed off the dock, Melville called out, "Remember, it's much harder for me to explore the canal with you if you're dead."

El Buscador answered Melville, who was increasingly out of earshot. "Indeed, I'll require a different ferryman to take me across that river."

El Buscador began his journey back to the subway station, which was quite the walk since Red Hook was not connected to the underground. At Carroll Street, he picked up the godawful G line that zigged and zagged from Brooklyn into Queens like some lost out-of-towner. Where the G ended, he hopped on the M, crossing over to Manhattan, getting out at Lex and 53rd to pick up the 6 downtown. He avoided the shortest routes, the stations he'd often frequented, the spots were Tolland's men could pick up his trail. No, Tolland's men would only follow the trails he wanted them to, and they'd be on one of those paths soon enough. He took the 6 nine stops to the chaos of inundated Canal Street, then stepped onto the Z train, appropriately to end his journey at the furthest stop east on the Lower East Side at Delancey and Essex. The hour and half wending journey gave him plenty of time to plan and, more importantly, plenty of time to think of what he would say to Jeanne. As usual, the planning came easier than the words.

Heading down Essex and then east onto Grand Street, he avoided the temptations of Kossar's Bialys and the Doughnut Plant and just kept walking, cutting through the Projects and finding his way to Corlears Hook.

As he spotted Pratt with a burlap sack in one hand and a rat trap in the other, El Buscador was exasperated and amused. "You just couldn't help yourself, could you?" El Buscador filled his voice with disgust.

"Keep your shirt on. I did what you asked, although for the life of me, I don't know why."

"You're no longer sleeping at the Worth Street station, right?"

"No, I left once they flushed you out of the city hall station," Pratt now grinned at El Buscador, "just as you advised." Unspoken was the little jab of see, see, El Buscador, I do listen to you. Emulating his mentor, Pratt had lived in his own abandoned subway station, although if the old city hall station evoked an atmospheric abbey, the Worth station felt more like a penal colony for crazed graffiti artists.

"Good. And nobody knows where you live?"

"Not even you." Pratt smiled. The man was in a damn good mood. Then again Pratt always seemed to be when he was catching rats. "So now you're telling me the Russians think you're living at Worth?"

"Word is being distributed that I've moved in." Pratt understood that meant El Buscador had shared the information with his many whispering friends, who shared the location with his sometimes friend Thackeray, who couldn't help but share that information with Tolland, who shared that information with the Russians. El Buscador tapped his pants pocket like he just remembered something and took out $200. "Here's for the trench coat and hat."

"Put your money away. I'm earning good coin from the Blue Rat media feeds I've got going, and Gotham Social says there's more where that came from. You need the money more than I do, now that you're out of the tour guide business." Catching El Buscador's wince, Pratt added, "at least temporarily. Anyway, the hardest part was getting the manikin. You do have a flair for the dramatics, don't you? Why not just sneak in here without all the theatrics?"

"I need to know that they won't be where I'll be right now. I can't take that risk."

"What are you going to do the next time you cross the river, keep planting decoys?"

"I'm not sure I'll ever be back."

"For God's sake, you don't expect me to visit you in Brooklyn, do you?"

"And I thought you loved me."

"There's love and there's Brooklyn. Do you expect me to risk being infected by a hipster?"

"Where I live Pratt, hipsters are not the most virulent of contagion."

"Then you inhabit a territory I cannot imagine."

"This coming from a man who spends his spare time tracking rats." El Buscador eyed the vermin in the cage. It was a good haul since seven of the nine were blue. "And while we're on the subject, I think it's time for a temporary halt of Operation Rat Dump." Operation Rat Dump had been their plan to drop blue rats in the basements of Tolland's multitude of associates. The approach was if they couldn't get to Tolland, at least his buddies would make him hear about the mounting consequences for his actions. El Buscador, Pratt, and Pratt's former colleagues at *The Herald* had pushed the district attorney as far as they could on the legal issues – the money laundering, the labor violations, and the obfuscations of housing regulations. While the real estate mogul was tangled up in the courts, El Buscador and Pratt had kept up the pressure by having the blue rats invade his associates' homes. Since the rich were unaccustomed to confronting vermin face to face, Operation Rat Dump had been quite effective. Thackeray told El Buscador that Tolland had been catching so much hell from his cronies that he was considering ceasing his blue rat activities.

"But I thought the program was going well," said a crestfallen Pratt. "Don't worry about not being able to help me anymore. I've got a good system now."

"Given what's been going on, I think we better lay low with the operation. There are a lot of eyes on us." Pratt looked like El Buscador had just gutted him. Pratt had repeatedly expressed his fears that Tolland's new project in Gowanus would be a major problem; his sources down at the rat pit said it was completely different than anything the mogul had attempted in his career. Even Tolland's most ardent architectural critics argued that the Gowanus project was exciting and innovative, something they could support. More than El Buscador, Pratt sensed that Tolland was gaining momentum, and if suddenly some of his foes (community leaders and critics) became his allies, then the movement against him was doomed. As he embarked on the trickiest act of his entire shady existence, El Buscador understood Pratt's anxiety, his fear that the battle was slipping from their grasp. The rat operations had become the central purpose of Pratt's life. El Buscador offered him a measure of consolation. "Hey, you can still bring the rats to the pit."

Pratt brightened. "That makes sense." Under the guise of Mike Mahoney, Nathaniel Pratt has been a regular at the rat pit on Madison Street for years. He'd found out his best information about Tolland there. Most of his employees, from the top executives to the lowliest clean-up crews, gathered at the pit to blow off steam. Since Pratt left *The Herald*, he had grown a big beard over his handsome face and no longer cut his hair, although thankfully he still showered regularly so that his unkempt appearance was more of a façade than an essence. "So what's the plan?" Pratt asked like he'd actually adhere to a rigorous methodology. Most of the time Pratt would merely pretend to coordinate with El Buscador.

"We're back in an information gathering mode." El Buscador pointed to the rats. "That means no more poking the bear. Stay out of the basements. Bring your rats to the pit. Keep your ears open. Send your tweets. Write the occasional column under your Blue Rat alias for the services. And most importantly, keep that hairy head of yours down for now. I can't have you out of Manhattan too."

Turning over the traps, Pratt shook the rats into the burlap bag, even the brown ones. "Do you want me to visit you?"

"Only if you'd like. Thackeray keeps hinting to me that Tolland's got big plans in Brooklyn, but you know Thackeray. Maybe this exile is a blessing in disguise."

Pratt threw the burlap bag over his shoulder, looking for all the world like a meth addict Santa Claus, and gave El Buscador a half a hug with his free arm. El Buscador whispered, "Make sure you're there at the appointed times. You just might spot me around the corner."

"I'll try not to shudder when I see you," said Pratt.

Using the few seconds when Pratt was distracted by stacking his traps, El Buscador took off into the projects, vanishing the scene like a ghost.

Just like the old days.

•　　　•　　　•　　　•　　　•

As El Buscador headed down the back steps of Jeanne's basement apartment, Mikhail, Demetri, and Maksim were gliding with military precision down the front steps of the abandoned Worth Street Station. True to their training, they were cautious and thorough, checking their flanks, first what was behind them and second what was before them. Even with their night vision goggles, they waited a good five minutes to get their eyes adjusted to the darkness before they moved silently forward with their Makarov pistols into the dirty, broken station, the walls graffitied forty years ago, seemingly nothing cleaned since. Yet clearly the place had been inhabited: the cot, the blankets, the water jugs, and the three paperbacks left no doubt.

Sitting in the corner in a chair against the wall was a man. He wore a fedora and a trench coat. A small glow emanated from the figure. Perhaps, there was a fourth paperback he was reading. Mikhail, the leader of the raid, smiled with satisfaction that he and team had been so quiet that the hushed peace of the bookworm had not been interrupted. He could think of no reason to draw closer to his target. As always, the clothes identified the man and the tipoff came from unimpeachable sources. Mikhail nodded to Maksim and Demetri. The sniper Maksim fired rounds into the skull while Mikhail and Demetri hit the chair, knowing the bullets would penetrate the body, all three moving forward while they fired. After each of them exhausted their twelve rounds, they moved right to the slumping, shattered head, pulling out backup Makarovs just in case.

From the figure's reaction to the shots, the absence of blood, the lack of dangling tissue and organs so common in such an operation, the team knew that they had executed something that wasn't human. As Mikhail studied the dummy, he initially feared the thing might be booby trapped, but soon concluded, if that were the case, the figure would've exploded from all the bullets it took. The wreck of a manikin had a note pinned to the right lapel of the trench coat. The bullet holes through it made reading a challenge. He pulled the note off the manikin and deciphered it: "Message delivered. You won't see me anymore. By the way, you work for a great man."

Maksim turned to Mikhail. "What's that?" Mikhail passed it to him. Maksim shook his head. "That doesn't mean anything."

"False," said Mikhail. "It definitely means something."

"What?"

"We are going to need more pay."

·   ·   ·   ·   ·

"Finally," said Jeanne. Down the back steps, she heard the familiar shuffle of Luke – none of that El Buscador nonsense, they'd known each other for too many years. She turned her wheelchair in preparation to confront the greatest source of stress in her life. As he entered through the door, she demanded. "What were you waiting for me to die in here before you decided to show up?"

"Look who's being all dramatic."

"I'm being dramatic? You're the one who became a fugitive, like you're John Dillinger or something. I'm here where I've always been. Where have you been, Luke?"

He thought better than to mock Jeanne for her archaic grandma-worthy Dillinger reference. He liked that she called him by his Christian name Luke, the only one still around who did. "I am so happy to see you again."

"Don't give me that bullshit," said Jeanne. "If you were really happy to see me, you would've never gotten yourself in this pickle. It finally happened. You stopped being Luke and became El Buscador." She said the name dismissively in the voice of a testosterone-laden Neanderthal. Then her tone softened slightly. "You happy now? You shouldn't even be here. They're gonna kill you."

"Yeah ... there's that. Can we just enjoy these moments together?"

"It feels like a funeral. It feels like a goddamn funeral. How about some Grand Marnier? You bought it for me, you might as well drink it with me."

Happy to be doing something and no longer looking into Jeanne's wounded eyes, Luke grabbed two brandy snifters. He poured three fingers, but decided it really was a four-fingered occasion. The viscous, amber liquid rose higher in the glasses than good form permitted. Fortunately, good form was not on Jeanne's list of agenda items today.

Jeanne asked Luke where he was sleeping; failing to mention getting kicked out of increasingly sordid hovels three nights running, he spoke of a spacious abandoned condo in Park Slope. Jeanne asked Luke how he was eating; neglecting to describe last night's supper of Cheetos, he talked about a cheap greengrocer where he feasted on souvlaki chicken with rice and beans. Jeanne asked Luke if he had rediscovered purpose in his life; avoiding an account of his worst existential crisis since he lost his wife and daughter almost 20 years ago, he explained how he was finally ready to let go of Tolland and to live the rest of his days in gentle scholarship and sweet charity.

Luke hoped Jeanne swallowed these lies as easily the Grand Marnier since the glass was losing fingers as quickly as a blind man working in a sawmill. The liqueur rendered Jeanne's lips wet and ecstatic. She rolled the wheelchair up to his spot on the couch, hooked the back of his neck with her strong hands, and pulled his face to hers. They were kissing like they had done this many times before but with an awareness that they might not do so again.

After Jeanne fell forward out of her wheelchair onto Luke's cushioning caress, the ensuing activities orbited in that same sphere of familiarity and urgency.

Usually, sleep followed, but not today. Jeanne knew she didn't want Luke to lie about the worst part of it all. "I know you can't come back right now. But I know something else. You made this mess; you can figure how to get out of it."

Luke brooded, not seeing how his liberation would ever be possible. "I'll do my best."

Jeanne sized up Luke. "Do me a favor. As you're doing your best, don't forget about me. I saw the way you looked at Mavis. I know in your weird way you brought her to my apartment to tell me something. You've never bought anyone here before, let alone an attractive woman."

Yeah, he knew he had problems hiding his feelings about Mavis. He wasn't used to being so romantically vulnerable, so compromised. "Look—"

"—Don't get me wrong," said Jeanne. "I know we've always had an open relationship. We're beyond all that nonsense. So have your fun with Mavis, but don't forget about me. Don't forget about me."

"Ah Jeanne, do you think that would happen?" To his credit, Luke had the grace to not even hint that he put his life on the line to come visit her.

"Let's hope not," Jeanne said. "Just find your way back, O.K.?"

"I will," Luke assured. "In the meantime, I'll make sure you'll have other visitors."

"Who? Mavis? Great. I mean she's nice and down to earth and all. But I'll have in the back of my mind what's happening. I'm human, you know."

"How about Pratt?" Luke ventured. "Now that's a handsome young man."

"He is, but with that beard he looks like a goddamn cave dwelling hermit. I expect a raccoon to crawl out from his chin."

"It's necessary for his protection." Jeanne frowned. Luke offered. "What about Alice? She's sprung from prison. She's good company."

"Great," Jeanne said. "Another woman who's given her life to you. Boy, sounds like a lot of laughs."

"I don't know," said El Buscador. "Suffering can be very funny."

"Yeah?" She rolled her wheelchair close to him. "Let me kick you in the balls and see how amusing that is for you."

"I'm glad your mouth works better than your legs." Jeanne's eyes opened wide and they shared a lecherous giggle. Then Luke's eyes turned moist and from all indications he looked like he would cry. Neither of them was ready for such a scene. Downing the last drops of Grand Marnier, he grabbed both snifters and washed them out in the sink.

"Leave them. You know I'm not a cripple."

Luke smiled and placed the snifters in the drain board. As he slipped toward the door, he waved.

"Find your way back, Luke. If you want to find your way back, you'll figure it out."

Shutting the door, Luke grumbled. Climbing up the steps and out onto this dangerous island, El Buscador kept his mouth shut and his eyes down, figuring out just how many subways it would be wise to take so he could return safely to Gowanus, a place where he had no job, no friends, and no bed.

Hell, he'd have to find his way there before he found his way back.

CHAPTER 5
UNA NONNA

Once again kicked out of his hovel by yet another squatter (it's a bitch to get housing in Brooklyn), this time south of the canal on Sackett, El Buscador would have another long night. The homeless man was kind enough to arrive late, at least letting him catch a few winks until two a.m. Perhaps tomorrow morning he'd find a quiet corner at the Red Hook branch of the public library where he could snatch a nap. He had awakened hungry, which made sense since he hadn't eaten all day. He crossed the canal at Union, with a great graffitied sea monster on the east side and Pig Beach, now closed for the night, on the west. He only knew of one place nearby which was open, so he took Union to Smith and headed west.

Even during his time in Manhattan, El Buscador had heard about Una Nonna's Pizzeria. Every year, lists would come out for the best pizza in New York City. Una Nonna's was never on it. Una Nonna's didn't deserve to be. In fact, it could well be the worst pizzeria in the city. It was without a doubt the worst of any pizzeria to stay in business for more than ten years. The force behind Una Nonna's was Nancy Castiglione. She might've been a grandmother, but she looked a few years too young. Still, decades of making bad pizza had rendered her haggard. She only served a cheese pie. Nancy had no toppings. She also served previously frozen spinach. She'd heat it in a pan; atop it was one whole clove of almost cooked garlic and a drop of non-extra virgin olive oil. No extras of either garlic or oil were permitted. The pie costs $20 ... no slices. The spinach came in one of those half-pound plastic containers more commonly found in delis and Chinese takeout joints.

A cheese pie and spinach. That's all Una Nonna's served. If you wanted anything else, you were out of luck. Even her name made clear her limitations. Una Nonna meant a grandmother, not *the* grandmother or grandmother *number one*. Outsiders of Gowanus shook their heads and wondered how she stayed in business. But the locals understood. She was open 24/7, open even on Thanksgiving and Christmas. She kept this continuous operation running with only one employee, JoJo. JoJo might've been her husband, her brother, her third cousin. No customer had the nerve to ask. They were not the friendliest of servers. JoJo was the widest man El Buscador had ever seen who was not also obese. Standing about 5'4", he was almost as broad as he was tall. He clearly didn't lift weights, just born that way, although lifting pizzas might have kept him firm. Dark and balding, JoJo stood in direct contrast to Nancy's pale skin, wiry frame, and brown hair, hair far too long for someone her age.

No matter when a customer walked in, one of them was sleeping. The other one was explaining that they didn't have pepperoni and that they didn't make grandma pies. The customer at the counter in front of El Buscador asked, "How can you call yourself Nonna's when you don't have a grandma pie?"

Over JoJo's snoring in the corner, Nancy explained, "My grandma's pizza happens to be a plain cheese pie."

"So let me have your grandma's pizza."

"Good. I have one right here." El Buscador noticed three cheese pies of questionable warmth lined up. Nancy gave the customer before him the pie that looked the most like the others. "Want any spinach?"

"Spinach? Here?"

"It makes for a balanced meal."

"Sure, throw in the spinach. How much is the damage?"

"Thirty bucks."

The customer had the courtesy not to stagger a little. Instead, he took out his Visa card. "Here you go."

"Cash only."

The customer was not surprised. He handed her $35, perhaps the extra $5 was for the sleeping JoJo, to give him more pleasant dreams. Their round-the-clock service of soggy pizza and wilted spinach for too much money gave Gowanus what it needed, if not what it wanted. The scrap metal hauler who hadn't eaten all day spotted the dim neon sign and filled his belly at midnight. The restaurant pastry chef at the Michelin two-star in Carroll

Gardens, signing off work at two in the morning, stopped in for humbler cuisine. The Park Slope security guard punching out at four came to Una Nonna to have a last meal before slumber. The portapotty cleaner down on DeGraw arrived for breakfast at 6, and the emergency room nurse appeared an hour later.

All of them had a cheese pie that was shockingly bad. No matter how many times they returned, they still could not believe how awful it was. My God, this was Brooklyn after all! How was this possible? And yet they returned, sometimes adding the spinach out of morbid curiosity. Maybe it had to do with it being the only place on that barren stretch of Smith Street that lured them in, that ugly awful section strewn with bulky industrial debris that looked like glacial landforms deposited during an apocalyptic ice age. For some reason, the section was called Eileen C. Dugan Boulevard, but it should have been called Una Nonna Way.

Part of El Buscador wanted to walk out to avoid the suffering. But he had to order a pie. No other option presented itself. Neither El Buscador nor Nancy was happy he ordered that pie. Now, she would be down to just a single tepid one on the counter and would have to make more. Even a bad pizza took some time to craft. El Buscador then asked a question. He prepared himself for rejection. "Do you have anything to drink?"

"I can give you a glass of tap water," she said. "But you have to return the glass."

"Can I return it tomorrow?"

"You promise to return it."

"Yes."

She turned on the spigot of what looked like a slop sink – what looked like her only sink – and held a glass below it. "Then here you go." Cleanliness was not a top characteristic of the glass. El Buscador contemplated Una Nonna's business model. Universities might study it for years to come. JoJo continued to sleep, thick right forearm serving as a pillow for his head.

Handing Nancy a twenty, El Buscador took the pie and the glass of water. He walked east on Smith, cutting in toward Bond. He marched up the street holding the glass in his left hand and the pizza box propped high in his right, along his shoulder, like a waiter carrying a tray. He had not seen a soul until a big woman in a yellow hoodie walked toward Bond Street at President, where a faded strip of cobbles rolled toward the canal. She nodded to him the way someone who belongs to the communion of three-in-the-morning wanderers would.

Then she snatched the pizza box from El Buscador's shoulder and ran down President.

Shaken from his placid state, El Buscador put down the water glass and chased silently after her. He waited for her to turn into the storage lot on the right before he glided closer, his eyes peering out from the corner. She opened the top of the pie box on the hood of a beat-up El Camino and poked around inside with her index finger. Closing the lid, she cursed once and scooted to the back of the canal toward the Carroll Street Bridge.

She left the pie on the hood.

El Buscador had to decide whether to chase the woman or grab the pizza. He took the pie, walking away, constantly checking whether she would follow him. With a yellow hoodie, she'd be hard to miss. Even as he kept an eye out, El Buscador let his thoughts spawn many questions. Why did she steal his pie? (in all his years in the city remarkably no one had ever stolen his food). Why did she leave the pie on the hood? Was she saving it for later? Did she change her mind? Was she disappointed? (she did curse). Did the curse indicate disappointment or did it hint that she was simply not right in the head? Who steals a pizza? Was she disappointed because it was an Una Nonna's pie? What other pie would be available in these wee hours of the morning? Did she expect to see something other than a pie? And if she wasn't following him, chasing down the pie, what was she doing now? Was she hanging around the Union Deli, waiting for it to open so she could snatch some poor slob's bacon, egg and cheese sandwich?

As he sauntered the couple of blocks until he reached Sackett, perversely hoping yellow hoodie would track him down, he was disturbed how small his questions had become. What ever happened to El Buscador the searcher, the deep thinker? He walked Sackett's old cobbled street until its dead end at the canal. To the right was a scraggly dogwood, aproned by a tiny patch of grass. A sign announcing Green Streets marked the little boxed spot. Its presence was patently absurd as it was swallowed up in industrial buildings and debris. Even more absurd was the little park bench up against one of the more noxious segments of the canal.

El Buscador knew that this rotten little bucolic oasis was the perfect place to indulge in the worst pizza in all of New York City. As he dug in, El

Buscador flushed with a glimmer of hope, not because the pizza was any good, mind you. It was truly, astonishingly awful: the red sauce was sweet and syrupy, the dough undercooked, unleavened, and flaccid, the cheese more ductile plastic than dairy fresh. Even the temperature was impressively tepid, as if Nancy had slipped him a pie that had been sitting on the counter for hours. Yet El Buscador brimmed with burgeoning optimism.

If Nonna could make it here, then who couldn't make it here?

El Buscador ate deliberately. Only someone with a death wish devours a whole Una Nonna's pie. As it was, with half a pie still in the box, he couldn't lift himself from the park bench, the meal inspiring a languorous muddle of indigestion and inertia. Next door, Pygmalion continued to paint along the ledge, with her palette in her right hand and her tiny brush in her left. This time her careful strokes were forming an osprey, its talons clutching the edge, a mackerel in its beak, a fierce, predatory gaze rising from its eyes.

He sidled over to her, pizza box in hand. "I'd offer you some, but since you're a local, I don't want to insult you."

Her radiantly dark skin barely visible, she nodded, concentrating on a speckled wing.

El Buscador ventured again. "So when you go home hungry –"

This time Pygmalion finished his thought, "he'll always have a fish."

El Buscador was tempted to say more, like it's nice not being alone, but Pygmalion's subversive smile as she picked up another tiny brush made any further words pointless.

The bench facing east, he peered beyond the soaring osprey into the rising sun. Although El Buscador had sunk low, he wondered if the problem was that he'd not sunk low enough. He would make sure the word would spread of his newfound appreciation of Tolland. Melville would deliver missives; even Pratt, who wouldn't be happy about it, would whisper of El Buscador's allegiance to the higher power.

CHAPTER 6
LOOMINGS OF THE GWAKEN

El Buscador couldn't figure out what attracted him to the Gowanus Canal – maybe the fascination manifested from the awareness that despite its contamination and its perverse addiction to stagnation, the canal was connected to the East River and the big city and, beyond those aspirational boundaries, New York Harbor and the grand Atlantic. He would open his nose bravely waiting for the stench to blow out past Red Hook and for the sweet, salt sea to sweep over Governor's Island and roll onto the humble, industrial banks. That vigil was often many hours as El Buscador fought his way to the water's edge, his path all too regularly blocked by pesky fences, guard rails, and the less than welcoming razor-ribbon fencing. Still, his insomnia-fueled peregrinations made him increasingly adept at straddling along the canal's brink, tiptoeing and stumbling like a drunken tightrope walker. Sure, the last thing he wanted to do was fall into the canal. Yet the hazards along the shore demanded attention too – the strange random hunk of torn-up cement, the brutal sticker bushes that thrived in the opulent fertilizer so generously donated by the sewage system, the baroque industrial equipment hanging over the water's edge.

El Buscador wasn't sure how he ended up on the south side of the canal – maybe he crossed the 9th Street Bridge after staring up longingly at the F train, a part of him tempted to hop on the subway westbound and slip back to his beloved Manhattan. Yet in Gowanus he remained. He found his neck stretching out through the murky darkness toward the oddly welcoming lights of the massive Whole Foods marketplace. He peered down into the 4th Street basin, which in the old days was a dumping ground for dead horses. Focusing on the dark water in the darker night, he realized the basin was roiling. Water uncharacteristically lapped against the banks. Of course, bubbles rose, but in the canal they always did since chemical reactions abounded: the past and present toxins intermittently making love or making war.

But something else was churning in the Gowanus. A current coursed across the surface with a force that El Buscador knew was the stuff of life. He witnessed a rise in the water, a thin, elegant crest moving from the basin out into the main canal. Determined to follow the gliding water, El Buscador picked up his pace and shuffled in a rapid side-step around the awkward, broken back of the basin, abutting Third Avenue, and turned left, wending his way past an impressive mound of debris, rushing to the canal front by Whole Foods, past the oyster restoration project, to once again spot the ghostly specter gliding through the middle of the canal.

Witnessing a swish that approximated something like a tail, El Buscador had decided he was following a larger beast. It could've been a big fish or an alligator or a giant sea turtle or a small whale or maybe even a school of smaller fish that traveled as one. Whatever it was, he determined the entity was a creature, a creature swimming through the most contaminated place on earth. The creature left a wake of ripples in an ever-expanding Vee, creating its own tide, as if it possessed lunar powers. Indeed, the creature brought energy to the murky and torpid canal.

El Buscador followed the undulating splashes of sea foam. To get a better view, he hopped to the center of the 3rd Street Bridge. Even as he stared into the swelling waters, he still couldn't see the creature that infused the sullied canal with life; all evidence of the creature was indirect, its motion beneath the surface tugging the current with irrepressible potency. Crossing to the north side, El Buscador continued to follow the rolling spray eastward, along the final numbered streets 2nd and 1st. The journey broke into a genuine ease, as he picked up the civilized path of the waterfront park, a park that gawked up at the outrageously priced apartments of the spanking new Lighthouse building. El Buscador felt a kinship with the creature as it restlessly thrashed through canal while he staggered along the banks. Now he could indulge in a leisurely stroll, his movement mirroring the gentle rolling through the lavender waters.

Stepping on the cobblestone apron of the Carroll Street Bridge, he heard a great splash below as if the creature waited for the cover of the tunnel to breach the surface. Sprinting to the east side of the bridge, El Buscador thought he caught a glimpse of a submerging tail, but he couldn't be certain, especially given the gathering weariness in his eyes and the odd lights surrounding the bridge that implausibly detracted from one's vision. If that ghost of the tail was any measure, the creature could be ten feet long, quite the beast for such a small body of water.

Returning to the north bank of the canal, he continued east of Carroll Street even though, following its descent, the creature left no ripples in the water. It had ceased swimming just below the surface, ceased leaving the lapping, foamy wake. It had either decided to rest in the black mayonnaise depths or to swim on in a self-forged channel many feet below. El Buscador's instincts told him that the creature was still moving forward, so he kept pace. His aggressiveness was rewarded with what sounded like another leap in the tunnel of the Union Street Bridge. The splash was strong enough that it could well be mimicked by tossing the body of a small mob figure into the canal. This time the creature didn't descend. Instead, it glided just below the surface, enough to confirm it was a living specimen of sea life, but not sufficient to identify what the hell it was.

Now El Buscador returned to the unpleasantness of climbing over and around fences to follow his prey. He traversed the dead ends at Sackett and DeGraw. The creature was heading into the canal's last block where the pipes came out of the Gowanus pumping station and flushing tunnel, spewing brown bubbles that left a stomach queasy. The creature seemed no more pleased than El Buscador with the new conditions, tipping its torso so that one end broke the water surface. Although El Buscador could not be sure which end, he suspected the head because he spotted what seemed to be whiskers.

And then the creature disappeared.

El Buscador waited at the Douglass Street dead end a few minutes. When the creature didn't resurface and the canal waters turned eerily still, he spun back westward retracing his steps hoping to see the creature again, maybe even the mere current it infused in the canal. But the canal fell flat and silent. He wondered if the sludge at the flushing tunnel was too great even for such a powerful creature. Was the creature now as lifeless as the canal? And what creature had whiskers? A seal maybe? A giant catfish? Though catfish only liked freshwater. Festering in the stew of chemicals, the

Gowanus was quite brackish. Despite their apparent stoicism, the tides of the Atlantic found their way from the East River to this incursion into Brooklyn. So a seal then? But the wake didn't feel true to the slick glide of a seal. No, it seemed like a big fish. And not a peppy fish like a dolphin or even a marlin, but a big, steady, deliberate fish with whiskers.

El Buscador needed to sleep on this mystery. That is, once he found a place to sleep.

CHAPTER 7
MAVIS AND EL BUSCADOR

Mavis Wellington headed down the F train steps at 9th Street, crossed the smelly canal, and walked up to the back entrance of the designated rendezvous point. As always, El Buscador had arrived early and was waiting for her.

She handed him an envelope. "I must say I was a bit amused to get an actual letter in the mail. It seemed old fashioned and charming." Mavis's smile was supplanted by a scowl to signal a transition. "But you've gotta be kidding me with the note."

El Buscador rolled his head ruefully. "I thought clear and simple was the best approach."

She took back the envelope she'd just handed to him and pulled out the napkin enclosed. She read the words as incredulously as the first twelve times she had perused them: "So let's see what you sent me: *'Gone to hell. Be behind Bat Cave at 6:53 every morning for whatever mornings I have left.'* This from the man who the last time I saw him gave me a scone and promised me brunches in places no one has eaten before." El Buscador furrowed his eyebrows to give the impression he was remembering. "And I thought we were going to plan the move together."

El Buscador looked down – his version of a shameful apology. That brunch promise was over the top and the note wasn't his finest work. Best to change the subject. "Tolland planned the move for me."

Mavis was skeptical. "How's that?"

"He finally sent his men to kill me."

Mavis would not be emotionally manipulated. "And why didn't they succeed?"

"I jumped on the back of the train. You would've enjoyed it. They used real bullets. I felt like a superhero."

Warming up to him a bit, Mavis waved the note before his face. "Looks like that delusion hasn't worn off. By the way, did you expect me to burn this note or something?"

El Buscador lifted his eyebrows. "Well, that would have been appropriate. It would've followed proper procedures."

Mavis chuckled. "Procedures? Are you kidding? I'm framing this thing."

El Buscador opened his arms and Mavis stepped inside of them. "It's really good to see you, Mavis." He gave her an embrace that whispered awkwardness and affection.

"You too," she said. "A small part of me was worried about you. It was the second little toe on my right foot, but that toe happens to be very sensitive and tender."

"Well, that can always be amputated."

"Ah, you have the soul of a poet," said Mavis. "So where are we going?"

"To walk the canal."

"Not again. I'm starting to worry about you. I was hoping we'd go to Prospect Park."

"Too artificial." Mavis snickered. El Buscador pressed ahead. "Anyway, I want you to help me find something."

"In the canal? You're messing with me again."

"There's something in there," said El Buscador. "I saw it last night."

"What?" asked Mavis. "A body? I can believe that. It won't be the first or the last found in there."

"No, this thing's living." El Buscador proceeded to tell Mavis of the movements in the water and that glimpse of whiskers before the creature disappeared for good.

For the first time since they met today, Mavis studied him carefully. Hell, she'd been so worked up to lay into him about the note that she couldn't bother with anything else but to get that out of her system. She was worried about how deeply she was falling for this trainwreck of a man, and now looking at him, she noted his haggard raggedness, one that spoke of sleeplessness. "Why do you think you'll be able to find this thing?"

"I'm pretty sure it's been sleeping where it submerged and it's probably getting ready to rise soon," said El Buscador. "We better get moving."

"Sure you don't want to show me the Bat Cave before we go?" asked Mavis. "What happened to the Tour Guide I used to know and love?"

"He decided he better lay low for a while. It's harder to give tours when people are shooting at you."

Mavis frowned at him. "That's not the only thing I've heard that's different. Word's out that you've decided you're in love with Tolland."

El Buscador smiled. "Yeah. I've heard that word too."

"That means you agree with it?"

"For the moment." El Buscador's countenance was consciously enigmatic.

Mavis smiled at him. "I guess you have some elaborate plan up your sleeve?"

"Well," he answered. "Not really elaborate."

"That's what I was afraid of."

"Yeah, well, I'm going to need more of your faith."

Mavis laughed. "That means we're both screwed."

El Buscador chuckled. They returned to the business at hand. He hoped to tour again, continuing to unearth secret spots in the city, even if it would now be in this most inner of the outer boroughs.

Mavis tried to buck him up a bit. "But the Bat Cave sounds right up your alley."

"Later. The creature awaits."

Mavis could tell El Buscador was in a rush because he didn't take her on his usual journey along the canal, which required much tedious twisting and turning past the countless obstructions of fences, wires, barriers, and miscellaneous debris. Instead they crossed 9th Street, picking up Smith Street, which pushed off many yards from the canal and followed along the ominously elevated G train. Stepping aside rubble and random delivery drop-offs, they entered the segment of Smith renamed Eileen C. Dugan Boulevard, not exactly New York at its most picturesque.

Mavis couldn't help but comment. "It fires the imagination as to what fiendish crime Ms. Duggan committed to have such a foul stretch of roadway named after her."

El Buscador snorted as his form of a laugh. They followed Bond Street all the way to Douglass to reach the dead end that marks the head of the canal. Here the Pump Station and the Flushing Tunnels were spitting and spilling brown foam everywhere. Mavis pointed, "Doesn't take a detective to figure out what that is."

"At least it's been treated."

"Looks more like it was mistreated to me."

They waited a while. Mavis updated El Buscador about what was happening at *The Herald*, their current investigations of Tolland, and the legal status of his old friend April Huo. Mavis asked him if he needed anything from his former confines at the abandoned city hall subway station.

"No, not really. I don't have any place to put my books right now. Luckily, I had all my cash on me."

"You couldn't have much left. Can I give you some money?"

"I have about ten thousand." Mavis whistled. "That should last me a while."

"Jesus, it's amazing you haven't been mugged. But then again you don't look like you've got a pot to piss in. Actually, you don't. With that money, and the way you live, you might be able to make it a couple of years."

"But since you're asking," El Buscador paused to make sure he had Mavis's full attention. "I could really use a big favor that I feel terrible asking you."

Mavis knew this wasn't going to be good. She exhaled and muttered with a tone approaching dread, "What is it?"

"Given the way I had to leave, I couldn't well take the turtles with me."

"You want me to bring them to you."

"Well, I don't even have a place for me, so I really can't take care of the turtles. I guess I could dump them into the canal."

"And kill them?"

"Well, unless you're willing to take them."

"You son-of-a-bitch. I told you those turtles were your responsibility."

Just as El Buscador girded for the inevitable onslaught, the canal breathed in a non-industrial way. Not the trickling, dribbling, spilling from the pipes that jutted from the sea walls like so many oozing sores, but a robust crest, singularly from the movement of the large and the living. Perhaps it was the daylight or maybe the creature decided to be a bit more forward, but now El Buscador could make out a form.

So could Mavis. "Will you look at that?" Mavis gave El Buscador a hard stare. "Don't think I've forgotten about the turtles, but I've gotta get this." Mavis pulled out her phone. She clicked a few shots and switched the camera to record mode.

"Hey," said El Buscador. "You're not going to show anybody this?"

Mavis was losing her patience. "You do remember what I do for a living, right?"

"Mavis," said El Buscador, a hint of pleading in his voice. Mavis had to admit she liked when he called her by her name. "You run a story on the creature, and every hipster will be down here in Brooklyn feeding it meat pies and hurling axes at it."

Mavis giggled. El Buscador sometimes could be a funny bastard. "You old fool. You think you're the only one with eyes. You think no one's going to see this thing. And stop calling it a creature. It's a big fish."

El Buscador looked carefully. Examining its long, scaly, narrow form, he wanted to believe it was something more exotic than some mere fish, that it was a mythical beast. "I was hoping it was a gator. You know an ancient lizard. I like the idea of a prehistoric creature invading these post-industrial waters."

"Honey, you may have gotten your wish. Look at that thing."

El Buscador was looking, but he still wasn't sure what he was seeing. Kindly hovering a mere couple of inches below the foamy, russet surface, the fish had to be about eight feet long, the thin, elegantly curved back fin four fingers above the bubbles, and a second fin a foot closer to the main body teasingly pierced the surface. Its snout was extended and narrow, and its submarine body glided with the inevitability of inertia. As Mavis continued filming, her arms out steadily following the fish's movements, El Buscador now spotted what he thought he saw last night. "Do you see the whiskers?"

Mavis laughed. "Honey, you're not looking at whiskers. Those are barbels."

"Yeah, yeah." El Buscador loved being corrected, "That's what got me first thinking last night that maybe it was a catfish. But catfish can't live in brackish waters."

"You're right about that, but then again, I didn't think anything could live in these waters. I think I know what it is."

"Yeah?" As he continued his observation, El Buscador thought he was gawking at the most fantastically alien creature in the world. "Look at those crazy scales on it." The bony plates stuck up and out of the torso like they were riveted in, like they were prehistoric plates.

"I think they're called scutes," said Mavis.

"Who died and granted you a degree in marine biology?"

"I don't need a degree. I watch David Attenborough."

"The guy in *Jurassic Park*?"

"No, his brother. He made millions of nature videos." El Buscador looked puzzled. Then Mavis understood. "Sometimes I forget that you haven't watched TV since the Twentieth Century. Anyway, I watch all of David Attenborough's shows about the sea. I watch them over and over again. They help me relieve my tension." El Buscador could think of better ways to relieve tension. "If you're told something enough times, you tend to learn it, although I'm not sure that educational strategy has been very effective with you." El Buscador wasn't paying attention at the moment. "So those four whiskers are barbels – that means we're looking at a bottom feeder here because they drag those funky whiskers along the riverbed to find their grub. The bony plates are scutes. That's not too common. That's what makes the fish look prehistoric. It's an ancient protection. You've got a very old species here, so you've got your wish."

"So what the hell are we looking at?"

"Don't quote me on this, because I'm not a hundred percent sure, but I think what we have here is a sturgeon."

"Sturgeon, huh?" El Buscador rubbed his chin. "Don't they get fancy caviar from sturgeon?"

"Sure as hell do, although I wouldn't trust the roe from this one."

"You think this fish is a female?"

"I do."

"What? Do you see some markings?"

"No, but it's big. The females are usually bigger. And it's clearly brave, another feminine characteristic."

El Buscador eyed her carefully. "You know, I was starting to believe you for a minute."

"You better believe me."

A dog walker was coming to the dead end of Douglass looking for a place for his schnauzer to further befoul the Superfund site. El Buscador whispered to Mavis, "Can you stop filming? I don't want this guy spotting the creature." Mavis frowned, preparing to deny the request. Then he added, "Let's give the sturgeon some privacy while we still can. Let's do that for her." El Buscador's acknowledgment of not only the species, but the gender, did the trick. Mavis returned the phone to her purse, grabbed El Buscador's hand, and strolled casually like they were lovers.

Seemingly sensing the reprieve, the sturgeon dropped below the surface, perhaps returning to the black mayonnaise bottom so that its barbels could scrounge up some breakfast. As they left the canal and wandered up Bond Street still holding hands, playing parts that neither was willing to accept nor relinquish, El Buscador asked, "What do you think she eats?"

"I don't want to know."

"Can you do me a favor?"

"Another one!" Mavis let go of his hand. She was happy about that, more comfortable yelling at El Buscador than playing handsies with him. "What now? Don't think I've forgotten about the turtles."

"Tell you what. How about you bring the turtles to me? I'll take care of them. It's time I found a place anyway."

"Well, that's the first sensible thing you've said all day. Boy, this new favor must be a doozy."

"It is." El Buscador swallowed. "Can you not run a story on the sturgeon?"

"What are you crazy? Just because you're," here she made air quotes "*secret boy* doesn't mean the rest of the world squirrels away information like they are golden nuts to feed on next winter."

"How about this? Can you wait until someone else sees the sturgeon?"

"And ruin my scoop?" Mavis eyed El Buscador. The man looked scared and excited. She determined that this sturgeon was the best thing to happen to him in years. Yes, she would've preferred that she occupied such an honor, but hell, the man was strange, broken, and pure. Mavis answered "Alright" before she knew why. "But once it comes out, I'll be all over this story."

"Fair enough."

Mavis saw gratitude in his moist eyes and wondered if deep affection rested behind them. "Will you walk me to the subway?"

"Sure. Will you come back tomorrow?"

"I might." Mavis was glad El Buscador looked crestfallen. Good, maybe he'd get a sense of what it was like to live with the uncertainty that filled every waking moment of her relationship with this vexing, moderately exciting man.

After he saw Mavis off at the subway turnstile, kissing her sweet mocha forehead as a farewell, he understood that his ignorance of the sturgeon left him hollow inside. He would spend the rest of the day at the library learning everything he could about the ancient fish. He would not leave the library to eat or to sleep until closing hours. He knew he could well miss another appearance of the sturgeon. But he needed to learn and after the library lights clicked off, he needed to get to the Red Hook waterfront tonight to flag down the passing Melville. It might be time to get another set of eyes on this mystery.

CHAPTER 8
THACKERAY, FAR FROM HOME

Thackeray was not a happy man. He'd gotten so comfortable on his barstool perch at Delmonico's that he was convinced he'd stay there until his dying days. For years, everyone came to him. Even El Buscador. But today he had to venture to ... Brooklyn. However, he had a funny feeling the journey would be worth it just to see El Buscador's reaction.

They met by the Carroll Street Bridge at Lavender Lake, the bar's name adopted from the long-tinctured color of the canal, stirred through with rich unnatural hues from dye factories that hugged the coast. They could've met at Pig Beach, which had quite the festive outdoor seating right on the canal, but that place owned a popularity that both Thackeray and El Buscador found inconvenient. Sure, Lavender Lake had its own outdoor seating, but its nondescript entrance and indoor niche of a bar were more to Thackeray's needs, if not to his liking. Simply put, it was a hundred years and four levels of class below Delmonico's. Yet, making the best of his first time slumming since semi-retirement, Thackeray stroked his immaculately groomed salt-and-pepper beard and asked, "Do they make sidecars here? Please tell me they make sidecars here."

"They'll make what I buy and you'll like it."

"Oh, look at El Buscador in full hard-boiled detective mode." Thackeray eyed him from the brimmed hat to the busted shoe leather. "Been watching old movies lately?"

"Only the ones spooling through my mind."

"Oh jeez. It's going to be one of those conversations."

The drinks arrived. They were in highball glasses with three cubes. Thackeray could look past the cloudy froth and the sprig of mint on top to know that the cocktails had plenty of booze. Lifting his glass in sync with El Buscador's to perform an air toast, he asked, "With what poison are you plying me?"

Before answering, El Buscador took a sip and nodded his approval. "It's called Hipster's Crisis."

Sipping and grinning, Thackeray mused, "I didn't know such a thing was possible."

"Which? That condition for hipsters or the drink?"

"Oh, definitely the drink. That's all I care about. Almost makes it worth coming here. Why couldn't you meet me at Delmonico's?"

"You know why."

Thackeray grinned again. He was surprised he was in such a good mood. "Well, I would've liked to have seen you try."

"You would've liked to have seen me dead. Manhattan is no longer the friendliest of confines for me."

Thackeray stroked his beard smugly, "And after all those years of rambling around footloose and fancy free."

El Buscador did not enjoy the way Thackeray poked at the ashes of his dying embers. He knew the former triple spy would make him pay for taking the trip to the boroughs. "You have the plans?"

"So much for niceties," said Thackeray. "Shouldn't you ask me about the family?"

"Unless you've turned over a few rocks, you can't have much to report."

"Oh, you needle me with your prickly wit." El Buscador knew that the last time Thackeray had been truly wounded, emotionally or physically, was twenty years ago, when a Chechen agent drilled a bullet in his thigh. He suspected that Thackeray's limp was an unnecessary affectation just to remind all he encountered that he had a colorful past.

"The plans?"

Out from one of his many deep pockets, Thackeray pulled a rolled 9 by 12 envelope. "I don't think you're going to like what you see."

"With Tolland, I never like what I see." In front of Thackeray, El Buscador needed to continue to act disdainfully toward Tolland. Although he had indeed remained disdainful of Tolland, he'd been sending out messages that he was warming up to the real estate mogul. However, the only way Thackeray would believe that El Buscador was softening his view would be if the old enemy continued to act defiant. The dance had to be nimble. If El Buscador was changing his views on Tolland, he would not tip his hand to Thackeray. Thackeray would be the last person he'd show his true feelings. El Buscador inwardly smiled in his knowledge that for him to seem credible to Thackeray was to act like he was lying as he was telling the truth.

Thackeray finished his Hipster Crisis and signaled the bartender for two more, beyond certain that El Buscador would be paying. "This time, it's because you'll be surprisingly impressed."

"How's that?"

"Tolland's got new architects."

"No more Lud, Gib and Nirob?" That architectural firm infamously designed for Tolland some of the great offenses to the eye sockets ever to grace the Manhattan skyline, droningly monotonous edifices on a grand scale.

"Tolland decided he needed a new sensibility for Brooklyn," said Thackeray.

"Tolland needed a new sensibility the moment he slid from the womb. What does it matter? I'll let you in on a little secret: Lud, Gib, and Nirob is not the only firm capable of architectural abominations."

Thackeray offered a smug, sly smirk that shot through El Buscador. He knew that Thackeray must've had a doozy up his sleeve. "What if I told you that Tolland's hired the Graffiti Sisters?"

El Buscador was silent, and Thackeray drew great pleasure from leaving his old frenemy speechless. The Graffiti Sisters had created a half dozen impressive developments in the city in the last two decades, specializing in transforming old industrial and factory spaces into residences and parkland that captured much of those places' history and character without the rotten smells and grating noises that had been also part of the past. "Why would the Graffiti Sisters take his business?" asked El Buscador. "Tolland has the worst of the Midas's touch. He turns everything into money even though he makes everything look like shit."

"But what if he gave them complete artistic control?" Thackeray's questions had an especially haughty tone today.

"He wouldn't," said El Buscador.

"Well, let me tell you the deal and you tell me if he has."

"Fire away." El Buscador focused, attending carefully so he could shoot down Thackeray's case.

"Well, it's simple," said Thackeray. "After some pretty agile wheeling and dealing, Tolland owns five city blocks on both sides of the Gowanus. He instructed the Graffiti Sisters to create five thousand condo units of nine hundred square feet apiece in any way they so desired. With that one minimally constraining condition, they can design the rest of the project whatever way they deem fit, including placement of buildings and location of parkland."

"What are the restrictions, the provisos, the budgets?" asked El Buscador.

"There are none," said Thackeray.

"There always are some."

"Not this time."

El Buscador reminded, "This is Tolland we're talking about."

"A Tolland who's trying to resurrect his image," said Thackeray. "You know about his image, don't you? You've only spent half your life trying to destroy it."

"Don't remind me," said El Buscador. "It makes me feel like I wasted the other half before he arrived on my radar. Yeah, and whose getting tossed out of the buildings?" El Buscador still picked at the open wound of Tolland's throwing his parents out of their rent control apartment in the East Village almost twenty years ago. After, El Buscador's parents moved to Florida. He hadn't seen them since. Instead, he spent his time making sure Tolland would suffer consequences for his many inhospitable acts.

"That's the beauty of it," said Thackeray. "The buildings had no residents. They were all industries and factories, and those businesses have moved to the next wastelands with cheaper rents and rundown warehouses." Thackeray rolled an ice cube around his tongue and smiled, savoring the opportunity to enlighten his usually well-informed associate. "Tolland's been on his game on this one. He's been planning the district for years. He's already completed the environmental impact studies, received permit approvals, and handled the zoning. He's even made a deal with the mayor's office about affordable housing. He's ready to roll."

El Buscador sipped his Hipster Crisis and stewed for a minute or two. "Still, that doesn't mean the plans are any good."

Thackeray stared into the depths of his highball glass and contemplated a third. He was not used to drinking so far from home. He'd have to get an Uber to take him back across the river. Still, the journey was worth it just to watch the internal conflict emerge in the sallow trench-coated breast of El Buscador. "C'mon. When's the last time the Graffiti Sisters' architects made anything that wasn't a grand slam?"

El Buscador could not think of one failure. In fact, he might be their biggest fan. "Well, I'll tell you what I'm afraid of ..." as he said these words, both he and Thackeray knew he wasn't really going to say what he was afraid of, which was that the Graffiti Sisters were the perfect architects for Tolland's Gowanus plan. Instead, he paused long enough to come up with something, anything. "... I'm afraid that they're going to make a neighborhood that looks like Disney World. That the life force and the grittiness of the place will be scrubbed away and sterilized."

"I was going to leave and let you peruse the architectural plans on your own, but I think I'm going to enjoy your looking over the designs." He pointed to the bartender for another round of Hipster Crises. "This way I get to hear your lies with a bald-faced blatancy I've yet to encounter from you." Thackeray gave a subtle head shift to the envelope.

El Buscador obliged and opened the plans. He studied the blueprints, his right index finger meticulously following the details.

Thackeray grew impatient. Fortunately, the next round arrived. Still, after two sips, he blew out air from his cheeks. "Forget the blueprints, just look at the architectural renderings and tell me you don't love it."

El Buscador obliged. He knew immediately he had a major problem. The design was intricately charming, practical, livable, and lovely. Straddling both sides of the canal were parklands crisscrossed by humpbacked bridges with a couple of bars and restaurants mixed along the turning basins and the side inlets. Sure, he could detect traces of Venice and Amsterdam, but, hell, what dominated the design was old Gowanus itself. The renderings featured cobblestones to nowhere, brick industrial buildings like the old pump stations, and splashes of graffiti that played off the reflections of the green water. One section of sea wall on each side of the Fifth Street Basin would be made completely of glass, so visitors could not only peer through the murky canal waters, but also look into a huge aquarium tank that capped the head of the basin. The best part was that the residences were so set back from the canal that the Gowanus would be returned to the people of New York. Trees, bushes, and native grasses edged the waterway, creating layers of roots to absorb runoff when the rains came.

After ordering an Uber to deliver him from this hellhole, Thackeray did not speak again until he was down to the ice cubes. "What do you think?"

"I'm not sure," said El Buscador. It was not the grand lie Thackeray expected, but still satisfying. "I have to study the plans some more."

Thackeray tipped his glass to taste the melting whiskey residue on his tongue. "You go ahead and study all you like, but you know where you're going to end up." Thackeray grabbed El Buscador's half-finished Hipster Crisis and took a sip.

El Buscador raised his eyebrows. "Should I order you another?"

"No, I just wanted a little more. I'm done. Anyway, what I want to see is how the famously self-righteous El Buscador is going to handle this one. This Gowanus Project could well be the greatest contribution to the city since the High Line. This project is everything you believe in and the only individual who can pull it off is the person you hate the most in the world."

"You know he tried to kill me last week."

Thackeray eyed El Buscador's glass, tempted to take another sip. "I might've heard something about it."

"He invaded my home. I can never go back."

"Do you think I'd have graced this godforsaken borough if I thought you could've come to me?"

"No, I don't believe so."

Thackeray was taking his time, soaking up the moment, stroking that damn immaculately groomed salt-and-pepper beard. "What's nice about all those developments is that you have more reason to hate the man than ever." Thackeray pointed to the architectural rendering. "But, pray tell, explain to me how are you going to hate this project? Will you try to deny the city this marvel of design and planning? Will you deny this to the city that you love almost as much as you hate Tolland?"

El Buscador decided it was a good time to finish his drink before Thackeray got his grubby hands on it. He signaled the bartender to pay out.

Responding to his buzzing phone, Thackeray said, "Ah, there's my Uber." While his hands did a fine job in helping lift him, protruding belly and all, from his barstool, they were no help in searching for his wallet. "If you figure out how to make your way safely back to the real city, you might see me again."

"Gee, that's quite an incentive."

Thackeray laughed heartily. "For my part, you're staying away would be quite a tragedy. I prefer to see you suffer before my eyes. Tragedy from a distance leads to too many false impressions. It hints to a nobility more common in myth than in substance."

El Buscador was too busy paying the bill to notice Thackeray's departure. He knew that for the rest of the day and night he would walk the canal, particularly those blocks that would soon be dubbed Tolland's District. He'd walk the canal and imagine. He'd walk the canal and try to find answers to questions that had not seemed possible minutes earlier.

CHAPTER 9
THE GWAKEN RISES

Mavis arrived behind the Bat Cave with a sloshing portable turtle cage dragging low in her left hand while her right hand brandished a rolled-up newspaper like a weapon. "I told you I should've published the damn story." El Buscador opened the front page of the *Brooklyn Eagle*. There was a full banner headline in a huge type size, the kind normally reserved for declarations of war. It read: "The Gwaken Has Come!" Mavis muttered phrases like "I don't know why I listen to you."

El Buscador tuned out the grousing and read the story authored by someone who called himself Slim Whitman.

We've had porpoises and seals and even Sludgie the Whale, but is the Gowanus Canal ready for what locals have already dubbed the Gwaken?

What is the Gwaken?

Well, that depends who you ask. Some say it's a whirlpool swirling below the canal, sending strange ripples and waves on the surface of the water. Some say it's a giant turtle. Some say it's a big fish. But most say it's a mighty sea monster that grows larger and stronger, feasting on the gunk that has gathered on the canal floor for more than a century.

"It's big and scaly and scary," said Ryan McCauley, a Bond Street resident. "I saw it rise out of the water with something disgusting hanging from its mouth. The beast doesn't surface very often, but when it does, it gives you nightmares."

Residents started reporting the presence of the Gwaken about a week ago. Most eyewitnesses described a sleek swelling of the waters that looked like something moving very straight, leaving a trail behind it, sometimes even a wake.

"It was tough to make out what it was," said Olivia Benjamin of the Lighthouse Apartments right on the canal. "The Gwaken seemed shy. But the lucky ones have seen its tail. Nobody knows for sure what they're looking at, but everybody who has spotted it has said they've never seen anything like it."

Local naturalist and a regular canoer on the canal Herbert Coffey said there have been too many sightings and witnesses for the Gwaken to be dismissed as an urban legend. Even Coffey in his explorations has caught a glimpse.

"Just because the Gwaken has been named after that mythical sea monster the Kraken doesn't mean it isn't real," said Coffey. "I can say with confidence there is a big creature in the canal. What it is, I can't tell you for sure, but I'm certain someone will figure it out soon."

That question and just what the creature eats looms heavily on the horizon.

Stay tuned and keep your eyes peeled. The Gwaken lurks!

El Buscador looked up. "Do you want me to help you with the story?"

"Isn't it a little late for that?"

"But you've got much better pictures. Look at that blurry mess." El Buscador pointed to the front cover image of dark water and an outline of something that could as easily be an oil slick as a sea creature. "And you can post your video. Plus, you know so much more. I had Melville come by. He confirmed it is a sturgeon."

By Mavis's scowl, El Buscador knew he had made a grievous error.

She grabbed the newspaper, rolled it, and offered a vaguely obscene, unquestionably threatening gesture. "I can't believe you had to get the Gwaken checked out with Barnacle Bill the sailor to verify it's a sturgeon. I already told you it's a sturgeon."

"Funny, you mention barnacles," said El Buscador, backing up. "Do you know that many a watercraft in New York Harbor used to take a detour into the Gowanus Canal to clean off their barnacles? The water was just that pernicious."

"Don't try to distract me with your trivia, fun-fact bullshit," said Mavis. "You didn't trust my judgment."

"It's not that I didn't trust your judgment. You should know as a journalist that it's always good to corroborate evidence."

"Uh huh, and you are not a journalist." Mavis slowed down her sentences to make sure El Buscador didn't miss a word. He knew he was really in trouble by her refusal to use contractions. "You are barely a person. You did not trust my judgment after I told you about all the nature shows I watched. After I told you that I know these things."

"You did, you did," said El Buscador. "And you were right. You were the first to understand what the Gwaken really was."

"Do not patronize me, you old fuck."

"I'm not patronizing you. Let's just say I was impressed that you knew and depressed that I didn't."

"Now you're getting closer to it, aren't you honey?" said Mavis. "Your pride's been hurt. First you lose your home and have to run away from Tolland. How humiliating. Then you end up in Brooklyn and you can't find any place to sleep. You're no longer the cool, elegant, underground El Buscador. Now, you're just some Brooklyn hobo with an outsized vocabulary."

Mavis could see she'd wounded him. He asked, "Can we talk about the sturgeon please?"

She pulled back. "Sure we can, honey. I'm sorry. I know you might not be thinking straight right now and maybe having Melville give you a little reassurance was good for you."

Her apology wasn't comforting. He thought he'd remind her he was good for something. "I think I know what the Gwaken eats. I read that sturgeon like oysters and there's this big education program where schoolteachers are seeding oysters all over the Gowanus. I even spoke to a middle school biology teacher as she was counting the tagged oysters in the cages. Most of them are surviving and have their own seedlings. I bet you the Gwaken is feasting on those oysters. They keep putting more in since it's supposed to help clean up the canal."

Mavis smiled slyly. "That's not a bad little nugget." They walked to the edge of Douglass where there was an absurdly placed park bench next to the razor ribbon … absurdly yet very practically placed for El Buscador to keep a Gwaken vigil while Mavis tapped away at her laptop, writing a lead that explained with great confidence her unveiling of the beast's true identity. Typing furiously, she asked if she'd be OK quoting Melville, as an esteemed member of the Explorer's Club, confirming that the Gwaken is indeed a sturgeon.

Upon giving his approval, El Buscador ventured, "So now you're happy I contacted Melville?"

Without looking up from her frantic typing, Mavis answered. "You'd be wise to shut the hell up."

CHAPTER 10
THE GRAND CAPITULATION

El Buscador studied the architectural plans repeatedly. The Graffiti Sisters had done something memorable here. He'd been fighting Tolland's projects for so long ... he questioned his own judgment that he actually liked this proposal. He could go to Pratt and Mavis to get their opinions, but he knew in his gut that everything about being El Buscador was arriving at decisions all by his lonesome. He palpably understood that he had to make a peace offering to Tolland which must be fashioned as a commitment to sell his soul. As he mused, he observed the gathering groups at the Third Street Bridge by Whole Foods. They were looking for the Gwaken.

Crossing the street, he stepped into the back of the Gowanus Canoe Club, where members were discussing the Tolland District. As one of the leaders said, "We really can't talk about it because we've seen so little."

Here El Buscador raised his hand and for the first time since he was a university professor 20 years ago, he spoke before a large crowd. "I have seen the plans. If you'd like, I can show you." The club members welcomed his input and put El Buscador in front of the map. "What the architects are going for is a little taste of Venice while keeping the canal's industrial roots." Murmurs from the crowd indicated approval for both Venice and industry. "That means charming, humpbacked footbridges crisscrossing the canal and big abandoned hunks of equipment being converted into public sculptures. That means cars will be far away from this project and walking paths will reign. That means the scale of the apartments will not exceed four stories and little streams and fountains will play off the intimacy of the canal. That means more oysters will be seeded and the flush tunnels below will be built so the slow, unpleasant cleaning of this Superfund site will continue. That means more people than ever will be invested in Gowanus because they will live here and walk here and embrace the lovely personal scale that makes the best of Brooklyn something Manhattan can't offer – a place that has been neither sanitized nor bowdlerized."

Having studied the architectural plans enough to commit them to memory, El Buscador pointed plot by plot, basin by basin in the section of the canal stretching east of Whole Foods on the canal's south side and expanding out to Smith Street on the north, all the way west to the subway at 9th Street. He spoke of thousands of native plantings, vegetation that would serve as the lungs for the district, and of the permeable paving that would further enhance drainage. He even showed the playful serpentine paths that would lead commuters in and out of the subway into the very soul of Gowanus. Better than the plans themselves, El Buscador laid out a vision of what could well be the most charming and funky neighborhood in the big bad city.

When he ended his impromptu presentation, he was surrounded by canoe club members who peppered him with questions. After he patiently answered all of them, he tossed out, "Does anyone here know Timothy Terrance Tolland? I mean do you talk regularly to him?" Receiving a few nods, he clarified. "I mean would you feel comfortable calling him and telling him what I said today and asking whether I could have a brief meeting with him?"

"I can," said attractive young Brooklynite, of dark olive skin and many heredities. She looked straight into his eyes and said, "But I have to ask, who are you?"

"I am El Buscador." He pronounced his name like she would recognize it. She clearly did not. He had to repeat it.

She walked out to the canal as if only the Gwaken was permitted to hear the phone conversation. Returning ten minutes later, she said, "He said to show up at the Tollandia at 8 and don't wear any disguises."

"Thank you so much."

"Can I ask you," she said, "El Buscador, is it?"

"Yes."

"Are you wearing a disguise right now?"

"Naturally," he said, still grasping for any aura of mystery he might preserve.

"Oh, thank God," she said.

As he wandered away from the crowd of Gowanus, a short, bearded man wearing gray slacks and a checkered button-down smiled at El Buscador, recognizing him. Grabbing El Buscador gently by the arm, he said, "Allow me to introduce myself. I am Irving Steinman." When El Buscador merely nodded, Irving continued, grinning, "I just want to tell you that you are not a traitor, just because you betrayed every person and every conviction you held dear." Then Irving released El Buscador's arm, shook his head in acknowledgment that their conversation was over, and moved away quickly as if trying to avoid contracting cholera. El Buscador wondered why his strong commitment to what he was doing did not render his innards any less gutted.

·   ·   ·   ·   ·

El Buscador thought the chances were pretty good he'd be shot on the way to seeing the real estate mogul at the Tollandia. If Tolland still wanted to kill him, El Buscador had just made the hit a hell of a lot easier, to the point he was sure Tolland would ask for discount rates since he basically earned the finder's fee.

And yet not one bullet flew toward him.

El Buscador was a little saddened by not being assassinated. He couldn't help but feel he was a traitor embracing the project of a man who did more to destroy the architecture of his beloved city than even Robert Moses. Tolland was famous for trying to intimidate his guests on their visits to his signature buildings. When Edmund J. Coppa met with the real estate mogul, he was greeted by crossbow demonstrations and other feats of weaponry. El Buscador's one visit to the penthouse, in the guise of a renowned Mayan explorer, featured a javelin piercing what appeared to be a rare tapestry, the blade dramatically impaling the heart of a unicorn.

But today intimidation would be replaced by waiting in the outer chambers for two hours, followed by something more concrete and brutal. When he was finally let into a nondescript office (no penthouse access today), El Buscador was welcomed by a rabbit punch to the kidneys. The blow came from one of Tolland's associates, the ensuing kicks to the belly and head of the collapsed figure were delivered by Tolland himself. A personal touch is nice.

If he could have gotten the words out, El Buscador would have noted that Tolland's assault on him was as original as his buildings. He could've beaten El Buscador with anything, from a butternut squash to a Statue of Liberty figurine, but he went with the predictable. Hell, Tolland was famous for his tendency to steal quirky behaviors from eccentrics of the past. All he needed to do was recreate the scene in *1984* of a rat crawling through a glass tube to gnaw on the victim's face. If he'd used a blue rat, Tolland might've presented a sweet moment of poetic justice. Instead, he just beat up an aging man. One wouldn't think there would be much satisfaction in that, but Tolland practically oozed ecstatic gratification.

El Buscador ventured, "Are we good now?"

"We'll never be good. These are the terms. I arrange daily meetings with city council members, community board members, residents, and assorted potential pains-in-the-asses. Then you give the tour. Make sure they're oohing and aahing the way the canoe club posers were when you started chatting up the project. Let's say you'll do it every day at noon, so it intrudes on any plans you might make and keeps you out of trouble. You stand at the 3rd Street Bridge. I'll make sure there are maps and architectural renderings in case you can't paint a pretty enough picture with your words. And no subversive shit or you're done. Got me?"

El Buscador nodded.

"Good. Now get out of here before I change my mind."

From the moment he'd entered Tolland's office, El Buscador had walked into a bad movie, tired dialogue and all. He was more than happy to rush out of that theatre.

He took the F train down to Jeanne and told her what he had done. She cried. He couldn't tell if the tears were of tenderness or of disappointment. The next thing he knew she was falling out of the wheelchair pushing him onto his back, kissing and grabbing and moving her hips in ways few paraplegics can.

By the time she was done with him, she dropped into slumbers and started snoring. He carried her to the bed.

Awakening, she asked, "Luke, are you leaving, my lover boy?"

"Yeah. I need to catch up with a few people here now that I'm less likely to be shot on this island."

"Enjoy it while it lasts."

"What do you mean?"

"You know you're going to blow the whole thing up. You won't be able to help yourself. Why do think I took you right here and now? Cause I've gotta get the gettings while the gettings are good."

"So now that the gettings have been gotten, are you tossing me to the curb?"

"Nah. Let me ask you something, are you going to live back in the old station?"

"Not for a while. I've got to take care of some things in Gowanus."

"Yeah, you'll be dragged down in the lavender filth like everybody who goes there." When Luke had nothing to say about her prognosis, Jeanne asked, "When will you be back?"

"As soon as I can."

"Just remember I'm waiting for you."

•   •   •   •   •

El Buscador found Pratt in his usual spot, checking traps below the FDR Drive. At first, Pratt was happy to see his old friend, but once El Buscador told him about his arrangement with Tolland, he grew so angry that El Buscador feared Pratt would do with his cache of blue rats what Tolland lacked the imagination to consider.

Pratt's voice was low and venomous. "You're the last person I'd ever figure to be a traitor."

Projecting not an ounce of shame, El Buscador looked into Pratt's eyes. "I know this doesn't look good, but I'm asking you to trust me."

"Do you know what you're doing?" asked Pratt, unconvinced.

"I think I do," said El Buscador. "This one will be trickier than anything I've done before, but I think I can pull it off." Pratt looked at his friend, seeing plots spinning around in his head. "Give me a couple of weeks. If I fail, I'll be happy for you to feed me to those rats."

"Remember something," said Pratt, "Unlike Tolland's men, I know how to find you."

El Buscador laughed. "I wouldn't have it any other way."

Pratt could detect no trace of nervousness or guilt in the countenance of El Buscador. All he could see was profound commitment, which was strangely reassuring. "Yeah, just don't disappointment me. I'm not psychically ready to handle the devastating effects on my perception of the universe."

"I won't ... as long as you do me a favor."

Pratt chuckled. "I can say one thing, you haven't lost your nerve."

"What can you find out about this Tolland District in Gowanus?" El Buscador asked.

Pratt raised his eyebrows. "You mean the one you're praising to the heavens."

El Buscador nodded. "The very one."

"Does that mean you don't believe the claims you are making?"

El Buscador decided now was the moment to speak about himself in the third person. "El Buscador is not that big of a fool."

"You might be right about that," said Pratt, peering into his burlap sack of rats. "I've always pegged you for a lesser fool."

"Well, find out what you can for this fool in the rat pit."

"What makes you think I don't know a lot already?" asked Pratt.

El Buscador smiled. "Because I'm certain a good friend like you would tell me right away."

Pratt tied up the sack of rats and gave his full attention to his shadowy mentor. "I wasn't going to tell you until I nailed the information down, but since I see that you might still be more than a PR flak for Tolland, I would poke around the American Concrete Company if I were you. When the boys around the rat pit say the company's not exactly on the up and up, then you know there's some shady business going on."

El Buscador adjusted his fedora. "Are they working for Tolland?"

"They have signed the biggest contract for the District."

"Good," said El Buscador. "Keep digging."

"I will," said Pratt. "Just don't turn into Benedict Arnold."

"My young protégé," said El Buscador, "sometimes a bit of deception is necessary for the larger cause."

"Yeah," said Pratt. "I hear you, but don't you dare become Benedict Thackeray either."

El Buscador grinned, stroked an imaginary beard, and left the underpass of the FDR Drive, away from Pratt's bag of rats toward others of an undetermined nature.

CHAPTER 11
TWO PIES, THREE BIRDS

When El Buscador arrived at Una Nonna's at four in the morning, Nancy was still behind the counter and JoJo was still sleeping in the corner.

Nancy had one pie left, which was too bad, since El Buscador was hoping she was out, so he'd get a fresh, hot one. A pizza, even an Una Nonna's pizza, had to be better straight from the oven, right? Right? Yet with Nancy's limited pie-making skills, he wasn't sure. He gazed upon her smiling visage, then down to her house dress, flour dusted over it like a prominent case of dandruff, and asked, "Don't you ever sleep?"

"I'm sleeping right now."

"That explains a good deal."

"Explains what?"

Nancy was so pleasant and friendly on this very dark Gowanus night, there was no way he would insult her. "It explains why walking into this place feels like a dream."

Nancy beamed at El Buscador. "Exactly! You feel it too, don't you?"

"I do." Since he didn't, El Buscador decided it was best to get down to business. "How about I buy one of your wonderful pies? But I see you only have one left."

"That's OK. I can make more. This one's been sitting here for hours. It's been slow. I'll make some fresh ones."

"Oh, you don't have to make a fresh one for me," he said, piling lie upon lie.

"Don't worry, I won't. The rule is the pies are served in the order they're made."

"That's fine." He inwardly groaned. "It'll be good just heated up."

"Heated up?" Nancy laughed. Her giggle was curiously charming. "We don't reheat pies. That would ruin them."

El Buscador wanted to her ask, just how in God's name does one ruin the worst pie he had ever eaten? Instead, he nodded apologetically, "You're right. I don't know what I was thinking." After Nancy boxed and passed the pie and he handed her the twenty, El Buscador should've followed the path of what every other Una Nonna's customer had taken for the past dozen years and rushed out the door. But instead, he lingered. He took out the glass from his trench coat. "Here's your cup, but before I return it, could I have more of your fine water?"

"Of course," she said.

As she filled from the tap, El Buscador tried to imagine the water pipes stretching as far away from the canal as possible. He stood at the counter because the quality of the seating was commensurate with the quality of the pizza.

Nancy took out the round barely risen discs from the metal containers, sprinkled them with flour, and started slapping and tossing the dough about. El Buscador was astonished how awkward, even spastic, she was in her dough throwing. No wonder all three came out in disparate sizes and thicknesses. "It must take an awful lot of practice to reach your skill level," he said, an impressive measure of earnestness in his voice.

"I was very lucky since I'm a natural." She swirled the sauce on the three pies, the amount dramatically different on each, the mozzarella following with a similarly splattered clustering. El Buscador understood that he was witnessing the most egregious quality control procedures ever to exist in an established, successful business. Apparently, Nancy wasn't paying attention to what she was doing and her next question served as compelling evidence. "Do you know anything about real estate?"

"A decent amount. Why?"

"A guy came in the other day and offered me $2.5 million to buy the place. That seemed like a lot."

"It is," he acknowledged, "but Gowanus is hot right now. Are you going to sell it to him?"

"That's the thing. I told him, 'No.' He came back today ... well, I guess it would be yesterday by now, and offered me three million."

El Buscador whistled. "Whoa. Did you take it?"

"I don't want to take it, but …"

"Three million dollars is a lot of dough."

"That's not it. I don't want to sell this place for anything. I've got something special here."

"You really do." This time El Buscador was telling the truth. It was an entrepreneurial marvel. "So what's your concern?"

"He gave me the impression that it would be a really bad idea not to take his money."

"Oh." El Buscador waited.

"He reminded me of a tough guy from the neighborhood," she said. "But he wasn't from this neighborhood. I think the neighborhood he comes from makes even tougher guys than the ones who come from here."

"So are you going to take the three mil?"

"No. I just can't." She threw the pies in her ovens.

"I think I'll have one of those pies too." El Buscador pointed, leaving no doubt.

Nancy waved her hand to the far left of the oven. "You'll have that one, since it's the pie I put in first."

"Good."

Like a bear out of hibernation, JoJo rose and stretched, rambling over to a big pot on the kitchen stove. He turned on the gas for the burner and put a wooden spoon in the pot.

Seeing the spinach in a separate frying pan, El Buscador was curious. "What are you making there?"

"Clam chowder," said JoJo. "New England."

"You adding that to the menu?"

He laughed heartily and Nancy joined in. "No, this is our dinner."

"Don't you eat pizza?"

"Nah," said JoJo. "Pizza's for the customers. I make chowder for us or get takeout."

"But why not make chowder for the customers? It sure smells good."

"It does, doesn't it?" said JoJo.

"The chowder is for us," said Nancy.

"I see."

JoJo disappeared behind a curtain and returned a few moments later. His prodigiously wide torso (a large delivery box could fit inside his chest) was shirtless and he wore swim trunks. With a towel draped off one shoulder, he walked out the back toward the canal.

El Buscador turned to Nancy. "He's not going in the water, is he?"

"Every morning."

"Why isn't he dead?"

"You kidding? The more he swims in the canal, the stronger he gets."

El Buscador imagined JoJo as a pencil-necked geek prior to his daily ablutions. "He should be suffering from toxic shock."

"That's the problem with people today. They're too afraid of being poisoned. You can't develop immunities if you're too pure."

El Buscador doubted her medical advice, but then again JoJo was quite a specimen. "Excuse me for a moment," El Buscador said to Nancy. He had no choice but to witness the plunge.

As he followed with his sturdy shoes, El Buscador wondered if the swim was the most treacherous part. Through the pall of the lonely darkness and the awakening sun, the barefoot JoJo stepped over coarse chunks of concrete, jagged twists of rebar, angry, heavy machinery parts, and hostile shards of glass like he wandered along a sandy beach. At the sea wall, he dove in without hesitation and broke into a good-looking crawl, the curved arms propelling forward, the legs kicking lavender mist, and the mouth turned upward toward the pungent air. El Buscador feared the resurgence of the Gwaken, although to look at the JoJo, perhaps the Gwaken should be the one afraid. He crossed the canal for what must've been ten laps, hoisted himself back onto the sea wall, and threw the towel across his shoulders, his back so large he looked like he was drying himself off with a hand towel.

"Doesn't that bother your lungs?"

"No," said JoJo. El Buscador studied his blemishless skin.

"Does the canal have any effects on you at all?"

JoJo thought for a good minute. El Buscador could tell the swimmer felt like he was disappointing his questioner. Then his eyes brightened. "The canal wakes me up."

"Wakes you up," El Buscador muttered. "Have you ever tried coffee?"

JoJo laughed and slapped him on the back. El Buscador thought his toes would shoot out of his mouth. When they arrived back at the pizza shack, JoJo headed behind the curtain while Nancy slid out the first pie. It was unmistakably underdone. El Buscador knew there was nothing he could say to convince Nancy to put that pie back into the oven. This Greek tragedy would just have to play out the way the fates allowed. Some part of him desired a parallel universe where he would receive the second or, better yet, the third pie, since they would have a few extra moments in the oven, especially since Nancy took an extraordinary amount of time to get each pie into a box. Instead, he smiled and said, "Now I know why the guy offered three mil for the place."

Nancy looked even happier than usual. But then a frown followed. "What do I do if he comes back?"

El Buscador was uncertain why she sought his advice but knew at a time when he seemed increasingly worthless, he liked it. "I'd act like you're taking his offer seriously. It'll buy you some time. If you want me to come around more often, I'll try to find out who the guy is."

"You'd do that for me?"

"Of course I would." He said it like they were lifelong friends. Then again, besides Pygmalion, she was his only friend in Brooklyn, so that did give Nancy honored status.

He took the pizza from Nancy, piled it atop the other long-cooled pie, handed Nancy another twenty, and headed out into the sunrise. Through the window, he saw JoJo and Nancy gathering at their little table. He decided that must've been their dinner, with lunch following at the regularly scheduled time, and breakfast arriving in the evening. He imagined JoJo on the other side of the canal grabbing egg sandwiches from a sketchy deli and returning by means heroic and disturbing.

As the sun prepared itself for the day, El Buscador walked back to Sackett along the cobbled street to his spot on the bench overlooking the canal. He took the older pie, sluggishly ate a slice as a point of comparison, and then tossed the rest in the beat-up metal can that seemed left just for him. Then he opened the fresh pie and yanked away a gooey section. The pizza could have used ten more minutes in the oven and the slice sagged until it flopped under the weight of its misery. The newly fashioned version was worse than the one he had just eaten and the one from the day before. It was remarkable.

Ben Franklin said hunger is the best pickle, indicating that everything tastes better when you're famished, and that famished condition tends to bring out the flavors in any dish. Old Ben clearly never had an Una Nonna's pie.

Yet El Buscador continued to eat the fresh pie out of morbid curiosity and out of the strange feeling that anything this bad tasting must be some form of medicine. He was adopting a warped version of JoJo's unusual health and wellness philosophy. He knew with this pie weighing down his belly, falling into the canal would mean sinking into its black mayonnaise depths. He would not rise like JoJo or the Gwaken.

So lost in his own world, he didn't recognize Pygmalion until she spoke to him. "I'm starting to wonder about you and that pizza."

El Buscador frowned. "I've been known to indulge in masochistic idiosyncrasies."

"I kind of figured that," she said. "Why else would you keep ending up here?"

El Buscador smirked. "Don't sell yourself short, sister. Watching you paint is the best part of the day."

"Yeah?" said Pygmalion, skepticism in her voice. "That's why you didn't even notice me since you got here." Funny how Pygmalion had grown fond of his attention. She liked the purity of his gaze as it cast upon her work rather than upon her. Normally, the glisten of her espresso brown skin and her arresting green eyes tended to send an observer into a dreamy trance. She was glad to see he did finally show up, since she was proud of the parrot she had added to the ledge. She considered her intricate brushwork capturing the fuchsia, vermillion, and cerulean of the bird's plumage the best she'd ever done. He noted its quality right away and then started asking about her involvement with local groups. He seemed particularly interested in her role at the Gowanus Art Cooperative. He asked for an introduction to the chairwoman.

"O.K.," Pygmalion said tentatively. "I'll introduce you, but it'll be strange seeing you during full daylight."

"Don't worry," El Buscador assured. "I won't really see you during the day. I'll just talk to you. I'll only really *see* you at night." He waved his arm across the growing menagerie to leave no doubt as to his point. Somehow, he got away with such hokum. He was feeling more comfortable in this fresh green breast of the new world.

For the first time since Tolland's men shot at him, he sensed a plan developing his head. It would require relying on many others – something he did not desire, but he had no other choice.

As Pygmalion put the finishing touches on her dazzlingly colorful parrot, he knew he'd better rise from this bench soon. He'd keep an eye out for the man who wanted to overpay Nancy to buy Una Nonna's. He had a strange feeling that man might be someone who had recently fired bullets at him.

CHAPTER 12
THE RETURN TO DELMONICO'S

Thackeray was so happy El Buscador was willing to meet him in the cozy confines of Delmonico's that he embarked on the shocking initiative of paying for drinks. The triple agent had no idea that El Buscador for the first time in his long, earnest life had embraced the guise of a double agent. Hey, even the ever oppositional El Buscador was surprised he could appear so completely compliant in his backing of Tolland's Gowanus District. He wondered if he was more sincere in his support than his conscience suspected. Whichever the case, he presented an authentically conflicted persona to Thackeray.

"No matter how many times I look at the Gowanus plan I can't find problems with it," El Buscador told him. "There is nothing to poke holes through ..." which is why he had needed not only to get the Russian mafia hit removed from his back but also to sidle close enough to Tolland to unearth the insidious corruption in the project, even as he had to show outwardly his unreserved support. El Buscador grudgingly acknowledged to Thackeray, "Tolland's really bestowing something quite wonderful unto the city of New York. Frankly, it's exciting."

As he sipped his sidecar, Thackeray was fascinated by El Buscador's turnaround. Normally, he would not have believed the rebellious underground figure could be so malleable. Then again, a few bullets flying past one's head tends to make even the dissident rethink his positions. El Buscador didn't look like a man playing some game or working an angle. In contrast to the debonair ease of Thackeray who casually stroked his immaculately trimmed salt and pepper beard, El Buscador emitted waves of nervousness. Dare he say, for the first time in Thackeray's long relationship with him, El Buscador radiated weakness. Inwardly, El Buscador warmed with satisfaction that Thackeray conveyed a surface nod of pity and an underlying note of disgust. Tolland would only believe in El Buscador's abject capitulation if Thackeray confirmed his craven descent.

Their drinking down the street from where El Buscador had become an underground celebrity further advanced the cause of unmitigated humiliation. After being only afraid of this one man in his communications, afraid of the legend's famously vigilant zealotry, Thackeray relished in the understanding that a broken El Buscador was good for his blackened catfish soul. Lifting his elbow ever so slightly, Thackeray ordered two more sidecars and regaled El Buscador with a tale of his youth when he first knew that spycraft was his line of work. The CIA had shipped the inexperienced Thackeray out to the Uruguay office and his Russian counterpart Yuri had targeted him and recruited him. Even then, Thackeray oozed corruption. Yuri quickly learned to trust the intelligence Thackeray fed him, chiefly because the information was true – triple agents need to tell the truth 95 percent of the time for the valuable lie to really stick. Thackeray had to be a committed traitor to transcend his treachery.

He knew what a traitor looked like, and El Buscador not only fit the profile, but, more importantly, he drank like one. El Buscador polished off the sidecar with an uncomfortably rapid assault on the glass, relegating his compulsive, guilty mouth to the seasoned ice, the barely melted naked ice.

Thackeray pointed to El Buscador's glass, "Are you having a rough time living with yourself?"

Avoiding his companion's eyes, El Buscador peered through the frozen cubes. "Of course, I am," then fearing he might be laying it on a bit thick, added, "Don't you?"

Thackeray smiled. El Buscador noted inwardly that the triple agent never looked more gleeful. "Me? Oh, no. I've always had a pretty good idea of who I am. But for you, this must be a shock to your system."

El Buscador decided a touch of defiance was in order here. "Not really. As you pointed out when you so kindly agreed to have a cocktail with me at Lavender Lake, Tolland's Gowanus project is so good that if I was truly a man of principal, I had to get behind it." In response to Thackeray's arched eyebrows, he threw in, "Does it feel strange to be on the side of Tolland, my sworn enemy for all these years? Of course it does. But right is right and Tolland's project is right for the city."

Taking just the tiniest sip of his sidecar to impart that, unlike El Buscador, his emotional state did not require compulsive quaffing, Thackeray whispered, "I'm certain that the threats on your life had no influence on your decision, my dear El Buscador."

El Buscador saw this last jibe as his greatest test. He could not overcook his response. He answered, "I'm sure you know me better than that." El Buscador uttered his reply with a suppressed hint of shame, just enough to suggest that at this point Thackeray could not know who he was since El Buscador had never been more uncertain of the direction his moral compass pointed.

Thackeray made little effort to conceal the bubbling vapors of disgust as his head-shaking façade of pity guided them to the dining room for two prime New York strip steaks. Thackeray's parsimoniousness lost a battle with his titanic propensity for *schadenfreude* in paying for the meal after all the years of letting the eminently well-informed, incorruptible El Buscador foot every bill in this century. El Buscador's finest acting job of the evening was hiding his rich enjoyment of the steak dinner, especially as he compared its sturdy, textured tenderness to the flaccid nightmare that was and always will be an Una Nonna's pie. Oh, an Irish coffee followed. Why not? Might as well have this betrayal supper soak fully into the gills.

As Thackeray prattled on from Montevideo to Berlin to Vilnius, El Buscador plotted. He would have to ask more than ever from Tanvi and even more from Pratt, but ultimately Mavis would have to carry the burdens that he had never asked of another in his tattered, compromised life.

First, he'd have to pay a visit to Edmund J. Coppa, since, unlike the others, Eddie had no idea yet of what El Buscador would require of him. Out of the front entrance of Delmonico's, he walked north. The Pint O'Plenty could not have offered a greater contrast to the refined mahogany and the elegant murals of the fabled restaurant. Upon his entering the keg-drenched dive, El Buscador confronted the stale beer and worse riding up the soles of his shoes. He endured two shoves and a belch before he spotted Edmund J. Coppa in the corner of the bar. Even with the sidecars and the Irish coffee,

Eddie's red eyes and blue slouch told El Buscador that his old friend was way ahead of him.

Still, the rest of Eddie looked significantly better than his swelled and bandaged hand. Slapping Eddie on his shoulder and signaling for two pints renowned for their plentifulness, if nothing else, El Buscador asked, "What'd you do to your finger?"

Wrapped in gauze and medical tape, Eddie's left index finger wagged with a startling gout of blood on the cotton nub. Although he claimed he had no idea of the cause of the injury, Eddie understood with troubling clarity that the tip of his index finger had been permanently removed by the teeth of a fellow imbiber who did not like Eddie's description of his mother. Eddie gave El Buscador a shrug like they'd seen each other yesterday instead of the months separation necessitated by his old friend being on the run. "Occupational hazard" was all Eddie offered.

"Which occupation?" Even though he asked, El Buscador didn't want the answer. Hell, what did it matter? Better to get right down to business. "Forget that. Let's try this instead: Could your next occupation be construction? You certainly are no stranger to the tool belt."

"You're not lying." Given his ne'er-do-well existence, Eddie had taken on almost every blue-collar job out there and was good at most of them. "But since when did you start working for an employment agency?"

The beers arrived and El Buscador slid one in front of Eddie. "Since I could use someone at a Tolland construction site."

Eddie rolled his eyes. He'd been involved in El Buscador's best scheme against Tolland and the real estate mogul knew his weathered face, permanent five o'clock shadow and all. "Me? Are you shittin' me? Tolland would never let me onto the site."

"He won't know. You think he concerns himself with such trivial details?"

"And suppose I manage to get on his construction crew. Where would I be heading? I thought all Tolland's projects were shut down." El Buscador smiled in acknowledgment that he was a main reason for Tolland's recent inactivity.

"You're going to Gowanus."

"Brooklyn? Friggin' Brooklyn?"

Trying to hide his amusement, El Buscador shrugged. He had no recollection of Eddie ever venturing off the Isle of Manhattan. "Oh c'mon, don't be a baby."

"Don't be a baby? I've got to go to Gowanus with this?" Eddie brandished the bloody finger like he'd lost a limb.

"Ah, it'll be fun, although you might want to put a new dressing on that thing. Bleeding applicants are generally less appealing to most employees."

Eddie took a healthy slug of his beer; then he did the same with El Buscador's. "Listen to yourself." As he spoke, Eddie gesticulated wildly, the bloody finger dancing like a red conductor's baton. "You don't believe a word of it." Then Eddie chided El Buscador. "Why don't you come with me, hotshot? Let's see how much fun you'll have in Gowanus."

El Buscador grinned. "I'm living there now."

"You're shitting me. You? You're the only guy I know who belongs there less than me. I'd heard the rumors, but I refused to believe them." This time Eddie's arms flailed a bit too wide and he cracked the brute next to him on the cheek.

As Eddie was tossing out an apology, the brute was yelling, yelling like his anger might've been steroid induced. Given the brute's attitude, Eddie withdrew the apology and indicated he might be happy to smack him again. Since he'd been roped into Eddie's ring of hostilities too many times, El Buscador stepped forward, bought the brute and his buddies a round, apologized to the brute, explaining that his friend had been heavily medicated, and deftly ushered Eddie out of the Pint O'Plenty.

He guided his friend straight to Duane Reade for more gauze, ointment, and medical tape. His trip to the pharmacy had the desired effect as Eddie couldn't help but be reminded of the time El Buscador saved his life. On that occasion, El Buscador found Eddie outside the Pint O'Plenty bleeding from many parts of his body. Even as he scowled over the thought of working in Gowanus, Eddie knew he could not refuse El Buscador, as once again he was under his shadowy friend's care. Taking Eddie to the Cedar Local and ordering two Guinnesses from the bar, El Buscador led his friend to the bathroom and redressed his wounded finger. The loss of the index's tip was bad, but the smashed blackened fingernail looked much worse. Back in Gowanus, El Buscador would have to buy more supplies and make sure Eddie changed the dressing every day. One infected finger could spoil the entire operation.

Returning to the dark, foamy pints, they took to the barstools that offered respite for their elbows and their asses. Looking down at the wound, El Buscador nodded at his friend. "Eddie, I need you for a different type of fight."

Eddie took a sip of Guinness, froth coating the bottom whiskers of his mustache. "I'll be there, but my experiences with you tell me I'd be much better off having another finger hacked off."

CHAPTER 13
NEWLAND ON THE BLOCK

Cynthia Newland was only moderately alarmed when the handsome young man approached her. Before prison, the occurrence was common. Although her fortieth birthday marked an emotional earthquake during her incarceration, constituting shocks at the highest needle point on the Geiger counter, Cynthia remained beautiful. And she had been very rich, which once upon a time made her more beautiful. With her fortunes dramatically diminished, she did not expect to see such a handsome face above an impeccably cut suit within a month of her freedom.

When Pratt put on his dark gray Armani this morning, he was pleasantly surprised how damn good he looked, just like the old days when he was the most famous columnist in New York and CNN booked him whenever they needed a bump in their ratings. And today, even the well-trimmed beard (for the first time in months not rat-pit scraggly) could not hide his youthful magnetism. His greeting to Cynthia was simple. "I just want to thank you for the remarkable buildings you have given to New York." To say Cynthia Newland's skyscrapers were remarkable was quite a stretch, although any observer would have to admit that they were not nearly as awful as Tolland's. But he needed an excuse to greet Cynthia as he softly slipped the note into her hand. When Pratt disappeared from the Midtown streets, she took the liberty to read the message, thinking it might be a dinner invitation.

She was wrong.

The scrawl was elegant.

I will start with a disappointment. I am not the dashing bachelor who handed you this note. My apologies for the bait and switch, but you will find that in the end more baiting and switching will ultimately serve in your favor. I have a proposition for you that will give you a golden opportunity and allow a mutual enemy to suffer greatly. We must meet away from the security cameras. At 8 p.m., I will be waiting for you in the Ramble of Central Park. Bring a flashlight and follow the tags at the bottom of the lampposts. Each lamppost lists the approximate cross street and how far you are in the park's interior from the avenues, going east to west. I'll be standing at the lamppost tagged 77.41 - or if you need old-fashioned directions, that's around 77th Street, in the middle of the park, slightly to the east. You'll recognize me by my trench coat and fedora. Feel free to bring whatever weapons you'd like to feel safe, just don't bring anyone else with you. We have one shot at making this work.

From the note, she was going to meet either El Buscador or someone pretending to be El Buscador. Whichever the case, it wasn't good. If it was someone pretending, then Tolland had set a trap. If it was the legend himself, then Tolland could still have set a trap, especially since the news had got out that El Buscador had just sold his soul to the real estate mogul and was now giving glowing tours for investors of the new massive Gowanus project. She went anyway, since she was desperate enough to take a risk based on this note, a note which smelled of roasted nuts.

•　•　•　•　•

Cynthia had to beam her flashlight onto a dozen different lampposts before catching El Buscador's trench-coated silhouette, his fedora casting angular shadows across the mist-ridden evening. Something about El Buscador hurtled any encounter back many decades. Yet she could not be swept up in the romance of the rendezvous.

"Were you sent by Tolland to set me up again?" she asked, hardened, her right hand in her own trench coat, a Burberry limited edition, significantly darker and a few thousand dollars more than El Buscador's. She acted like she held a pistol, which made El Buscador feel more secure – she prepared herself for traps; caution would be a friend to both them. "I heard you turned to the dark side."

Acknowledging the gun outline with a subtle nod, he said, "I see. Word travels fast."

Cynthia smiled, her lipstick glistening. A slight toss of her brunette locks gave El Buscador the impression he had encountered a more animated Kardashian. "Yeah, when the biggest enemy of my enemy joins Tolland, I tend to notice."

At one point, Cynthia and Tolland had been lovers. After their romance fell apart, Cynthia was determined to gain majority ownership of his flagship property, the Tollandia. She was very close, 49th percent close; she almost bought the final needed two percent from New York's other great captain of real estate Matt Aruba. She envisioned that the crowning achievement of her life was to change the name of the Tollandia to the Newlandia. However, when Aruba rejected her advances, Tolland not only squeezed her out, but planted enough oxycodone on her to get her imprisoned on the first crack.

After she was released, Cynthia had some reason to hope. During her prison time, El Buscador and *The Herald* had blocked Tolland's monstrosity on Canal Street and severely damage his reputation, particularly through the revelation that Tolland ran a rat-breeding operation downtown. Even better, Matt Aruba began courting Cynthia from the moment she was released from prison. He too had been burned by Tolland in a real estate venture and now regretted not giving Cynthia the controlling two percent. Naturally, El Buscador knew all about Cynthia's rekindled relationship with Aruba (thanks to a four Moscow Mule lunch with Thackeray).

From his years as the Tour Guide, he had a way of speaking one-on-one that gave the participant the impression she was the smartest person he'd conversed with in years. "I know you're the sharp businesswoman. The word even in my underground world is that there's nobody better. I want you to think carefully, like you were negotiating a big deal, which I would say right now you are. You are talking to El Buscador. You know what I have done. I want you to think through the many reasons I might join up with Tolland."

He watched her evolving expressions. She was really quite stunning. Another man might've had romantic notions. El Buscador had something else in mind. "I see," she hesitated, "some possibilities."

"Only a man with Tolland's ego could think he could change El Buscador." He tapped the rim of his fedora, the same hat he'd worn for years on his very same head.

She nodded, her dark eyes sparkling with something that approached acceptance. "What is it you want from me?"

He met her gaze. "May I take you on a secret tour? I want to talk to you about some things nobody else knows."

"Not Tolland."

"Well, he doesn't know now, and I assure you when he does know, he won't be happy."

"Then lead on."

He guided her up and down the many hilly paths of the Rambles, telling her tales of how the designers of Central Park, Olmstead and Vaux, sought to make this section of the park resemble a mysterious trek through hidden forests and babbling brooks. Then they crossed 79th Street and cut just west of the massive structure of the Met, Cleopatra's Needle rising up to pierce the night, the ancient obelisk giving El Buscador a whole new tale to tell of the dramatic voyage from Egypt to its erection at this very site.

He kept telling stories as they made their way north following the reservoir on the east, then cutting west of the Harlem Meer, traversing more than thirty blocks to get to their destination, where business could be engaged. At a mighty stone structure, he pointed and pronounced, "Here we are. Welcome to the oldest building in Central Park."

Cynthia raised her eyebrows. "I thought you just told me that Cleopatra's Needle was the oldest in Central Park."

"Oh, so you were listening to me. Cleopatra's Needle is indeed the oldest edifice in Central Park. Who can beat the Egyptians, right? The Blockhouse is the oldest structure actually built in Central Park. Originally it was hastily constructed for the War of 1812."

"You took me all the way up here to see this?

"No, I took you all the way up here to go inside."

"Do you have a permit?"

"I am El Buscador."

"And you don't need no stinking permits."

He did not answer. He simply walked to the iron gate and she followed. Pulling a Bogota pick from a small case, he took about thirty seconds before he popped the lock (he had practiced last night). Cynthia followed him as he talked about the garrisons stationed here, about the munitions that had been stored.

Cynthia was much more interested in the two folding chairs and the screw-together table in the middle of the fort. "Is that for us?"

"It must be, since you're the first person I've taken here." El Buscador pulled a chilled bottle of Sancerre from his backpack and two wine glasses, placing them on the cocktail table. From his pockets came packets of waxed paper with cheese wedges from Bourgogne and Umbria. From the backpack emerged two thin, small baguettes, which he promptly broke apart, and a corkscrew, which he promptly applied to the Sancerre. He even pulled out an old inn lantern and lit it on the table, transporting them back centuries.

"I'm presuming we have arrived at the business portion of the tour."

"We have indeed. But first, let's have a toast." He poured the Sancerre, which he had chilled so ruthlessly that it created fog and even a rebellious bead or two on the wine glasses. Lifting his glass, he pronounced. "To friends, forged from an enemy."

"Let us hope," said Cynthia, clinking her glass to his and sipping lightly.

"How much do you know about the Tolland District?"

"I've heard Tolland say it's a real departure for him, that's it's going to change the course of architecture for the entire country, no the entire world. Blah, blah, blah."

"Yet Tolland would be right if the architectural plans designed by the Graffiti Sisters for him are realized."

"So you *have* switched teams."

"Hear me out. The architectural renderings are magnificent, so magnificent that not only will Tolland have a very hard time financing the project, I am certain he has no intention of spending that kind of money. Even if he thought it is as wondrous as I think it is, I know he is genetically incapable of spending that freely. Let's just put it this way: the New York City public and the people of Gowanus will benefit from the proposed district much more than Tolland ever will."

"So why are you supporting it?"

"Because I think the project can be completed without Tolland being in charge of it."

"Yeah?" she asked, her eyes hardening. "And how do you imagine that?"

"Well, this is the part where you come in and requires you to move very quickly if you're on board. I would need you to work with your business associates, especially the ones with deep pockets," both of them knew that Matt Aruba's name would not enter this conversation, "and quietly buy up shares of Crystal Enterprises, which is the financing arm of the project. You and your associates cannot have their names attached to the purchases. In fact, if those purchases could look like they've been snapped up by a Saudi prince or a Russian oligarch or a Chinese technocrat, all the better. But you have to move quickly because the share prices are tremendously low."

Cynthia smiled and sipped some Sancerre. "And whose fault is that? Between you and *The Herald*, the hedge fund guys think Tolland is *persona non grata*."

"But when the architectural designs are made public in the next few days all that will change. Don't be alarmed when you hear me sing my praises for the Graffiti Sisters' plan, don't be alarmed when I give credit to Tolland for his daring risk. Don't be alarmed when the *Times* architectural critic describes Tolland as the most serious contributor to New York since Rockefeller,"

"Share prices will shoot through the roof."

"In a few days they will, which is why you need to make sure you and your associates snap up as many shares as you can. Tolland thinks that thirty percent is enough for a controlling interest. I would tend to think the only percentage sufficient would be 51 percent. If you get close to that number, I am confident there will another time when the price will drop dramatically again."

"Did anyone ever tell you that you remind them of Thackeray?"

El Buscador grabbed his chest. "Are you trying to wound me?"

Cynthia's answer was a giggle.

El Buscador pretended to be exasperated. "Would Thackeray take you here and serve you wine and cheese?"

"He might if he could figure out a way to remove his rear end from the barstool at Delmonico's."

"Thackeray?" He paused, "of all people, why him?"

"You seem to do a lot of plotting."

"Much more than I used to. Tolland tends to require all types of Machiavellian machinations."

"I get it."

"Are you on board?"

Cynthia took another sip of wine, finishing the glass. "You know what, I think I am."

"Good. Can we meet again in a week?"

"A week? What on earth for?"

"This all is going to go down must faster than you think. There are a lot of moving parts to the operation."

"Am I one of the moving parts?"

"Cynthia, you are most important moving part of them all."

She lifted her glass and El Buscador poured more Sancerre. "Look at you. What a charmer. I've heard half the women who take a tour with you fall in love."

"Yeah, and the other half ..."

"They want to drop you down a hole and pour hot oil in until you're fried to a crisp."

"Jeez, good thing I don't rely on Yelp for my business."

Cynthia sprawled back in her chair, calm and relaxed, like she was on vacation. She broke open the end of the baguette and slid in a wedge of Bourgogne. "We can hang out here for a little while, right?"

"Of course, what's the point of entering a hidden place if you're going to rush right out of it?"

As El Buscador listened to her speak of time in prison, they killed off the Sancerre and he pulled out a flask of Grand Marnier. "Sorry. I failed to bring snifters."

Pushing her glass forward, Cynthia conceded, "I guess I'll have to rough it." As he poured, she commanded, "Tell me a story, mystery man. Everyone says you have wonderful stories. Why haven't you told me one?"

"I don't have to tell you a story." He opened his arms. "The story is right within these walls. Are you up to rising for a moment?"

Trying the Grand Marnier, Cynthia blinked and answered, "Why not, that is as long as it's not too far."

"No, it's not too far. Could you pick up that lantern and walk it to that wall over there?" He pointed to the left. "Then look down."

Last night, El Buscador planted the artifacts like he had for so many other secret tours. "I see a scalpel and a pair of tongs," Cynthia said. "Did I miss anything?"

"No, you've found it. Bring them back here and I'll tell you all about the brief time when the Blockhouse was a scientific laboratory."

"Really. I find that unbelievable."

"Yet true. Back in the beginning of the previous century, the scientist, one Yuri Breslow, had developed the first rhytidectomy technique, more commonly known as the Face Lift."

That hooked Cynthia, especially since she'd been contemplating one herself (her good friends told her she should get one before her looks started to fade). "Did he invent it for his wife?"

"Funny you should ask that," said El Buscador. "In fact, he had no interest in giving his wife a face lift. Georgette, that was her name, was such a beauty and twenty years his junior that a face lift for her never entered his mind."

"Oh," said Cynthia, slightly disappointed.

"But she had an entirely different problem."

That rallied Cynthia. "Do tell," she said, doing her best sophisticated doyenne routine. "What problem could a beautiful young woman have?"

"Well, despite her perfectly cut figure, her sparkling eyes, her sweet little nose, and her luxurious auburn hair, she possessed a little birthmark on her right cheek disrupting her otherwise flawless alabaster skin."

"I don't get it. Was the birthmark ugly? Most people consider a birthmark sexy."

"Not Yuri Breslow. No, the birthmark was not ugly. The few who got close enough to Georgette thought it looked like a cute little hand. But not Yuri."

"And what did Georgette think of her birthmark?"

"At first she was happy with it." El Buscador lifted his glass and clinked his Grand Marnier with Cynthia's. "But Yuri kept staring at the birthmark, initially with minor dissatisfaction and later with scarcely repressed disgust. Ultimately, Georgette begged Yuri to invent a procedure to remove the birthmark."

"I think I know how this story ends."

"You just might. You want to give it a shot."

"Sure." She lifted her glass and El Buscador emptied the flask. He started to wonder how he was going to get her home. Cynthia took a sip and nodded with blissful approval. "Yuri is overconfident. He thinks after the facelift that this procedure will be easy. But the operation goes terribly wrong.

Georgette is horribly disfigured, her beautiful face scarred beyond recognition. And then she throws herself into the Harlem Meer, drowning away the disgrace, the judgment, and the expectation of perfection that all women must hold deeply within their breasts."

El Buscador lifted his glass to her. "Boy, that's remarkably close to what actually happened. In fact, I like it better than the truth. Georgette never got a chance to see the results because she died right on the operating table. In the end Yuri couldn't figure out if Georgette died because she didn't want to live without her birthmark or whether something in that birthmark was vital to her very survival. Had the little hand come from a greater force beyond her?"

"Ah, you brought me to the Blockhouse to tell me about how an obsessively controlling man ruined a young woman's life."

"No, my dear Cynthia, I brought you here to discuss with you how we can bring down an obsessively controlling man who ruined one beautiful woman's life, at least temporarily."

"I see," said Cynthia.

Overall, El Buscador was pleased with how the evening transpired. Hearing the story would assure that Cynthia wouldn't get cold feet tomorrow. Good thing nobody read Hawthorne anymore. He had a feeling she'd be on the computer buying Crystal Enterprises stock tonight.

He led her back out of the Blockhouse, closing the big iron doors and snapping the lock, and found a cab for her right at 110th Street, giving the driver a twenty. He offered his usual regrets, that he wished he could escort her back to her apartment, but the secrecy of this operation made clear they could not be seen together.

When the cab drove off, he was tempted to return to the Blockhouse and sleep there. But Gowanus was now his home, so he walked the 50 blocks south through the park to 63rd Street until he headed east to hit the F train at Lex. From there, after waiting twenty minutes for the train, he'd only be on the subway for 16 stops. That was the easy part though. When he returned to Gowanus, he'd have to find some place to sleep.

CHAPTER 14
THE JOURNEY TO THE UNSEEN

To get a break from the desolate loneliness that research investigations often require, Mavis started showing up at Jeanne's basement apartment. From her leather briefcase, she pulled out thick reams of documents downloaded from city files. Meanwhile, Jeanne scrolled around the internet forever searching for dirt on Tolland, just then lasering in on Gowanus. Casting a wider net, Mavis scrutinized all of Brooklyn, trying to unearth hidden properties that Tolland acquired.

Neither Mavis nor Jeanne would perform the daring feats of El Buscador, who'd hop over a chain-link fence or break into a building without thinking twice. They didn't sneak about hidden underground corridors or have secret rendezvous with long-legged women and short-bearded men. Instead, they doggedly perused, endlessly scrolling and turning pages, work that left them exhausted and hostile.

After the exposés *The Herald* had run on Tolland, the real estate mogul stopped putting land and projects in his name. But Tolland being Tolland, he couldn't resist titling each of his operations as a tribute to his ego. Originally, peacocks and rats appeared prominently. Now he had moved on to other terminology. Jeanne and Mavis were struggling to adjust to the new company names.

"What do you think of *megastructure*?" asked Mavis. "You think he would use that?"

As Jeanne grew increasingly frustrated, she turned proportionately surly. "Don't be stupid."

Mavis wanted to duct tape her mouth. "I'm not being stupid. It doesn't hurt to throw out a few names. Better than groping in the dark like you do."

Jeanne pointed her crooked index finger at Mavis's noble head. "I'm the best groper in the dark in this entire city. And that's saying something."

Mavis scoffed. "As long as you're groping yourself."

Jeanne grumbled and scrolled, pouring over lists and documents in every direction. Now it would be a race. She would be damned if Mavis would find a Tolland property before her. But she required some fortification, so she wheeled back from her desk toward the liquor cabinet. "How 'bout a taste?"

"Whattaya got?"

"What do you care?" Jeanne asked. "When have you ever turned down a drink from me?"

"Just curious," said Mavis.

"Uh huh." Jeanne pulled out two glasses and took out some Sambuca. She tended to rotate from Pernod to Ouzo to Sambuca, a wobbly licorice carousel. Sometimes after she poured a glass, she made a point of forgetting which bottle she grabbed, so she could try to identify the liqueur by taste alone. She spilled five fingers in both rocks glasses – Jeanne didn't mess around when it came to cordials. "Here, grope this."

Mavis snickered and toasted. "Here's to stupid questions for stupid friends."

Jeanne clanked her glass to Mavis's and said, "You ain't kidding sister."

Mavis sipped her drink and looked back down at her intimidating pile of listings, her finger gliding along, line by line, looking for a name that could be something. What confused her the most was his naming Crystal Enterprises the lead organization for the Tolland District in Gowanus. That didn't fit into his other patterns. The name wasn't macho enough. Jeanne didn't have the same concerns Mavis did in her research; she kept scrolling on the computer, searching for the hidden spots where Tolland gained financing and which crews he'd hired. With enough exhaustive effort, Jeanne would eventually find what she was after and deliver to El Buscador the ammunition he would need if he wanted to uncover the skeletons buried in the Tolland District. But as Mavis stared at entry after entry on page after page, she murmured the names of dry, miserable capitalism: Friendly Equity, Elegant Fiduciaries, Admissions Incorporated, and Unexpected Company. So many names unattached to Tolland. She wasn't sure what she was looking for, except she knew the man, and she would recognize whatever term he fashioned.

Then, she read a business name she didn't understand; Venandi Inc. had just the right combination of familiar and distant that compelled her to look up the word. She first tried to translate *Venandi* from Italian on Google. When she came up empty, Mavis grumbled. Moments later, her eyes opened wide. "I wonder," she said. Then she translated the word into Latin and got "hunter."

"Bingo," she said. While Tolland wasn't exactly celebrated as a sportsman, he was renowned in his efforts in trying to convince people that he was a great white hunter. Now flagging the property right next to the Barclays Center, she scrolled about furiously until she discovered Jagermeister Realty. Just to confirm her suspicions, she translated *Jagermeister* from German to get Hunt Master – the term was more than a painful liqueur. That property followed an intriguing path on Atlantic Avenue about a quarter mile from the other.

Those two discoveries sent Mavis on a furious scouring for the next hour, scrolling and searching. She looked up all the names for hunter in the European language – *cazador* for Spanish, *chasseur* for French, *kynigos* for Greek, even *okhotnik* for Russia – but none of names surfaced in her investigations. God, it was frustrating. What the hell did Tolland have up his sleeve? Even two more refills of Sambuca did little to soothe her.

Mavis needed to get some fresh air. Hell, for some reason, she wanted to stare at that dirty canal. Her attentions moved from the indifferent printouts to the hostile, yet active Jeanne. When Mavis asked if she'd like to come out with her, Jeanne almost fell out of her wheelchair. Mavis told her she'd help her up the stairs. They were in this together. Mavis asked again. "Would you come out with me, Jeanne?" The way Mavis asked moved Jeanne. She seemed vulnerable, like she really needed the companionship. As Mavis waited for Jeanne's response, the softness in her eyes made her more beautiful. Luke never asked Jeanne to come out.

Jeanne answered, "Why not?"

For the first time in ten years, except for trips to the doctor's office, Jeanne left her apartment. She did her best not to act out of place or seem excited. Mavis hired a Lyft driver to take them over the Brooklyn Bridge, across the river, toward Gowanus.

That brought an end to those three minutes of warmth and sweetness. Jeanne groused. "I finally agree to go out and this is where you take me? Not

Broadway, not Lincoln Center, not even to Saks or Rockefeller Center. But Gowanus? Are you out of your goddamn mind? No wonder you're attracted to that idiot Luke."

As usual, Mavis ignored Jeanne's rantings. "I thought you might like to see the Gwaken."

"A sturgeon? That's what you're showing me? Why don't you just take me to the aquarium in Coney Island? At least I'll see a few seals in the bargain."

Mavis shook her head and pointed out the window. "Do you have any idea what time it is? I know you haven't been out since Reagan was president, but I think you can still recognize darkness. I'm not sure you know this, but the aquarium is usually closed during these hours."

Jeanne snickered. "You're telling me that we're going to see a sturgeon in the dark?"

"Well, they've installed these new instruments called streetlights, so we should be able to see the Gwaken. Hey, I think they even had it in your day – they were gas flames back then."

"Boy, you can be awfully snotty when you want to be, Mavis," said Jeanne. "Your reporters must hate working for you. Oh my, I can't wait to see the sturgeon." Mavis kept quiet for a minute, so Jeanne filled up the silence. "A sturgeon. What an awful fish. They're only good for caviar. You couldn't take me out for caviar, could you?"

"No, I couldn't." Mavis spent the rest of the time thinking about what she would do once they got out of the Lyft and propped Jeanne back into her wheelchair. It wouldn't be too hard to roll Jeanne right into the canal. The driver dropped them at the apron of the Carroll Street Bridge. Mavis made a special effort to wheel roughly over the cobblestones. If Jeanne was going to be miserable, then Mavis would do it right.

They crossed over toward the Bond Street apartments and the adjoining the canal walk where the Gwaken rarely appeared. Mavis rolled her around there just to build up the suspense and show Jeanne that she'd have to earn her chance to spot the creature. They then turned around and headed further inland up Bond Street, rolling on into each of the dead-end streets that terminated at the canal.

As she looked around at the industrial buildings with an expression of less than wonder, Jeanne muttered just loud enough for Mavis to hear.

"Well, I'm glad you took me here because if this is what I've been missing, then I think I'll be content with never getting out of my apartment again."

Mavis kept pushing Jeanne over the hemorrhoid-inducing cobblestones and Jeanne kept bitching. "And this is the shithole where Luke is living now? No wonder he's gone off the rails."

"But if you see the Gwaken, you will understand."

The journey continued in and out of dead-end streets, Jeanne grumbling all the way. Each time Mavis took Jeanne right up to the edge of the canal; they peered into the water and saw nothing. If both were honest, they spent as much time looking behind them, hoping to catch sight of El Buscador, as they did in search of the sturgeon surfacing before them.

When Mavis pushed Jeanne back out of DeGraw, a young male passerby noticed the sultry sway of Mavis's hips as she pressed the wheelchair forward. He said, "Mama, when you're done with that nursing home care, you can tuck me in."

Mavis gave him a stare the stupid would interpret as sexy, but the wise would understand as scary. "Tuck you in? That's my sister I'm taking care of. You best leave me alone if you want all your bones intact."

After the suitor disappeared, Jeanne reached back and patted Mavis's hand. "You called me sister."

Mavis laughed. "I've called you a lot of other things too."

Twisting in and out of the cobbled streets, they got a chance to observe the local population. Some were smartly dressed in business suits, others in more casual slacks, still others in stylish jeans. An unusually high percentage wore some form of hat. Almost everyone seemed neat and clean, but the nearly universal bemused expression that marked the faces of locals was what really stood out.

Their eyes smiled like they walked through a pleasant fog. Jeanne was the first to speak of the bizarre phenomenon. "I know I've been cooped up in my apartment for a long time, but does everybody in the outside world have such goofy, happy faces?"

Mavis nodded in recognition. "Only if they're stoned."

Jeanne twisted her neck to look back up at Mavis with genuine curiosity. "Are they?"

"We've run a bunch of stories on this new product that has become all the rage in this area," said Mavis. "They call it Ganja Ganache; it's made in one of the legal pot states. Some say it comes from Massachusetts; others say it's from as far away as California. Anyway, those who've gotten their hands on the smuggled Ganja chocolate bars claim they're the best thing they've ever eaten. They're delicious and they give the most pleasant high without much of a pot hangover. Millennials like it even more than spiked seltzer."

"Ganja Ganache," muttered Jeanne. "Stupid name."

"The cool cats call it GG," said Mavis, an ironic smile emerging.

"Jesus," said Jeanne, rolling her eyes.

"Although you have to admit," said Mavis, "walking around with all of these happy, stoned people is kind of a trip and a half, like we've entered into an experimental film."

Jeanne countered. "You have to remember that just being outside for me is an experimental film, so this is freaking me out a little."

Mavis wondered whether El Buscador noticed the spaced-out condition of the Gowanus citizenry. She meant to point it out in their walks, but El Buscador was always so focused on the business at hand, whether that be strategizing or conducting his bizarre version of flirting, that she never got the chance. Although El Buscador was incredibly observant in so many ways, he was prone to astounding bouts of blindness to the commonplace. No, Mavis decided that El Buscador had no idea that most of Gowanus had GG on them as surely as they had a Metrocard. In his world, he assumed everyone was tripping, so why would he notice something as dull and profound as communal contentment?

After about an hour wandering up against dead ends for a Gwaken that wouldn't surface, Jeanne turned her head back to her escort and asked, "Are you ready to give up?"

"No," said Mavis, "are you?"

"Me?" asked Jeanne. "Of course I'm ready to give up. I was ready to give up the moment you got me into that stupid car."

"But this will be worth the journey. How about we go to the bar for a while and then we'll come back out to see if the Gwaken shows up?"

"Nah," said Jeanne. "I want to go home."

Mavis relented and ordered another Lyft. As they returned to Bond Street, Mavis spotted one Edmund J. Coppa rushing toward 9th Street and the F train, clearly on his way across the river to the Pint O'Plenty. She told Jeanne of the Coppa sighting.

"Well, it's not the Gwaken, but at least it's something," said Jeanne, rallying a bit.

"You think so?" asked Mavis, encouraging Jeanne to state the obvious.

"Coppa's not here for the cheap beer," Jeanne said, smirking, "although you can never tell with Coppa. No, if he's in Gowanus, then Luke has been making plans, which is better than the aimless thrashing I feared." Mavis patted Jeanne on the shoulder reassuringly. It was nice to know that they weren't the only ones left to do the thinking.

As they rode back out of Brooklyn, Mavis pointed to some of the sights and buildings.

"You do remind me a bit of him," Jeanne said.

Mildly horrified by the thought, Mavis again kept her own counsel.

Jeanne did not. "I'm sure there is something allegorical that we can take from our journey today. And I'm sure your allegory will be completely different from mine. I think mine is to stop wasting your time looking for shit."

"Yeah," said Mavis, "and if we don't do that, what do we do?"

Earnest and exasperated, Jeanne looked at Mavis. "Hell if I know."

CHAPTER 15
CONCRETE BEATINGS AND SUBURBIA

El Buscador realized he had been growing reckless in his old age. To find out the information, he should've waited for Edmund J. Coppa, who, as a member of the construction crew, would know. Or at least he should've waited, like he had arranged, for Mavis, so they could investigate the grounds of the American Concrete Company together. But, hey, the facility was one block over from the canal, and he always believed in arriving early – El Buscador would never leave a lady waiting.

What did it hurt if he snooped around a bit before Mavis arrived? As always, he walked through the warehouse like he worked there. He didn't know what he was looking for, but if Pratt told him that Tolland signed a big contract with the firm, it must mean something. Most of the businesses around Gowanus were legitimate, but it'd be just like Tolland to find the exception.

The factory had its fair share of cement mixers and framing boards along with stone crushers and limestone bins. Rock dust rose to the rafters and rendered the air soft and hazy. He was contemplating how much more sand was at the facility than cement when the blow came. El Buscador involuntarily reached for the back of his head as he fell with a thud.

"What'd you hit him for?" asked one man in a hardhat.

"He doesn't belong here," answered the other.

"Shouldn't you have asked him what he wanted?"

"Nah. Let's drag him out back. Whatever he wanted, he don't want it anymore."

Light rain drizzled on the crown of El Buscador's bloody skull. He didn't dream of Edwin Clark Litchfield.

When Mavis arrived at the front of the American Concrete Company, she immediately feared something was wrong. El Buscador was always exactly where he said he'd be. She knew it was unwise to walk inside the warehouse. Instead, she strolled the perimeter. After ten minutes of trying her best to appear like she was taking a casual ramble through an industrial wasteland, she came across El Buscador, his bloody skull propped against a dumpster. She grabbed his neck, felt the steady throb, and then listened to his unhappy breaths.

Mavis considered an ambulance but knew that El Buscador would never forgive her. She couldn't contact Melville to take him to the Explorer's Club and get him patched up there, since he was sailing the East River. Pratt was too far away. Hypothesizing that his wounds were not life-threatening, at least not at this moment, she called her sister Regina who said she was willing to help. Then Mavis tapped on the Lyft app. The car arrived in five minutes. She paid the driver an extra twenty to help her get the man collapsed against the dumpster into his car. He gave Mavis a towel. "Make sure he doesn't get any blood on the back seat."

"I understand. Bloody seats are bad for business."

The car ride out to Long Island took longer than expected because it always does, what with the BQE and the LIE forever in traffic snarls. An hour and a half later, they arrived at Regina's home in Carle Place. As Mavis and the Lyft driver carried El Buscador to the couch, already covered with towels and sheets, Regina asked her sister, "You're not going to get me in trouble, are you?"

"Don't worry. This guy doesn't even exist. Just take care of him."

Regina methodically examined her patient, her years as an emergency room nurse and her subsequent office work as a nurse practitioner graced her movements with a calm efficiency. After she cleaned the wound and injected medications, Regina told Mavis, "The best news, he has very little swelling. I'm going to have to put a butterfly stitch on his skull. The skin's too thin for anything else."

El Buscador soon started thrashing and muttering, so Regina administered a sedative to quiet him. Mavis smiled, "Boy, I've been wanting to do that for months."

After a long night's sleep, El Buscador awoke to the whirr of cars. He did not know he was snoozing right next to the horribly misnamed Old Country

Road. Here, along a three-mile stretch, almost every chain store in America put down roots and the suburbanites brought their minivans and their SUVs to fill up their large houses with multipacks of comfort. Somehow the horn-beeping and brake-screeching made his city slumbers seem comparatively hushed in urban serenity.

Unfortunately, Mavis decided to visit El Buscador when he was in a quite a mood. "Where the hell am I?"

"On earth, alive."

"Are you certain this is earth? Sure looks like hell to me."

Mavis asked him, "Do you know what happened to you?"

"No," said El Buscador. "Where am I?"

"Long Island."

"Jesus Christ."

"You took quite a blow to your head," said Mavis.

"Really? Long Island? God, I think this is the worse place I've ever been to in my life."

"This from a man whose chosen home is Gowanus."

"There I can see the virulence," said El Buscador.

"What are you talking about?" asked Mavis, trying not to get too riled over his ingratitude. "You just slept here for 12 hours. I bet that's the longest you've slept straight in your entire miserable existence."

"That's because I thought I was dead," said El Buscador. "I didn't think there was a need to wake up from that. Apparently, I was wrong."

"If you don't shut up, I'm going to take you to the Roosevelt Field Mall later," said Mavis. "You think you're having problems adjusting here." El Buscador looked at Mavis in horror as she pressed her advantage. "It's right around the corner, only a mile away. That means with the traffic, it's just about a half an hour in the car to get there and another half an hour to park. I could rock your pathetic little world in an hour."

Tenderly touching the back of his head, El Buscador bent his chin downward. "Why don't you just start the car in the garage? I'll crawl out there and let the carbon monoxide do the rest."

"Jesus, who knew the legendary El Buscador was such a drama queen, an ungracious one at that."

Holding his head in shame, El Buscador realized that Mavis was right. What the hell was wrong with him? His knee-jerk reaction was to blame suburbia, but he knew it was something else. "Mavis, I am truly sorry. How'd I get here anyway?"

"I took you."

"I know, but how? You don't have a car and I was knocked out."

"I had the Lyft driver help," said Mavis.

"He took you here," said El Buscador. "It must've been a fortune." He reached in his pocket, happy to see he wasn't robbed when he was assaulted, pulling out a wad of twenties.

Mavis shook her head. "I don't want your money. I don't even want your gratitude. But I'd like you to stop being a jackass."

He laughed. "You're right. You're right. Again, I am so sorry. Thank you for everything you've done for me and thank your sister."

"You can thank her yourself, now that it seems you stopped acting like an asshole."

El Buscador smiled. When Regina entered, he had returned to his charming self, asking her about the physician she worked with and how often she visited the island's beaches. He asked where she would like a tour in the city; when she told him to decide, he spent the next hour quizzing her about her interests and likes, incrementally building an itinerary in his head. As he traversed Manhattan in his memory, he fell back to sleep and didn't awaken until the next day. That following morning he stared out into the suburban abyss and cried out for Mavis. When he insisted he had to return to Gowanus, neither Mavis nor Regina objected.

Still, the man transformed into a much more grateful and gracious patient as he rode in the back seat peering out onto one massive expressway after another. Oh, El Buscador didn't even balk when Regina stopped at the nursery on 3rd Avenue so Mavis could buy a whole bunch of plants. As Mavis told him, "Gowanus could use some beautification."

"You think you can just plant that on the streets?"

"You think anyone's going to mind?"

Remembering an alley off Nevins Street, El Buscador could see that Mavis might be onto something. He wasn't too happy she was sharper than he thought he was. The sisters dropped him off at Whole Foods and made him promise to chow down on *mei fun*. What the hell was happening to him?

As he wandered outside of Whole Foods, he tried to recall the chain of events at the American Concrete Company. He was disappointed in himself for not hearing his assailant. Yes, the place had been very noisy, but when was the last time he let anyone sneak up on him. Yet, a piece of him was glad for the beating. It signaled that perhaps Tolland was once again up to no good. Any concrete company that secretive must be awfully shady.

Stewing over a soba bowl, he contemplated what he should do next. He didn't like to admit how his virtual homelessness was wearing on him. He always thought of himself as a nomad. But if the truth be told, his temperament was better suited to wandering around the Roosevelt Field Mall than to riding the rails as a hobo. El Buscador struggled over whether to move into the old Coignet Stone Company Building. Compared to the hovels he'd been tossed out of, the place looked downright palatial and its next-door neighbor was, Egads, Whole Foods, the lovechild of suburbanites and vegan socialites, its all-purpose udder currently nursing him back to health.

Given his capitulations to Tolland, El Buscador suspected he was growing increasingly soft and bourgeois, a shadow of the gritty underground figure of old. Yet, truth be told, he couldn't find a dirty, rotten shack to occupy over these past weeks. Every grungy spot had been seized by hipsters who once were and by hipsters to be. How could he get a decent night's sleep when he was constantly being tossed out on his rear? Plus, the Coignet Building had much in its favor. As the oldest concrete structure in New York, the robust 1872 edifice was a worthy successor to his beloved city hall station. It boasted a bizarre hodgepodge of porticos, columns, and urns, originally incorporated to show off just how versatile concrete could be. The real kicker was that its subsequent owner was Edwin Litchfield, the man most responsible for breathing life into the Gowanus Canal. Indeed, El Buscador was fated to break-in and inhabit such a place.

The back entrance, conveniently shielded from public view, led right to the quiet and elegant basement. Surprised that the place showed no evidence of other squatters, he dropped his blankets between the ornate balustrades. For the first time since he arrived in Gowanus, he felt like he was home. That night he slept long and hard. He dreamt of Edwin Litchfield staring over the floodplains east of Red Hook, the eelgrass-dappled creek rippling in the wind. Litchfield straightened the wide lapels of his long coat, his upturned shirt collar framing his carelessly trimmed beard, and pronounced, "Somebody needs to clean up this mess."

El Buscador awoke with a start and knew he had to see Pratt. Fortunately, since he had fallen asleep at two in the afternoon, it was only ten now. If he hopped on a subway within fifteen minutes, he'd arrive just in time for Pratt to be leaving the rat pit.

CHAPTER 16
OF PRATT AND PITFALLS

The rat pit on Madison Street reopened four years ago, reviving a century-old tradition of debauched savagery. At first, Pratt shuddered and winced before this spectacle of blood and death. But the rat pit was the best place to learn about Tolland's activities, some legal, most illegal. Now, after four years, Pratt not only grew accustomed to gathering around the pit, but looked forward to these nights. Pratt wasn't happy about this admission. Then again, he had committed worse sins and harbored deeper regrets.

On the bright side, his sincere love of the pit made him above suspicion and Tolland's workers spoke freely around him. The breaks between dogs were the best time to pick up intel. A dopey and slow Saint Bernard named Bella took almost twenty minutes to kill the requisite one hundred rats, even though her massive jowls were capable of clamping down on three rats at a time. Bella stumbled far too much and lacked the lateral movement to get the job done any faster.

After a few jokes about Bella's folly, the boys in the crowd got back to shop talk at the construction sites. Since most the attention centered on the Gowanus Project, Pratt expected that all the buzz would be about Tolland's new architects, the Graffiti Sisters, but no one mentioned the name, nor did anyone talk of the stunning designs of the lovely humpbacked footbridges or of the glass sea wall at the 5th Street Basin, or of the elaborate, serpentine ramp to the subway station. In fact, the way the workers in the staging area spoke, he got the distinct impression that Lud, Gib, and Nirob were still Tolland's architects for the project. Pratt wanted to ask about cobblestone paths and the integration of artifacts from old gashouses and pump stations, but the famed terrier Hannibal was getting ready to hunt.

The beast held the speed record for killing a hundred rats, coming in at four minutes and 58 seconds. Pratt placed two hundred on Hannibal beating that time tonight. Short-haired and stocky, the terrier had the combination of hatred and efficiency that made for the perfect rat killer. From their barrel seats and rough-hewn benches, the crowd gazed at the silvery walls. They waited for the boys to come in with their burlap sacks of vermin. Muscles tensed behind the saloon doors. Hannibal rocked and drooled, growling and yipping in anticipation. Already sitting through almost two hours of carnage, the crowd stunk of spilled beer, but the most offensive scents wafted from their pores. Those aromas, mixed with gas and death, delivered a savage reek that could only be the love child of locker room jockstraps and dysentery wards.

Pratt didn't mind. A wiseass might even have postulated that he liked the smell. He definitely liked to watch Hannibal spring out of the shoot as a hundred blue rats dropped down from the vigorously shaken burlap sacks. The rush of energy, the brutish attacking force of the agile terrier, enthralled him. Whatever shame he would feel later for the bloodlust slept soundly in the moment. Pratt screamed like a maniac, watching Hannibal clamp down on one blue rat after another. When the terrier swooped in, he swallowed waves of the blue sea and, when Hannibal stretched for a leaping rat above, he inhaled the sky. Tolland was clearly onto something when he chose to turn the rats blue. The dead vermin scattered across the floor looked like so many deflated balloons, although the sprays of red made them seem more like ulcerated bladders.

In a scampering panic, the surviving rats squeaked and gibbered, their feet scraping and cycling furiously as they zigged and zagged. Hannibal clamped down on everything that crossed his path. True to the rat pits in the sportsman's clubs of the late nineteenth century, Tolland coated the walls in zinc to maximize the light and the sightlines – no spectator could lose track of Hannibal and of the blue rats trying so hard to vanish. Standing cheek and jowl with burly construction workers, Tolland's suits hollered and screamed with increased intensity just to assure their spittle-soaked neighbors that they too belonged here. Pratt, the one who truly least belonged in the room, made no such effort. He had become an aficionado and many in the room would turn to him for his counsel. He could tell how a dog would perform just based on the sweat on its legs. He knew by the lather that Hannibal would be on the top of his game tonight. Plus, the terrier was guessing right; half of the stray rats zagged into his awaiting maw. The tricky part was the end. With so many dead rats strewn on the sand and blood sprayed across the shiny zinc walls, it was hard to pick out the living, especially since by now a couple of rats were motionless, petrified by fear. But Hannibal still had a minute to break the record and he climbed over a pile of bodies to track down the final one with fifteen seconds to spare. The crowd erupted as the winners shook their chits and the losers tossed their tickets to the sky.

Pratt was careful not to win a big bet too often. Every move he made was calculated so that he didn't draw too much attention. He was generous with his expertize. The regulars at the pit knew he faithfully walked in with a sack of blue rats that he'd trapped on the nearby waterfronts below the FDR. Truth be told, the blue rats were an increasingly rare commodity in his cages. The feverish cadre of Tolland supporters across the five boroughs, an angry group of mostly white males who were put-out by the dynamics of the city they lived in and who saw the brash real estate mogul as just what we needed, had lost energy and focus. Perhaps they had moved onto another cause. Whatever the case, Pratt's role as a significant contributor to the rat pit now was much more demanding. When blue rats were plentiful, he used to toss the brown rats out. Now he had to take them to his basement apartment, which was gradually transforming into an elaborate dye factory. Blue filled his sink and splattered his rug and cabinets – damn, he was never going to get his security back.

Whatever the complications, he needed those blue rats to maintain his stature in the pit. As the bets were paid out and he slid two grand into his pocket, Danny Naughton clamped his big paw on Pratt's shoulder. "Looks like you've done well for yourself, lad." A mountain of a man, with an impressive belly and a gray handlebar moustache, Danny was one of Tolland's project managers and a fine source of information.

"It's been a good night," Pratt nodded quietly. He had an open, handsome face that drew people to him. The face served him well when he was the top reporter for *The Herald*, and now with his two-month-old beard and a haggard expression derived from late nights and a few beatings, he was even more approachable.

"Where you been trapping, Mahoney?" In the rat pit, Nate Pratt was known as Mike Mahoney, since Pratt would have long been fed to the dogs if anyone knew his real identity.

"Oh, still around the water here and there along the Lower East Side," said Pratt, aka Mahoney. "The rats haven't been so plentiful lately, so I've had to set traps right up to 14th Street. Where you working nowadays?"

"Gowanus, with everybody else."

"Yeah? I've heard that's supposed to be some project. You involved in making those crazy bridges and ramps."

"Nah, nah, nothing like that," said Danny. "The usual stuff, just shorter. I'm not used to going up only ten stories."

"Ten stories?" asked Pratt as Mahoney. "I heard six."

"Yeah, that's what you're going to hear. We'll start framing for six, but believe me, by the time we're done, it'll be ten. You know how Tolland works." Danny laughed and Pratt joined him.

They spoke dogs for the next half an hour before Danny said he better get some sleep. Pratt followed Danny out of the sportsman's hall. He spotted a shadowy figure in a trench coat and a fedora on the corner of Madison and Catherine. Pratt walked over to El Buscador and the two continued down Madison. Pratt nodded and asked, "To what do I have the honor of seeing your return to your old stomping ground?"

"Gowanus," said El Buscador.

"Funny, I was just talking about Gowanus."

"Yeah?" asked El Buscador. Pratt filled him in on how everything the construction workers and the project manager told him signaled that they had no idea about the ground-breaking designs of the Graffiti Sisters.

"You might be delusional." Pratt told him.

"I might be, but not about the Gowanus Project. I've seen the architectural plans in great detail. I've even been privy to the updates and improvements as the Graffiti Sisters talk to community and conservancy members."

Pratt smiled, "Which means ...."

"Which means some curious shit is going down," said El Buscador.

"Mmm," answered Pratt.

"Mmm indeed. You know what happens next, right?"

"I couldn't have less of an idea."

"That I need you in Gowanus."

"What about the rat pit?"

"You can still go a few times a week to keep your ears open, but your place is in Gowanus. You see, I have ideas."

Pratt gave him a skeptical groan. Then El Buscador whispered in Pratt's ear many, many secrets. Pratt listened, smiled, and asked, "And all you want me to do is stupid work?"

"That and make sure you listen carefully to everything around you."

"You really think there's that much to hear."

"More than you could imagine," said El Buscador.

They walked and talked plots and strategies for an hour as they headed uptown past the Manhattan and Williamsburg bridges through the Lower East Side all the way into the East Village to Veselka on 9th Street. Pratt could tell by their past-midnight sojourn that El Buscador was becoming so comfortable that he might not ever want to leave the magnificent island again. And now he was at his favorite 24-hour restaurant. Although Veselka was Ukrainian to its very soul, its bones were those of a diner. That meant a menu as thick as an economics textbook and a short-order cook who deserved a doctorate in the steel-griddle arts. Pratt and El Buscador sat at the counter so they could witness the chef with his left hand gliding his spatula along the heat and with his right clipping tongs to pull sides, condiments, and garnish from an array of tins.

Neither of them was in the mood for anything exotic. When El Buscador settled on eggs and bacon, Pratt decided that breakfast it is (time was always out of joint when they were together) and ordered challah bread French toast with sausage. Pratt stated the obvious. "You know you look like shit, right?"

"Yeah? You should've seen me yesterday."

"I don't think Brooklyn agrees you," said Pratt. "The Fatwah has been lifted. Why don't you come back home? I'm sure the city hall station misses you."

"If you see her, give her my regards," said El Buscador. "But things are looking up in Brooklyn. I've got a new place. It features a lovely view of Whole Foods."

"Jesus Christ. What the hell is it with you and Gowanus?"

"Tolland," said El Buscador.

"If he moves to California, would you move with him?" asked Pratt.

"Of course not."

"Then why follow him?"

"He's still in my city."

Their breakfast arrived. Considering that the chef had seventeen orders clipped above his head, that was an impressive feat.

"I think you need therapy," said Pratt.

"I promise to stop when he stops."

The sun was rising by the time they stumbled onto 8th Street to pick up the R train back to Gowanus. From the Union Street station, they had a mere five-minute walk to get to Nevins Street where they turned left at the old National Packing Box Factory building. That's when El Buscador showed Pratt the alley just west of Sackett.

Staring in wonder, Pratt said, "Holy, Moly." The alley was the stuff of New York movie scenes. A rusty iron staircase welcomed visitors to the warm brick walls that rose four stories in a narrow canyon. But it was the riot of wrought-iron fire escapes, cat walks, and top floor bridges traversing and crisscrossing the old factory building that hooked Pratt. "This is where you want me to work?"

Now that he saw Pratt was intrigued, El Buscador could safely warn, "It'll be back-breaking labor not worthy of your expansive intellect."

Pratt scowled. "How many times have you told me that my brains are overrated?"

"True," said El Buscador. "But you don't really believe that, so this grunt work might be rough on you."

"You just worry about where I'm going to put all the dirt."

"Pygmalion wants the dirt." El Buscador had to pause here to fill Pratt in on the graffiti artist; Pratt became increasingly intrigued the more he heard about Pygmalion, especially the exquisite ledge birds she painted. Not wanting to get sidetracked, El Buscador pressed ahead. "Anyway, she's been begging me to get the dirt. She's actually been disappointed that I won't be doing the digging myself."

Pratt smiled. "Is El Buscador implying that he is too good to dig dirt?"

"No, he's implying that he's too lame to dig the dirt. A number of guests with guns, pipes, and fists have made clear to El Buscador that he's not quite the superhero he used to be."

"Ah, another legend falls," said Pratt.

"Well, part of his brain is still working, and that has to be enough right now," said El Buscador.

"So has that brain figured out whether this Pygmalion chick has the authority to have a big dirt mound right on the edge of the canal?"

"As long as she turns it into the Gwaken, the art council will let her proceed."

"But it will look like hell until she finishes sculpting the thing."

"This is Gowanus," said El Buscador. "Big dirt mounds are no problem. The only thing the residents will wonder is why there's no burnt-out truck on top of it to give it the proper ornamental crown."

Pratt shook his head. The whole business was crazy. "Why would she want to use dirt? Why not steel or resin or wires?"

"She wants it to look natural, like it's rising out of the ground," said El Buscador.

"She wants a sea creature to look like it's coming out of the earth?" asked Pratt.

"Artistic vision. Anyway, you'll be bringing the sea to her." With that suggestion, El Buscador and Pratt both smiled as they envisioned the trench Pratt would dig in their moment of shared contentment.

"Indeed, I will," said Pratt.

CHAPTER 17
COPPA AND THE TOUR GUIDE

Edmund J. Coppa listened in the distance as El Buscador transformed into the Tour Guide. He was no longer the shadowy, underground figure who altered the plans of the mighty by forever entering through the back door. Now, he appeared to be a perfectly conventional, albeit deeply knowledgeable, docent for the curious and the confused. If Coppa didn't know better, El Buscador could've been a corporate shill. Yes, he delivered many fun facts about the canal, the gasworks that line the numbered streets, and the dye factories most responsible for the canal's nickname Lavender Lake. Better yet, his recounting of the retreat by the colonial forces in the Revolutionary War across what was then the Gowanus Creek was so riveting that the audience applauded the escape of Washington's men. Even some of Coppa's fellow construction workers said the Tour Guide's depiction of the Battle of Brooklyn should not be missed.

His representation of Tolland's new Gowanus Project was so spell-binding that Coppa was ready to plunk down his life savings to snatch up the tiniest studio offered. Surely, the Tour Guide's unadulterated commendations had gotten back to the real estate mogul, and what could be more intoxicating than for your hated enemy to sing your praises. By the time the Tour Guide was done weaving his vision, his audience was prepared to be immersed in a wonderland where the best of Venice and Bruges were given a New York makeover of funky industrial, Escheresque elevated ramps and hobbit-like bridges. Coppa understood that El Buscador was laying his entire reputation on the future of Tolland's Gowanus project, a reputation he knew, if El Buscador succeeded in what he wanted to achieve, would be totally and irrevocably destroyed.

Of course, this eavesdropping of the tour was exactly what El Buscador did not want Edmund J. Coppa to do. He should be listening and watching everything on the construction site. Procuring the job was more difficult than Coppa had anticipated, given his vast experience in the field. Tolland's construction crews were closed clans, and it took a vouching from Pratt in the guise of Mike Mahoney down in the rat pit for Coppa to secure the position. When he arrived at the job, Coppa did his best not to reveal how much he knew about construction – man, he could've been the foreman of the foreman. He wallowed in basic competence, doing his job reasonably well without drawing attention to himself. He summoned his self-control not to point out the shoddy construction techniques: if the foundation ended up square and straight, that would be a goddamn miracle. But what was worse were the mixers sent over by the American Concrete Company. Only the least experienced of workers would miss the inferior quality of the concrete. Clearly, too much sand and water were used in place of the proper proportion of cement, making the whole slurry a soupy mess. Sure, when the cheap concrete dried, it didn't look so bad, but anyone with half a brain knew the cracks would come the minute it had to withstand any weight. And worse than the cracks, Coppa wasn't certain the concrete would hold up if it had to bear much of a load.

Nor was he happy about the supports used to work around the sewer pipes. But he stayed true to El Buscador's request: "Keep your mouth shut and report back to me." So Coppa merely kept observing and recording the many sins of both the concrete company and the construction crew. He waited for the day to end, so he could walk back toward Union Street and pick up the R. He could cross the East River on just the right line to land closest to the Pint O'Plenty.

It was a Tuesday when Coppa had a real tale to tell at the bar, since only El Buscador and perhaps *The Herald* would be concerned about the shoddy workmanship at the Tolland site. He was watching his foreman completely ignore the adage "measure twice, cut once" (God, they were going to spend a few beans in fillers and spackling on this job), when the construction crew started wandering inward toward the canal. If he were on another job, Coppa would've stayed with the foreman to help him mismeasure the remainder of the frame, but El Buscador warned him not to act too conscientiously, since diligence tended to raise suspicions, so he joined the other crew members by the water.

"Will you look at that," said Marco, pointing to the large, slow moving fish that glided along the surface of the water, its small dorsal fin cutting into the gentle current. Since the other crew members took out their phones and snapped pictures, Coppa figured he might as well take out his. He tried to hide his expertize at framing and his adjustments on his camera settings as he calculated just how much he'd charge Mavis for the images. He had to step back to get all eight feet, from its dog-like snout to its narrow, severe tailfin.

"That thing is something," said Craig. "Swimming in these waters. That's one tough beast."

Coppa was struck how ancient the sea creature looked. The strange catfish-like whiskers made it appear to be a hundred years old, and the rough, armor-like scales spoke of a species that swam with the dinosaurs. Another group of people would've texted their friends to come down and take a selfie with the Gwaken, but Tolland's construction crews were so insular that they thought the sighting and perhaps the creature itself belonged to them solely, like all those blue rats in the pit. In fact, most of the construction crew harbored the suspicion that Tolland had released the beast in the canal. Leave it to Tolland, who had quite the reputation as the great white hunter with lion and boar heads gracing the walls of his hotels and offices, to find a creature that could withstand the toxicity of almost two centuries of industrial pollution. Taking the occasion as a moment of quiet celebration, the workers broke out their GG bars and leisurely nibbled away, air soon expanding their skulls and warmth rattling their bones. In fact, such generosity of spirit pervaded the crew that Coppa soon received offers for a GG bar, a bar that didn't come cheaply and usually not easily shared. Thanking his co-workers profusely for their kindness, Coppa declined, knowing the indulgence could well leave him less observant. Anyway, being stoned at a construction site was a fine way to lose a limb. Yet, he would make sure to tell El Buscador of his grand sacrifice for the cause, since he was certain many a round at the Pint O'Plenty would be purchased for him in gratitude.

The Gwaken steadily swam eastward, away from the mouth at Red Hook, deeper into the canal. The increasingly mellow crew tried to follow, but the waterway bent southward and the creature glided deeper. All that could be seen in the dark waters was his majestic wake of vectorial ripples. Their reddening eyes followed the surface motions until the water stilled and even the Gwaken's wake was swallowed in the murky depths. Evidently, the Gwaken had returned to sandwich his scutes and barbels in the black mayonnaise.

Scrolling through his shots of the Gwaken, Coppa knew he wouldn't accept less than five hundred from Mavis. These images were even better than hers, since he had the advantage of full sun and none of the barriers that normally made tracking the Gwaken so vexing. Tonight, he would only tell El Buscador of the shoddy construction and weak cement while his buddies at the Pint O'Plenty would hear of the legend that is the Gwaken. Tomorrow, he knew El Buscador in the guise of the Tour Guide would deliver tales of Gowanus's mighty sea creature, tales that would bestow unto the canal such a mythical cache that no investor could resist Tolland's Project.

After the financial beating Tolland took last year when the City Council halted his building on Canal Street, the well-heeled elite wondered where the real estate mogul could procure the resources for such an ambitious project in Gowanus. Many theorized that Tolland hardly had a dime, and he was counting on drumming up interest in the project to gather enough capital to keep the plan going. Some even suggested that he just had sufficient funds to get through each week and had to worry about raising money every day to pay for the next – a crazy way to proceed.

Yet El Buscador had transformed into his greatest fundraiser ... expanding financial backing for a project built on rotten foundations. At the Pint O'Plenty, with visions of the Gwaken still in his head and three mugs already in his belly, Coppa now understood with disturbing clarity what a dangerous game El Buscador was playing.

•   •   •   •   •

As the crowd thinned around El Buscador, Irving Steinman was always the last to leave. Irving would sidle up to El Buscador like he was his best friend, make a little dig, and then disappear. Last time, it was "You possess honesty in every form but integrity." This time his comment was even more dismissive. "The treachery of your nature is so great that there can be no purpose in speaking to you."

El Buscador tried to ask in response, "Then why are you speaking to me?", but Irving was already gone. Irving's comments didn't gnaw at him. The assessment of another local resident who must have recognized him, however, did. She was small and Hispanic, reminding him of Marcela Pachon, a Columbian woman he knew long ago. In his mind, when she started to speak to him, she was already Marcela. "I never believed in God." She looked straight at him, no straight through him, her dark eyes moist and world weary. "But at least I had you. Now I have nothing. Thank you for clarifying matters for me."

Marcela waited for an answer. He wanted to explain his plan, the necessity of his subterfuge, his dedication to right, but his silent response was the proper explanation. He understood how risky a proposition trusting in him was. The billboards along the G train still assured him, "You need to believe in yourself." He was shifting too swiftly to have any idea which El Buscador he should believe in.

Left alone with this criticism, El Buscador shuddered involuntarily in his awareness of standing out so publicly, being so exposed. He realized that he was being watched again, that he stood in the crosshairs. He always instinctively knew when someone pointed a gun at him. A minute didn't pass before he flinched from the breeze that shot through his fedora. Or was he reacting to the small, elegant bullet that sank into the concrete behind him, a few gray chips spraying onto his trench coat? The distant rifle shot whizzed by him so quickly that he didn't know what to make of it.

He thought about running, but he knew the exertion was pointless. If a sniper so skilled to deliver two perfectly positioned holes in the front and back of his fedora wanted him dead, he'd be dead. Taking off the fedora, El Buscador fingered the bullet holes on his hat with his pinky and peered out toward where he thought the rifle might be perched. The marksman had to be Maksim, since he knew no other Tolland associate who was such a crack shot. The message was clear: El Buscador could be exterminated whenever Maksim was told by Tolland to proceed. Of all the humiliations of becoming Tolland's shill, this consignment was the worst. He had never known public vulnerability, and having just gained a hint of it, he'd make sure after this miserable penance that he'd never put himself in such a position again. For the moment, however, he would just have to accept that whenever Tolland wished, Maksim would be on his perch, shooting holes through his hat.

Finding his way back to the shadows, El Buscador struggled to make sense of the thoughts slithering through his head like snakes on the hunt. El Buscador had always comfortably inhabited the paradox of carefully cultivating an image, yet not caring what anyone thought of him. Now, with his compromised, perhaps villainous, persona, he still tended not to care what others thought of him ... except for Mavis. He ruminated over Mavis's intelligent eyes and lovely curves, her alluring hostility and her stately grace. He didn't mind being in love with her. Hey, what can you do? But his infatuation, his preoccupation with her ... That was problematic. He found aloofness easier when he had played the role he'd performed for years: subversive, subterranean El Buscador, detached and enigmatic.

He needed the city to perceive him as a traitor. And even though Mavis knew better, she'd have to pretend she only saw the present incarnation of Benedict Buscador – a man who became a sycophantic, kiss-ass toady for Tolland, a craven quisling of the most abhorrent degree. Naturally, Mavis had been asked by the media about the new El Buscador, her former ally. She gave terse answers, pointing out that his choices have been unfortunate, that he'd been going through a difficult time.

El Buscador did not want to be with anyone right now, but he did want to be with Mavis. Even that desire felt traitorous, a heartless rejection of Jeanne. If relationships are founded on trust, then his bond with Mavis sat on jagged granite. Every day, he wrote Mavis a note. None were love letters. Today's read, *"At Fourth Avenue and President Streets, Public Bath #7 used to clean the poor and downtrodden. Today, it's a theater. The public baths of those days have now moved inside the apartments, so the show can spill out into the streets."*

Later, Mavis would read the note and mutter, "Jackass. Doesn't exactly know how to steal a girl's heart, does he? And yet ..." She kept all of his stupid-ass notes in Ziploc bags (she could read through the clear plastic without breaking the seal). She wondered if and when he would try to kiss her, like they were teenagers. She would probably have to take care of that too. El Buscador can talk about theater all he wanted, but she knew who'd be responsible for the orchestration. And if they ever slept together, where? Not in one of his hovels. Mavis thought of the Brooklynites eating those pot-laced chocolate bars, and she murmured, "Ganja Ganache." She nodded inwardly and decided she could really use one of those marijuana confections about now. She would even share some with El Buscador.

CHAPTER 18
OF PIES AND BONES

El Buscador had returned to visit Nancy and JoJo three times during the day. Unfortunately, in between the second and third visit, the man arrived, upping his price to $3.5 million, saying it was the final offer and he'd have to know today.

"What did you say to him?"

"That I'd tell him tomorrow."

"I'm sure that went over well. What did he look like? Did he have an accent?"

"I think it was Russian, but I'm not sure. Accents aren't my thing." Considering her pizza, El Buscador wondered just what was Nancy's thing? "He was small and skinny, not big and strong like JoJo." El Buscador wanted to say the body type doesn't matter much; as long as he is strong enough to grip a Makarov, size doesn't matter a bit.

"Did you get the impression he was threatening you?"

"Yeah. He stared at me a lot and didn't say much besides the money and the deadline."

"I'll be back later," said El Buscador.

"Don't you want a pie?"

"Later."

El Buscador picked up the F train in Manhattan all the way into midtown to the Tollandia. Before he entered the lobby, he checked his backpack for the most valuable item he still possessed. He walked into the Peacock room and deftly stowed it in a place he thought no one would look. Then he took out a piece of paper, an envelope, and a stamp (required items for a man without a phone or his own address) and posted a letter to Mavis. If things headed south in today's discussion, Mavis could retrieve the item.

With the help of Thackeray, El Buscador had been spreading rumors about a 28-inch femur bone that supposedly came from the 8-foot tall Eddie Carmel, the biggest man to ever live in New York. Carmel even appeared in a horror movie as a monster. In fact, El Buscador grabbed the bone from the burial grounds on Hart Island, but he pushed the story of how an ever-resourceful grave robber had dug up Carmel's coffin. Since he had other problems with the law, the grave robber had left town and gone into hiding, at least that's how the story went. He reburied the bone somewhere in New York for safekeeping. Apparently, the bone had been recently rediscovered. Since he knew he'd have to offer something if he expected Timothy Terrance Tolland to squeeze him into his extraordinarily busy schedule, El Buscador now would dangle that femur – the real estate mogul and adventurer really loved his relics. El Buscador had been saving the bone for bigger, darker plans, but the fate of Una Nonna's pizzeria did feel dire and that damn bone was all he had left. He wrote a note to the secretary of Tolland's secretary, explaining that this really was a once-in-a-lifetime opportunity for the femur. All El Buscador required in return was ten minutes of Tolland's time.

Even with this urgency, Tolland made him wait three hours, during which day turned to night.

When El Buscador entered the penthouse, Tolland greeted him with, "You've got some pair of balls. I give you back your life and you want more."

"It is not I who wants, but I who gives." El Buscador knew his manner was a little affected, but something about Tolland brought out the jerk in him. "You will have a giant's bone."

"When you say a bone, you better not mean a goddamn pinky."

On another day, a day when he could afford to piss Tolland off (which had been scores of days in the past), he would've pointed out that the pinky actually has three bones, but today was not one for lessons in phalanges, proximals, and metacarpals. "We're talking about the 28-inch femur here, and it took some serious digging to find it."

"And what is it you want from me?"

"I want ten minutes. You don't have to answer. You just have to listen and promise me you'll consider what I've said."

"And I get the bone when you're done talking."

"You get the bone when you're done listening."

"Is it in your bag?"

"Of course not." El Buscador knew Tolland was not above having security hold him down while the real estate mogul grabbed it.

"So you're wasting my time."

"Not really. We both know you're not going to let me leave this office until you have the bone."

"Then why should I bother listening to what you have to say."

"Because you like to make a good deal, and believe me you're getting the better end of this one, and I think a small part of you is a bit curious about what I'm going to say."

"Well, at this rate, we'll waste ten minutes talking about your ten minutes. Start talking."

"I know you've been trying to buy out Una Nonna's pizzeria to finish off the properties necessary for the Tolland District." Tolland held up his hand. "Again, I don't need you to say anything. You don't have to deny anything. Just hear me out. That pizzeria is a local institution."

Despite the rules, Tolland couldn't help but interrupt. "That place is a hole. It's got a one-star rating on Yelp. I'm doing the community of a favor getting rid of that dump."

"It's loved and they don't want to sell." Tolland lifted his eyebrows as if to say, they will sell, whether they like it or not. "Their presence will actually help your district. The Graffiti Sisters have worked so hard to integrate the local traditional elements into the project. Get them to work around Una Nonna's. It's only a little shack."

"All the more reason it should go."

"It'll give the development even more character and color. You will be lauded as a big-hearted, culturally sensitive real estate developer. The community will love you for it."

"You really think so?"

"I do indeed."

"OK. I'll talk to my architects."

"That's great."

"Now where's my bone?"

El Buscador had no idea whether any of what he said sunk in nor did he like how easily Tolland agreed.

"You have a guard down in the Peacock Room."

"I can get one there."

"Tell them to go to the couch by the lion and the bone will be under the middle seat cushion."

Tolland laughed. "You're not quite right in the head, are you?"

As they waited, El Buscador said, "Now comes the awkward moments before the guard finds it when you're wondering whether you'll be shaking my hand and beating me with a club."

"Excuse me while I get my club," said Tolland.

"If you'll indulge me with one further question while the sword of Damocles hovers above my thinning neck ..." Tolland nodded. "How many people do you talk to in a day whom you absolutely hate?"

"Including you? Hundreds. How about you?"

"One. But I talk to very few people."

"And society thanks you for that."

El Buscador was tempted to bring up Maksim and the two bullet holes through his fedora, but he preferred that Tolland think the target practice didn't faze him one bit. Instead, the two of them avoided eye contact and tried to look like they were busy contemplating very important matters. The secretary interrupted their cumbersome silence to confirm the discovery of the femur.

Tolland said, "You're free to go, although I was almost hoping he wouldn't find it. It better be the real McCoy."

"It is, and if it's not, you know where to find me. More importantly, if it's not, you know better than anyone what to do with a quality fraud."

"El Buscador, you are more right today than you have been for many years."

"You only said that to upset me."

"Like you're worth the effort," said Tolland. "Now get out of here before I stop being friendly."

"That was friendly?"

El Buscador left the penthouse with just a smidge of hope. The hope was indeed a horrible hope because if Tolland preserved the unbelievably awful Una Nonna's pizzeria under his counsel, he would never really be able to go to war with the man again. The bastard would hold El Buscador's soul in his very cold hands.

He stewed on the F train. If yesterday El Buscador fought for brilliance, today he championed mediocrity. Ah Brooklyn, it messes with the mind ... with its Gwakens, its swimming JoJos, its soggy pies, its Ganja Ganache, and its overcrowded hovels. How's a man supposed to think when he can't find a place to think and everything becomes twisted in the pernicious waters?

El Buscador returned to the Smith Street station and the characters there looked particularly rough tonight, as if the clientele all stood around expecting drug deals to go south. There were too many wrinkles and too few teeth. Ice ages seemed to creep down their facial moraines. El Buscador turned east on Smith, passing by that endless beacon of light that was Una Nonna (he really could not tell them anything of value from his conversation with Tolland), weaving right on 5th to Hoyt to 4th to Bond to 3rd where in the shadow of Whole Foods hundreds gathered, staring at the canal, keeping vigil for the emergence of the Gwaken. Even greater multitudes were collected at the park along the canal before 1st and 2nd. There and beyond at the Carroll Street Bridge and down further at Union Street Bridge and the cobbled dead ends capping to the canal's head, the locals peered in below their flat-cap hats, pointing and gesticulating, thinking, hoping that the stirring was the actual Gwaken and not an unlovely discharge rising to the surface. TV camera crews had the prime spots on the bridges, peering intrusively into the murkiness with their brutal spotlights. Many others, stumbling about with bemused expressions, were draining their phone batteries as they took videos, hoping they'd catch a glimpse.

The false alarms were many; the Gwaken was lying low. In fact, it took most of the onlookers many minutes to notice the flames to the west and north. El Buscador, who had been looking almost compulsively that way, started weaving back from where he came toward Una Nonna's. He cursed himself for his gullibility. He didn't believe Tolland would do it tonight. He thought he'd at least wait until tomorrow. He even wondered if sadly his appeal had actually sped up the arson.

He rushed to the flames. JoJo had a bucket of water from the canal that he tossed onto the inferno. El Buscador feared the baneful brew would only add to the conflagration. Instead, it appeared to do neither good nor harm.

El Buscador came up to Nancy who looked surprisingly serene. "How are you doing?"

"I'm OK," she said. She held onto the straps of a huge athletic bag. He couldn't help but wonder what was in there: clothes? money? pizza dough? Nancy followed his eyes to the bag and then looked back up at the flames. "Thanks for asking. I'm just trying to figure out how we're going to serve pizza tomorrow?"

As the little shack continued to burn and as the fire trucks blared in the distance, El Buscador nudged her. "Is that the most important thing to you? You want to keep the pizza going?"

"Yeah," she said. "And the spinach too."

"You grab the cash from the place?"

"Oh yeah, I've got some and JoJo grabbed the rest."

El Buscador smiled. These were his type of people. "You want to watch the place burn or you want to come with me?"

"I don't want to watch this."

"Then let's go. You think JoJo wants to come?"

"Nah," she said. "He wants to throw canal water on the burning shack. I think he's curious."

"That's reasonable. You ready to come with me."

"Sure. It's not like I'm making any more pies tonight." She lifted her heavy athletic bag and followed. El Buscador considered offering to carry the bag, but he could tell that there was no way in hell she would let go of her grip.

CHAPTER 19
APIZZA THE HUN

Assembled in the sprawling lot between the Union Street and Carroll Street bridges in that canal rectangle north of Nevins Street, the collection of food trucks might be the largest in the world. The trucks gathered here on off hours. But the lot also was a graveyard for failed businesses. Nancy raised her eyebrows only slightly when she saw how easily El Buscador picked the lock on the fence gate. He wouldn't be the only criminal she had served pizza to in Gowanus.

"C'mon," he said, waving her in.

Nancy stayed put. "I could get arrested."

El Buscador laughed. "Are you kidding? Every cop for miles is cordoning off the perimeter around your roasting pizza parlor."

"Good point." Lifting the bulky athletic bag, Nancy followed him in. They walked past many of the acclaimed food trucks of the city: My Dumpling Clementine; Deck the Halal; Dog Days; Green Eggs and Hamburgers; Fair Shake; Traffic Cones; Chili Forecast; The Kabob Sled. Then they came to the fallen trucks, ones where dreams rolled to a halt: Buns of Fun, Tic-Taco-Toe, Here Comes the Fudge, Good Shawarma, Fit to be Thaid, Wok of Ages, Arepa Caper, Kale to the Chief, The Macroony Bin. Finally, right back by the canal toward Carroll Street, El Buscador reached the food truck he had in mind. In what can only be described as a brutal Mongolian font, the sign read – APizza the Hun. Pointing to the sign, a huge smiling moustached figure, who could've been anyone from Marco Polo to Genghis Khan, held a steaming mozzarella pie on a silver platter. It was the most unappetizing invitation to dine since Burger King offered chicken parmigiana.

El Buscador waved his hand like a used car salesman. "What do you think, Nance?"

"That? Would you eat pizza from that truck?"

"Hey, at least your customers won't have high expectations."

"Got me there."

"How much is it going to set me back?"

El Buscador considered who he would have to bribe. Pygmalion said APizza the Hun had been operating a month ago, which meant the owners probably still had a functional permit. "If you give me $2,000, I should be able to get you open by twelve tomorrow."

"That's a hundred pies.

"True, true. Or two hundred tubs of spinach. Honestly, what are you going to do tomorrow if you can't make pies?"

Nancy grumbled, but then turned her back on him and unzipped her athletic bag. When she turned toward him again with the bag zipped shut, she slapped two rubberbanded stacks of twenties into El Buscador's right hand. "Can we change the name to Una Nonna's?"

"Not on the truck. The permits won't stick. But you could put a little Una Nonna's cardboard sign at the window." Nancy frowned. El Buscador tried to reason with her. "Look, the truck will be right next the smoldering ruins of the pizzeria, near the spot where Una Nonna's has been for years, and you'll be making the pies. Only an idiot couldn't figure out that they're eating Una Nonna's."

Considering her clientele, Nancy knew half her customers would give APizza the Hun all the credit. But these were extraordinary circumstances. The main thing was to stay in business.

And for El Buscador, he would have loved to be there when Tolland heard Una Nonna didn't miss a beat. He picked the lock on the food truck so he could show Nancy around. Surprisingly, the place had three ovens, the same as the pizzeria, although between the granite dough stone and the ovens there was hardly enough room for JoJo to rest his big forearms on a ledge.

Nancy sniffed. "God, it smells like basil." Considering her pies, El Buscador struggled to believe she even knew those leaves existed, let alone the odor. Reading Nancy's sour expression, he popped open the back window facing the canal, figuring the famous aroma of the lavender lake would strangely deliver relief. Grabbing a rag, Nancy started wiping down the counter like she already owned the place. Even as she cleaned, she kept the athletic bag by her feet, the straps hooked around her ankle. El Buscador was trying to decide whether the pizza from these ovens would be just as awful as the ones for which Nancy was justly famed when he heard turbid splashes in the canal.

He peered out the window, but the angle was not right to see the water. Slipping out the door, he curled around the back of food truck and looked down into the current heading toward the Carroll Street Bridge. The tail of the Gwaken cut the water with an elegant ease. El Buscador sucked in his breath. He was surprised how excited the Gwaken made him: a shiver pulsed across his shoulders. Given the time of night and the distraction of the still burning Una Nonna's, he had the view of the Gwaken all to himself. Sure, he could've called over Nancy, but he knew she would have no interest in such an extraordinary creature. As she wiped and rewiped the granite, she planned how she would have to meet up with the distributor to get fresh supplies of mediocre mozzarella and low-grade crushed tomatoes and underperforming yeast and overground flour.

Of the duo of restauranteurs, JoJo would be the one who'd have had an interest in the Gwaken. Hell, given JoJo's regular pleasure swims across the Gowanus, he may well have floated lung to gill next to the mighty sturgeon. But now, El Buscador could be alone with the Gwaken, like the first night he spotted her. He felt the terrible desire to follow JoJo's example and dive in. He would've too, perils be damned, but he knew the splash would be an unholy invasion. Instead, he carefully observed the prehistoric scales serrating the surface. As she lifted her maw, El Buscador could see two fishhooks dangling among the barbels. Typical. Yet instead of swimming away from these predators from above, the Gwaken stayed with the locals wearing the Keds and Vans.

As he followed the Gwaken, El Buscador felt a splattering at his feet and then an explosion of gooey wetness. He thought the Gwaken was under attack but was completely disabused of this notion by a sodden slap to the head, a cracked eggshell spraying sideways across his shoulders, neck, and ears, the yolk running down his cheek.

"Traitor," yelled the egger, who then ran off. Apparently, the attacker had only spotted the duplicitous El Buscador, not the trusty sturgeon. The incursion ended, El Buscador was now once again alone with the Gwaken, happy that he had been recognized instead of his canal mate. As it glided beneath the Carroll Street Bridge, the Gwaken lifted her blunt, cartoonish snout high enough so that El Buscador caught just a shimmy of her catfish-like whiskers, fishhooks and all, a last reminder as she swam out of sight that the sturgeon belonged to his grandfather's generation.

El Buscador needed some sleep if he was going to be sharp enough tomorrow morning to make the necessary deals, so that he'd have keys in hand and Nancy could drive the APizza the Hun food truck across the canal to its new home next to the dying embers of Una Nonna's. Chivalry required that he ask if he could walk Nancy back to watch the last of her pizzeria burn, but he knew she would stay in the truck and organize the kitchen, organize her future.

Fortunately, his increasingly comfortable basement home at the old Coignet Stone Company building was only a couple of blocks away. Tonight, he would pick up his dreams of Edwin Litchfield and the turning basins he envisioned, but El Buscador knew he'd wake up many times thinking of Tolland, plotting what moves he needed to take next. Yes, he took Tolland's attempts on his life personally, but this act of arson on Una Nonna's was much more provocative. You don't destroy the worst pizza parlor in all of New York City and get away with it. If El Buscador was certain of anything, he'd make Tolland pay for this unpardonable sin. As he rested on his cot, he realized that he had nothing to eat tonight. He had planned on pizza. Now he decided he was happy that he'd gone hungry.

CHAPTER 20
TANVI AND THE GWAKEN

The kayakers were out in full force on this lovely Saturday clogging up the canal so completely that there was hardly any room left for the debris, no room for the tractor tire, the discarded sink, the amputated arm. Certainly, no room for the Gwaken. Mavis had sent her crack reporter Tanvi Khotari out to Gowanus as an unspoken punishment for making fun of her belief in the Gwaken. Mavis ordered Tanvi to write a light, humorous story about how the canal community was reacting to that extraordinary creature. Tanvi didn't do light and humorous; she was, however, quite good at dark and grim.

Naturally, Tanvi had been expressly prohibited from writing a dark and grim story about the Gwaken, but, hell, the locals whom she interviewed didn't know that. Along the edge of the sea wall and over the bridge at Union Street, protestors were shaking the most extraordinary signs. The largest one read, "Don't Clean Our Canals to Death." A sign next to it clarified the daring suggestion: "No Contamination, No Gwaken."

Suddenly, Tanvi decided this punishment assignment might have been worth the trip on the D train. After scoping out the place and eyeing up who might be the most amusing to interview, she landed on cornering the leader of the newly formed Black Mayonnaise Civic Association, Barbara Kornberg.

Going old school, Tanvi took out at pen and a notepad, just to make clear to Barbara she would be quoted. "Let me get this straight, your association would like the Gowanus to stay contaminated? Hasn't the community been fighting for years to clean the canal up?"

"Contamination has been a concern for us, but not as much as people think," said Barbara. "Those of us who have lived here all our lives don't mind the stink, and now that we have the Gwaken, we don't want to do anything to mess with its ecosystem."

"Uh, huh," answered Tanvi. She looked around at the other protestors in the association and pointed, "Well, I guess your comments make more sense than that sign." Held up by a guy in a mob suit, it read, "Take the Cannoli, Leave the Gwaken."

Barbara smiled smugly, "It's from *The Godfather.*"

"Yes, I know," said Tanvi, who had the annoying habit of seemingly knowing everything. "But what does it mean?"

"It's from *The Godfather.*"

"Ah," said a smirking Tanvi, "Now I understand." She didn't.

Barbara stuck to her talking points. "We need to preserve the contamination. A clean-up will lead to the destruction of the magnificent Gwaken."

Tanvi was in the mood to play. "Yes, the mighty Gwaken." She looked down at her blank notepad and pretended she was reading off a script. "An eight-foot Atlantic sturgeon feasting on the oysters seeded here to clean up the canal. More than two feet wide, scale encrusted. One of the world's ancient creatures, it goes back to the Triassic era." Barbara nodded, confident that Tanvi was finally seeing the situation from her perspective. Then the reporter asked, "Are you saving something that doesn't exist?"

Barbara's first instinct was to howl in protest of the unthinkable. She thought it'd be better to keep the conversation simple. "If we are talking about it, it exists."

Although Tanvi knew her editor would never let her run a story questioning the very existence of the Gwaken – a creature Mavis claims to have seen with her own eyes – Barbara didn't know that, and she decided a healthy dose of skepticism was appropriate. "Seriously?"

"What's so hard to believe about the Gwaken? A few summers ago there was a porpoise in the canal. A dozen years ago, there was even a whale, remember. Everyone called him Sludgie."

Barbara frowned. She did not like Tanvi. Tanvi never concerned herself about such nonsense. Instead, she expanded on her central theory. "Isn't it true that almost everyone in the neighborhood has been gorging on Ganja Ganache, also known as GG?"

For the first time Barbara smiled, "So?"

"So ..." answered Tanvi, "Don't you think a bunch of stoned residents claiming they saw a creature in the canal raises suspicions?" Clearly having enough of Tanvi, Barbara found something else to occupy her attention.

Tanvi wandered, collecting quotes from a dozen residents, all determined to keep the canal as toxic as ever. She had her share of conversations about the prevalence of GG, although none of the interviewees agreed with her connection between the product and the sightings. More than a few pointed to the benign effect of Ganja Ganache, produced from the finest ingredients in a legal factory out in California. Still, despite this angle producing little copy, the story was shaping up nicely since Tanvi could never have predicted that so many locals would want to maintain the canal's polluted state.

Yes, she got the obligatory rebuttal from Lynn Morales, the leader of Gowanus Conservancy. Lynn had ambitious plans, from plantings to sludge storage to recharge zones, for cleaning up the area – plans that had been slowly and painstakingly grabbing hold of the community until Gwaken fever swept across the lowlands like cholera. But Lynn's measured thoughtfulness was drowned out by the pop-up stores and t-shirt vendors selling icons and images of the Gwaken. In a second attempt at fairness, she also quoted a representative from the Gowanus Dredgers Club, which had been trying to clean up the canal for decades. Naturally, that sensible comment could not compete with the feverish full-frontal embrace of the mucky, filthy status quo championed by so many onlookers. Tanvi could not help but recognize that the glory days of sludgy chic were splattering across the Gowanus.

Among the kayakers, the adventurous stuck and shook long poles into the black mayonnaise, stirring up the coal tar in hopes of rousing the giant from the canal's depths. Tanvi knew even if the Gwaken did exist that the last thing any sensible creature would do was raise up its fin to join this shit show. After she spotted more a half dozen indulgers of GG, most nibbling at the chocolate bar without any attempt to hide their mildly illegal activity, Tanvi decided to wander westward, beyond Whole Foods out toward Tolland's massive construction site, swallowing all the area from the canal to Smith Street, down to the subway station.

Even more curious than the gigantic holes in the ground was a food truck operating besides the still smoldering ruins of a lost shack. Next to the food truck, two men were bouncing in and out of a small electrician's van to hook up power from the truck to stand-alone outlets. While mildly intrigued about whether Con Edison was aware of this new customer, Tanvi was more interested in what they were serving at APizza the Hun. She was disappointed to learn that she could only order a pie – no slices – and settled on an outrageously expensive half-pound of spinach.

Handed a spoon and a napkin, Tanvi took her plastic container of spinach, which at least felt somewhat warm, and made her way toward the construction site, not letting any of the plywood doors or the pesky locks get in her way of checking out the grounds. As she walked the perimeter, she found an opening up against the edge of the canal. Evidently, the construction crew did not anticipate intruders from the waterside. As she popped her head in, she didn't hear any activity at the site. It wasn't like Tolland to let all his crews off on Sunday. The first thing that struck her was how close much of the construction was to the canal. Yes, some of the work could have been the footings for the humpbacked footbridges to crisscross the canal, but nothing would be the size that she beheld. The foundations looked like they were being set for a skyscraper, not some modest, low-slung development. Then there was the water that swamped sections of the site; it was like a few pipes had broken or the workers had struck an underwater spring.

Tanvi tried to enjoy her spinach, but soon discovered that effort was impossible. She could not remember a time when she had spinach this greasy. She sat on the ground, took out her laptop, and banged out her story about the burgeoning preservation movement of contaminated old Gowanus. As the sun began to set, she looked out to see a figure perched up on the construction site platform against the canal. He sat there with the stillness of a stork waiting for the tide to wash in minnows. Without anybody having to tell her, Tanvi knew she had spotted the rarest of creatures, even rarer than that damn Gwaken, the shadowy El Buscador. He wore his signature trench coat and fedora and was deep in thought. The bullet holes through his fedora seemed like they had always been there.

On another day, Tanvi might've opened her arms wide to the construction site and asked him what the hell was going on here. But Tanvi had the sneaking suspicion that El Buscador was less interested in answering her question than doing something about it.

CHAPTER 21
MAVIS AND PRATT

For two straight weeks, Pratt had been digging out the alley between Union and Sackett Streets. Starting at Nevins Street, he planned on clearing a four feet wide and four feet deep channel right to the canal. El Buscador told him he eventually would refill the bottom foot with six inches of clay followed by six inches of sand, but El Buscador was still working on getting enough sponsors to pay for the clay. Seems that a few of the guests on his tours of Gowanus had deep pockets.

For one man with a shovel and a wheelbarrow, Pratt had made impressive progress. He had about fifty feet cleared. When he mentioned that a backhoe would be much faster and easier, El Buscador argued this simple example of pure human industry would be inspirational for the stages that had to follow. Pratt chided, "That easy for you to say since I'm the donkey who's doing the grunt labor."

El Buscador offered a grin that he only delivered when harboring many secrets. "While I am certain I am not working as hard as you, I can assure you I am involved in very unpleasant and illegal activities to assure the trench you dig will be given its proper treatment." From El Buscador's response, Pratt figured that involvement included breaking into numerous buildings and playing around with many pipes. No, overall Pratt would rather stick with his digging. He only took breaks to trap and dye his rats, so he could return to the pit on Madison. He was glad he didn't give that up since Danny had received a slew of blueprints from Lud, Gib, and Nirob and not even a single sketch from the Graffiti Sisters. When Pratt relayed this information to El Buscador, he hardly seemed surprised, even as he continued to lay out the inspired Graffiti Sisters' vision for Gowanus.

Most of Pratt's existence consisted of carrying away dirt from that alley. Pygmalion was quite pleased with the mound Pratt accumulated just east of the Union Street Bridge. She was shaping her Gwaken – here about four times the size of the already formidable original – catty-cornered to loom over the canal. She had already carved the severe back fin and had begun to sculpt the armor-like scutes and the modest dorsal fin, roughing the middle of the creature as Pratt continued his dirt deliveries. Initially, thinking Pratt was merely some handsome brute, Pygmalion treated him with condescension. After the first wheelbarrows arrived at her installation site, she said somewhat flippantly. "Thank you, dirt man."

Pratt smiled at her. "Plato said that people are like dirt: they can either nourish you to help you grow or they can stunt your growth to make you perish."

Pygmalion quivered slightly from Pratt's rugged erudition. Her dark slender exquisiteness generally fed her aloofness: she was used to being the one who sends anyone nearby into a romantic tizzy. Yet from that day forward, she greeted him with gratitude and a friendly challenge. "Thank you, wheelbarrow man."

Again, Pratt delivered an easy-going twinkle. "William Carlos Williams said so much depends on a red wheelbarrow glazed with rain water beside white chickens."

Pygmalion sighed with an aching happiness. "What a lovely notion."

"Except when it's not," said Pratt. That straightened Pygmalion's posture. "In *Moby Dick*, the heroic cannibal Queequeg doesn't know the purpose of a wheelbarrow so he carries it on his back. So sometimes I am a wheelbarrow man who lets it carry my burdens; at other times, I know I must shoulder its heavy load."

As he wheeled the barrow away, she admired his broadening shoulders. The next day she greeted his dirt delivery. "Thank you, canal man."

Pratt paused for a minute. Pygmalion thought she stumped him. Then his eyes grew alert. "Thomas Jefferson said that people generally have more feeling for canals than education."

As he turned the wheelbarrow around and headed back down the alley, Pygmalion yelled out, "So claims the man of education."

With each passing encounter, Pygmalion became increasingly determined that some late night she would sketch Pratt and his wheelbarrow on one of the large factory walls facing the canal since he too was another magnificent creature of the Gowanus.

For Pratt, Pygmalion was a treasured artifact from a history he'd abandoned. He hadn't put in the effort to charm such a beauty in more than a year. He struggled to figure out how often he should take his former self off the shelf and fiddle around with it. During these ruminations, he was visited by a ghost from his earlier life: his old editor Mavis showed up at his trench with two dozen blue flowering hydrangea bushes. Pratt chuckled and wondered just what El Buscador couldn't convince one of his friends to do. Clearly here on her day off, Mavis was dressed for toiling, although she was the only person he'd ever seen who looked elegant in a pair of jeans.

Placing four hydrangea plants in Pratt's now empty wheelbarrow and tossing a small garden shovel over her shoulder, she followed her former star reporter into the alley as it gradually sank to four feet deep. Along the trenches' banks, Pratt had inadvertently created small raised mounds. Those mounds were quite handy for Mavis as she dug holes and added peat to her plantings. After a few hours of labor, Mavis had the hydrangeas in the ground, edging most of the banks of the completed trench.

Pratt admired her work. "Boy is that a beautiful vision. But let me ask you something: Do you think the alley gets enough sun for them to survive?"

Mavis shook her head. "The alley gets some sun, especially since it's an open shot to the canal. It has some southern exposure. But I made sure I got a shade-loving variety. To tell you the truth, I was more concerned about whether they'll keep their flowers because they tend to bloom in late spring. The nursery must've had them in the greenhouse."

"You're in luck there," said Pratt. "I can tell you with great certainty that this alley is awfully warm. The tenants of these buildings must have some Con Ed bills with all the heat that escapes."

Mavis looked up at the wondrous array of fire escapes, catwalks, and bridges that teetered above the alley. A funhouse designer couldn't have installed a more atmospheric and playful cluster of platforms. She nodded. "El Buscador was right about one thing. This place does have character. And if he does what he thinks he can do and if you move all this dirt, boy that'll be something."

Reminded of the stakes, Pratt took off with another pile of dirt toward the art installation. Mavis gathered up all the empty plastic pots and dropped them in the trash. Upon his return, Pratt asked, "So will you be back?"

"Next week, on my day off with another two dozen hydrangeas, so you better keep clearing."

"Yeah, yeah. I'm going."

Right after she called a Lyft on her app, Mavis told Pratt. "Thank you for the dirt." Naturally, Pratt once again delivered the line from Plato about how people are like dirt and they can nourish you or destroy you. Mavis was slightly less dazzled than Pygmalion. "You think I'm supposed to be impressed because Plato said that. Any asshole could've said that. The same thing could be said about water or rope or even chocolate cake. Do me a favor, the next time I thank you for the dirt, say you're welcome."

Pratt decided to shift directions. "Those hydrangeas sure look lovely."

"I'm glad you think so. I think they'll hold the soil too."

Pratt rattled his brain to think of other things that hold the soil, but all he could come up with was vegetation. Damn Mavis and her specific way of talking. Damn Mavis and her editor's mind. At that moment, Pratt determined he needed to draw Pygmalion away from molding her giant Gwaken for a few choice encounters, so he could regale her with other pearls of wisdom. The next time she asks how he's doing, he might go a bit cosmic, answering something like, "Oh, just to trying to formulate the square root of infinity." Perhaps she'd like to find out if he could do more his hands than haul dirt and more with his tongue than utter poetry.

CHAPTER 22
MORE TOURS AND CONSTRUCTION

Landing at a nearby helipad, Governor Rosenthal came to the Tolland project site with aides and officials from the Department of Environmental Conservation in tow. Breaking away from the press, Rosenthal studied El Buscador warily, shook his hand, and told him, "You're more cosmopolitan than I thought you'd be."

El Buscador smiled, "I was thinking the same thing about you, only in reverse." One look at Rosenthal and El Buscador could tell that the governor cursed like a sailor the minute the mikes were shut off.

Rosenthal laughed. "So it's going to go like that, eh? Let me just make a statement to the press, so I can ditch them. Then you can give me a tour in private."

After he spoke about his excitement for the project, about how many jobs it is bringing to the neighborhood, and about how it will provide much needed middle-class housing, Rosenthal refused to answer any questions about tax incentives. He left his aides to provide background data and the DEC officials to take water and soil samples.

El Buscador led Rosenthal behind the plywood construction walls and pointed to three spots along the canals. "Those are the sites for the humpback bridges."

"Ah, they'll be nice," said Rosenthal. "Tell me, my strange new acquaintance, what game are you playing?"

"Me?" Pointing his right index finger to his chest, El Buscador offered the most imperceptible of smiles.

"Yes, you," said Rosenthal. He looked around, suspicious there might be a camera on him. Damn, there was always a camera on him, so he held back the onslaught of profanities gathering on his tongue. "Last check, you hated Tolland. Even got the attorney general to light a fire underneath him, and now you're his shill in Gowanus?"

El Buscador spent enough years with Thackeray to know how to answer Rosenthal. "Shouldn't your question be what game is Tolland playing?"

"Maybe it should. What's he playing at?"

"Let me see ... Here's a man who hadn't built a skyscraper under ninety stories in this millennium, a man who normally believes the only tool his architects need is a T-square, a man whose idea of addressing community needs is to kick all the residents out, a man who has never constructed anything in his life more beautiful than a cinder block ... this is the man who has presented the most exciting and lively project in the city since the High Line."

"So, are you telling me you're suspicious of Tolland's plans?"

"I am not suspicious of the actual plans. The Graffiti Sisters have created a truly stunning vision and if it is ever executed, that version of the Tolland District would indeed be magnificent."

"What do you think Old Scratch has up his sleeve?"

"Do you remember the Barclays Center?"

Rosenthal looked confused. He obviously didn't remember the Barclays Center because he never knew about it, except that it was a sports and concert venue. He was too young, too damned young. "I don't follow." At least Rosenthal was no fool.

"I'd advise you to do a little research."

"I've got a whole slew of tax incentives that the Senate's been pressuring me to give to Tolland to get this District built. Do you see any reason why I shouldn't give them to him?" When El Buscador didn't answer, Rosenthal persisted, "Will tax breaks come back to bite me?"

"They won't if they're given for the District designed by the Graffiti Sisters. Any variation of the plans will lead to the forfeiture of the tax breaks."

Rosenthal raised his eyebrows. "That will be a tricky provision to craft."

El Buscador nodded to indicate that the governor should be up to the challenge.

Given what had transpired, Rosenthal should've been back walking all around Gowanus, shaking hands, painting a bright vision of the future, peering into the canal in hopes to catch a glimpse of the Gwaken, and assuring the locals that they'll have a place in the ever changing nature of the community. But he had a queasy feeling about what Tolland was up to and El Buscador certainly didn't put him at ease. "Do you think I should come out against this project?"

Touching the top of his hat, El Buscador looked at the governor earnestly, with even a measure of sympathy. "Right now? How can you? Has anyone on your team caught Tolland committing improprieties?"

Rosenthal put his head down, "No, no."

"You'll just have to go along. You don't have to jump up and down about how wonderful it is, though."

"No, I don't," said Rosenthal, a mischievous grin rising from the depths of his suspicions. "That's your job, isn't it?"

El Buscador smiled grimly, "Indeed, it is."

"So, the legendary El Buscador, just what game are you playing?" asked Rosenthal again.

"The game only I'm allowed to play."

Leaving the construction site and heading to a neighborhood slightly more agreeable, Rosenthal laughed and nodded, "If you say so. If you say so."

El Buscador was slightly taken aback that Rosenthal did not want to hear the whole spiel, about the veritable forest of trees and meadow of grasses, about the playgrounds and the serpentine ramp curling its way to the F and G train stop, about the facades that riffed off of Venice, Amsterdam, Bruges, Bangkok, and Gowanus's old industrial past. No, Rosenthal didn't want to hear any of that. For the first time in months, El Buscador could imagine something better than a tragic outcome.

Just to make sure happiness lived behind a door without a knob, Irving Steinman found his way next to him. Irving must have been lurking ... stalking. Irving did his signature elbow grab like El Buscador was his best friend, "I've never seen anyone who would labor so diligently for a cause without any commitment to its tenets, without any adherence to its principles."

El Buscador answered, "Maybe the labor is enough," but his reply was to a man who was no longer there.

He tapped his unfamiliar fedora, one sans bullet holes, and picked up his pace. His head was still adjusting to the new hat. Even El Buscador was surprised that he had taken the extraordinary measure of stepping into a consignment shop and buying a spanking new used fedora. Though the old hat had been a faithful friend for 20 years, he decided that walking around with two bullet holes just above his skull was a bad idea: an invitation to anybody with a gun to use his dome for target practice.

Unfortunately, El Buscador relearned that Maksim didn't need any such solicitation. Just like the last time, he could sense the sniper rifle had him within its sights. This time the bullet whizzed much closer to his thinning hair, sending a few strands up in alarm, knowing that the fresh bullet holes in this fedora decorated a mere three inches above the brim. For once, El Buscador was pleased that his head had flattened over the years.

Maksim was clearly enjoying himself.

El Buscador was not.

No, he didn't like giving Maksim any more chances to brush his hair. Hey, even a sharpshooter could miss by a lobotomizing inch. Fortuitously, El Buscador's days as Tolland's shill were ending. If he needed any encouragement, Maksim's haircut assured that he would be heading far underground, deeper and more shadowy than ever. The only people who would see him would be those whom he'd have seen first. El Buscador would return to the consignment shop to buy another fedora, and he would severely curtail his movements.

•   •   •   •   •

Edmund J. Coppa was more than a little surprised that Russo, the foreman, rolled the heavy telescopic crane onto the recently laid concrete slab that protected the water main. Even Russo must've realized that the substandard mixture of too little cement and too much sand would not have rendered the sturdiest of structures.

For once on the construction site, Coppa couldn't help himself and opened his yap. "You sure we should put that here, boss? It's asking a lot from the slab."

Russo scoffed. "Where the hell else should it go? What's the sense of having a slab if you don't use it?" Coppa didn't want to explain his concern. When Russo tossed in, "Hey, this slab is going to have to handle much more weight than a crane by the time we're done here," Coppa wanted to answer that at least he'd be long gone from the construction site by the time higher floors were erected.

And that was another thing: the crane was awfully big for a building that's only supposed to rise ten floors. When the crane rolled onto the slab, Coppa winced a little, fearful of what might happen next. When he didn't see a crack in the concrete, Coppa merely shrugged and returned to riveting in the braces for the steel beams.

He'd sink the braces for much of the day, watching and waiting for not only Russo to take one of his many coffee breaks, but for Craig and Marco to wander off too. Even when they were all away from the site, Coppa took no chances. He pretended he had pulled a hamstring as he adjusted a bracket, so he could wander about, trying to stretch his thigh and absorb the pain. He made two circles around the slab before he slowed at the blueprints and stared intently at his phone like he was reading a text. He tapped the camera function and clicked away. He stowed his phone back into his pocket and wandered around a bit more, feigning soreness, before he settled back down at the braces. The entire performance was for none of his absent co-workers, but for the specter of security cameras planted God-knows-where.

Coppa was happy that El Buscador wanted him to fire the images off to Mavis's phone, since the shadowman still refused to own a phone – you'd think with all the concessions he'd made lately that he might give in there too. Better for him that El Buscador remained in the previous century since his corresponding with Mavis was the next best thing to seeing her; perhaps, she might want to meet so he could offer his expertize about the specs. He'd make sure in his text he'd send her this evening to present a few choice meeting spots – the Pint O'Plenty was no place for such a lady.

The blueprints served as a fine confirmation of everything Coppa had suspected and had suggested to El Buscador and Mavis. Funny how Mavis hadn't published anything about the disconnects between the Graffiti Sisters' designs and the footprints developed at the site, even down to the building construction being much closer to the water than allowed by law. Mavis had taken pictures herself from the other side of the canal and ordered one of her reporters to break into the construction site on the weekend, shooting the angles so there'd be no doubt about the blatancy of the violations.

What in God's name was she waiting for? Especially with the blueprints, Mavis had enough to get a temporary injunction. Each day, Coppa checked the morning *Herald* to see if he'd be out of a job. Each day, he picked up his lunch bucket and headed to the site. He would keep working. They would all keep working.

CHAPTER 23
TOLLAND, SLEEPWALKING, AND THACKERAY

Timothy Terrance Tolland wondered where his next sleepwalking adventure would land him. Last night, it was in front of the boat house; the night before was the whirling clock at the gate of the Central Park Zoo. Every night, he ended up in the park. That had been consistent. But where next? A week ago he commanded Ingrid not to stop him when he rose in a trancelike state and walked out of his penthouse. Tolland locked eyes with Ingrid and said, "You can follow if you'd like," which Ingrid understood to mean, if you don't follow, you will be terminated.

Ingrid tossed her coat over her nightgown and trailed him through the Don't Walk intersections into the park. In another era, when the park was famous for its muggings, Ingrid would've been fearful of a lurking predator; now she only worried about her boss. Tolland wordlessly marched ahead, a midtown zombie in an uptown reality. Clambering onto those mighty boulders left behind by retreating glaciers, Tolland staggered and scrambled. Ingrid resigned herself that on this inexcusably premature morning he'd break his skull. Instead, he rose atop the grandest hunk of schist for a dozen blocks, raising a paw like he was King Kong and had just climbed to the peak of the Empire State Building, or even better, one of his justly infamous rectangular skyscraping abominations.

He clambered down the rocks and continued through many of the park's meandering pathways, guided by lampposts that cast ominous shadows on the budding sycamore limbs. He had forayed into the 80s until he circled back around to settle under the bridge at Inscope Arch. If Ingrid were less charitable, Tolland in his haunted state might have well reminded her of a troll in a fractured fairy tale.

Here for the first time on this ramble, he spoke. "Where have you taken me?" Ingrid grabbed his hand and methodically led him back to the Tollandia. He persisted with his questions: "What did I do?" "Am I really at fault?" "Did anyone see?"

She persisted in not answering.

By the time they returned to the penthouse, Tolland was fully awake, unfamiliarly proud of himself. For years, he'd been affecting and manufacturing a slew of eccentric ticks and behaviors, ranging from feeding the needy from a coffin to public urination in atriums, each quirk stolen from a wealthy oddball drawn from historical aristocracies. Even his current eccentricity, circling an area three times before entering any door, was inspired by the triple migrations of Nikola Tesla. But this unsettling sleepwalking was not calculated to feed the followers of his Twitter and Instagram accounts. He had no control over this behavior. He wondered what was driving this activity. He suspected it had something to do with the Tolland District in Gowanus, but for the life of him couldn't figure out what. In their unbridled creativity, the Graffiti Sisters fashioned a design that transcended anything he had ever considered.

In the moments after his somnambulation, he allowed for the possibility that his sleepwalking served as a manifestation of his internal conflict about those inspired Gowanus plans and what his construction crews were furtively preparing. Tolland knew those who could be bribed in the early stages had been taken care of, but the truth would soon come out. The minute the Graffiti Sisters arrived at the site, the harsh reality would be patently exposed. And that would be the time when Tolland would have to be at his very best. Yes, the Gwaken had been an unexpected gift. Beyond that mythical beast, he would provide his own share of distractions and so much more. All elements of the Tolland District, as signaled by the Graffiti Sisters, would remain – the long staircase to the subway station, the footbridges, the structures, but with less charm and poetry, more height and floors.

The sleepwalking too had been a serendipitous gift. The papers and the Twitterverse offered quite the glowing coverage, romantic visions of a developer who wandered in his dreams because he carried the burdens of the city's future in his subconscious. It had been his most successful act since he initiated the grass roots efforts to dye the city's rats blue. Only the goddamned *Herald* accused Tolland of pulling another derivative stunt. That horror Tanvi Khotari delivered a few acid phrases that seared in his memory.

She wrote: "Just as he has aped every warped rich duck who offered his eccentricities to the celebrity starved public, just like he stole the idea of dyeing creatures from the much more intriguing Lord Berners, Tolland has returned to his second-hand shenanigans, with his nocturnal operations expanding to sleepwalking in Central Park, a behavior he filched from the renowned author and artful dodger Charles Dickens, who somnambulated his way through London, perhaps spotting the ghost of Christmas past on his crossings. Back a century and a half ago, Dickens wrote, 'It was the best of times, it was the worst of times.' If Dickens lived today in Tolland's New York, he would abandon the first half dozen words, but embrace the last half dozen words with more conviction than ever."

Tolland almost called *The Herald* to protest that his sleepwalking was true, real, and earnest, but to what end? Would his profession of sincerity imply that his earlier acts been mere stunts - he'd never contacted *The Herald* previously. No, better to let his sleepwalking take its course and let the rest of the media and the nimble public relations arm of Crystal Enterprises depict Tanvi and *The Herald* as angry naysayers, as haters.

When he wasn't sleepwalking, Tolland advanced an aggressive agenda in Gowanus. Ironically, he would keep his face far away from the canal for now. Let El Buscador carry the mantle a bit longer. Might as well use him up until the moment he turns. Irving Steinman stopped by to confirm that El Buscador had indeed become the tireless advocate necessary for the project. Steinman told Tolland, "He's kind of broken actually. It's a little bit sad."

Tolland answered, "Not for me it isn't."

Thackeray would arrive at the penthouse any minute and the old conniver would expect cocktails, though eleven in the morning was early even for Irishmen. Ingrid, who still hadn't recovered from her nocturnal responsibilities, was stirring Moscow mules in small copper mugs when

Thackeray greeted Tolland with his usual, "so how is the master of the hounds this fine morning?"

To which the mogul gave his usual reply, "Just waiting to talk to you before I ride into the hunt."

Without asking permission, Thackeray sprawled himself out on the divan in anticipation of his mule's arrival, since the triple spy's deference to Tolland came in words rather than posture. "How is my good Lord today? From what the squirrels tell me, at least some of him was roaming the park in the wee hours the way the Hound of Baskervilles roamed the moors."

Tolland was happy that Thackeray caught wind of the night's sleepwalking which meant his peregrinations would be on Page 6 of the *Post* and seemingly everywhere else by lunch. "What have you been hearing about me?"

Ingrid handed the two collaborators their drinks, the stirred ice rendering the copper flushed and fogged. "Well, let's see. I've heard of your triumphant rehabilitation as the king of New York. That after you complete Gowanus, you should run for mayor."

Tolland laughed, "And give up all this power? What have you heard from El Buscador? Does he still adore me?"

"For the moment, yes. But if you have eyes for another tour guide, or maybe if the tour given is of a project gone, I'd say he will quickly become the spurned lover."

"Yeah, well. He's played that part before." Tolland would not explain to even a confidante like Thackeray that El Buscador will not have the chance to play such a role again. He'd make certain of it. "And the Gwaken? Will the DEC put a moratorium on the project to protect it?"

Thackeray sipped from the copper mug and turned his head from side to side. "No, they're not even sure the creature exists, and if it does, it's not a native species. Plus, the public is confident that you love the Gwaken and would do nothing to harm it."

"Damn, right. The Gwaken is great." Again, Tolland was in no mood to discuss with Thackeray his inexplicable desire to toss a spear into the Gwaken, pull it to the shore, and fry it in a pan.

Pivoting, Thackeray stroked his immaculately groomed salt-and-pepper beard. "Although I'd be concerned about the Una Nonna property. There's been quite a groundswell of sympathy and support for them, especially with the food truck up and running. You know how people love a fable about the tough, resilient New Yorker."

Visibly disturbed, Tolland took his first sip of the mule and fumed, "Don't they know how bad their pizza is? One and a half stars on Yelp! The stomachs of New Yorkers would be better served if Una Nonna served her last pie."

Thackeray was so luxuriously sprawled on the divan that he was in grave danger of sliding off. "Yeah? Tell that to the people donating to the GoFundMe campaign. They've already raised $200,000 to rebuild."

"Jesus," said Tolland. "Don't they know that, for reasons that can't be discussed in polite company, Una Nonna's has made extreme enemies with mobs from numerous families?"

Thackeray nodded. "Believe me, that information has been well distributed and communicated. There's not a person in Gowanus, not a person in all of Brooklyn, who has not heard of Una Nonna's connections to organized crime – how they had a snitch and an arsonist in one Butchie 'The Mongoose' Alberti stowed in the back of the restaurant for five days."

Tolland kept sipping away at the mule. He tried to remember if he even had breakfast yet. "Don't they understand that the mob was going to have to make Una Nonna pay? And don't they understand that the mob would be inclined to burn a place that harbored a monstrous arsonist?"

Smiling at Ingrid to indicate a fresh Moscow mule was in order, Thackeray enjoyed how well Tolland parroted the very talking points the triple spy gave him. He would not reveal to Tolland the role El Buscador had in the rapid return to business of the pizzeria through his procuring of the APizza the Hun food truck. Each interlocutor would receive just the information he deserved.

For the next twenty minutes Thackeray debriefed Tolland on the activities of his construction crews, including who was on the take and who was trying to unionize; then, he moved onto which members of the zoning board could be bribed and which could be blackmailed; then, he spoke of his competitors, especially his old flame Cynthia Newland and the reality TV star/entrepreneur/fledgling developer Matt Aruba. As Thackeray moved onto ways Tolland could hurt *The Herald's* bottom line so much that he could get the owner to sell the paper, Tolland signaled Ingrid to bring out the finger sandwiches.

With more than a twinge of tension, Ingrid nodded to Tolland as she exchanged Thackeray's empty copper cup with one heavy with booze and condensation. Now would come the most trying moments of Ingrid's challenging morning. Tolland and Ingrid had rehearsed the entire scene a dozen times yesterday. Since after the second practice run she believed they had gotten down the choreography, Ingrid couldn't help but feel a little violated. She was proud of herself for refusing to go with Tolland's initial plan that called for his using mouth-to-mouth resuscitation. But in the rehearsals he made her pay for her integrity.

Now she brought in the tray from the kitchen that Philippe had so artfully crafted. Yes, it was early for finger sandwiches, so Tolland told Ingrid to think about the performance as a morning matinee (she had come to New York to be an actress, after all). Thackeray licked his chops and accepted one smoked salmon and one cucumber while Tolland pointed to the ham and brie. Then Tolland announced, "Ingrid, you have had quite the morning. Why don't you put down the tray and join us? Have a finger sandwich or two."

As they had rehearsed, Ingrid flushed with surprise by the magnanimity of her handsome and charming boss. That she, a mere working girl, had been asked to join two of the most famous men in the country for a dainty repast. Feigning nervousness, she delicately grabbed a chicken and cranberry sandwich, her body quivering like the wings of a hummingbird. Sensing what was about to transpire, Thackeray discreetly took out his phone. Ingrid listened to Tolland and Thackeray compare high tea at the Pierre and the Carlyle as she bit into her sandwich. She tried not to chew too carefully.

For the first ten seconds of her seizing up and closing her windpipe, the two men did not notice her suffering, since they were deeply contemplating the flakiness of the currant scones among the Upper East Side establishments. Too bad, since Ingrid thought her suffocation was well modulated, moving from awkward swallowing to stifled gasping to throat-about-the-neck trickles of panic. No matter, when she dropped onto the Persian rug, Tolland rose with the authority of a man who knows how to take charge. Thackeray leaned back, phone now in camera mode, and pointed with the easy confidence of a suppliant who understand how to spread a story. Dizzy with suffering and lack of oxygen, Ingrid hardly noticed when Tolland lifted her, grabbed her from behind, interlocked his hands on her sternum, and pulled tight. She shot out the finger sandwich she had deftly lodged in the corner of her mouth and sucked in the breath of life.

Somehow in all their rehearsals and even now, Tolland's hands managed to rise above the sternum during the miraculous recovery. Ingrid could not remember a damsel ever accusing her rescuer of gratuitous groping, and she was in no position to set a precedent. Thackeray's pictures only captured the perfectly executed Heimlich maneuver. Indeed, Tolland had been well-practiced in the life-saving procedure: he had saved many pretty, young women from choking in the past.

After a few cursory moments of checking on the welfare of the afflicted, Tolland had signaled to all involved that he must attend his next appointment – alas he was a very busy man. Anyway, Thackeray needed to spread the images and whisper the words of Tolland's latest heroics, and Ingrid had to clean the copper mugs and the crumb-laden plates.

When Thackeray departed, Tolland picked up his copy of Dan Brown's *Angels and Demons* and headed into the bedroom. For the first time since college, he had been reading books, all of them Dan Brown's. He took three months to complete *The DaVinci Code*. He was not a fast reader, but he did possess an advantage most other readers could not even fathom: he could now imbed symbols into his buildings. Someday, Tolland was certain Dan Brown would write a book about his buildings. As he dived into the second chapter of the novel, Tolland said to Ingrid those dreaded words, "I think I'll take a nap. If I start walking, you might want to follow me."

CHAPTER 24
FLATS, TUNNELS, AND QUALITY CONTROL

At first, Nancy thought the shift in the food truck came from JoJo's moving to the right end of the cooler to grab more shredded mozzarella. But the list was so pronounced that she slid downhill. Now that she thought about it, Nancy heard noises that sounded like two gunshots. In Gowanus, many cracks and blasts resounded along Smith Street and the screeches and rumbles of the G Train didn't exactly provide sonic purity. Indeed, the aural quality of Gowanus had a warzone vibe common among most industrial areas, given their heavy equipment, busted trucks, and potholed streets.

As she took a pie out of the oven, she asked JoJo to look outside. The two left tires were as flat as flounders. He stuck his finger in the round hole of the front tire. They had not run over anything since the truck had been set up at five in the morning – they got the truck flushed out and the porta-potty disinfected between 4 a.m. and 5 a.m., which had traditionally been their slowest hour of the day. That was the time they took their showers at the Retro Fitness gym, cleaning themselves as the truck received its freshening. Anyway, if they had run over glass or some other puncturing debris, the flat tires would've come much earlier. The holes were so neat and round that they had to be from bullets. Even a skilled maniac with an icepick or a knife couldn't have made such precise perforations.

JoJo's ruminations received more conclusive evidence as he heard a whizz and a pop in the front right tire, then the back right, with air rapidly escaping. JoJo ran around to the front and sought cover near the doorway to make sure the shooter did not confuse his wide frame with a steel radial.

Inside, Nancy had noticed a nice leveling off of each side as the other tires flattened. She naively thought JoJo had rectified the problem. For some reason, she had not noticed she was sinking.

After waiting five minutes and concluding the shooting had ended (JoJo had a sixth sense about such matters), he reported what had transpired to Nancy. Thinking of the fire, Nancy theorized, "I think someone is trying to send us a message."

"That's a possibility," said JoJo grimly.

"Funny, I don't think the message ever arrived."

Laughing, JoJo stepped back out. He didn't have to explain that he was off to Gagliano's, since where else would he be going? He had put on his swim trunks for a dip, but now he'd get out on the other side of the canal. The owners of Gagliano's Tire Shop were his uncles; the guys who loaded the truck with Roadlux 216 Commercial Radials were his cousins. Riding in the back with the tires, JoJo returned and got Nancy out of the kitchen. Cousins Michael and Bobby had the punctured tires off and the new tires on in 15 minutes. The two customers who came during the repair decided to wait. Both had never seen shot-out tires before and thought this incident would make for a nice story to tell around the shuffleboard courts and the canoe ramps.

Michael and Bobby wouldn't hear about charging JoJo and Nancy a dime. They muttered something about Una Nonna's being an institution. Nancy tried to give them a pie. Clearly former customers, the cousins would have none of it, simply saying it was great that they could help keep this Gowanus icon up and running.

Nancy was relieved that JoJo could take care of the tire problem before El Buscador arrived to run the place for them. Una Nonna's always had one of them making the pies and charming the customers, but the bank needed signatures from both of them if they were going to get the new construction started. Even without receiving the insurance adjustor's reimbursement, since the arson investigation still had to be completed, they would plow ahead, hoping to break ground within a month, or if they decided to go with a prefab building, even faster.

Nancy had thought about shutting down Una Nonna's for the bank appointment, but El Buscador had already helped out several times. He was a butcher with the dough, but everything else he had down pat. She had tossed five doughs to give him a head start. Anyway, he said he'd bring help with him. Still, when he arrived with a statuesque, middle-aged black woman, Nancy was taken aback. She had expected someone else in a trench coat and a fedora like him. But whatever, both she and JoJo put on their best clothes and walked the seven blocks to Investors Bank as they prepared their future.

•　　•　　•　　•　　•

El Buscador had already given two tours of the Tolland District, painting pictures of an exotic fantasyland for stakeholders and potential buyers. Even though his schemes and plans were diametrically opposed to the full-throated support of the District that he projected, he still felt dirtied and sullied by coming off as a Tolland shill. However, that effort was absolutely necessary. His role as substitute chef at Una Nonna's was not. Yet ever since he'd had his first Una Nonna's pie, he'd been dying to see if he could get Nancy to make a better pizza. Even as she left to go to the bank, he tried to pitch to her what could be new procedures for pie-making. "You see the way you do it, where you don't measure anything, that can make the pizzas inconsistent."

"I don't make my pizzas with measurements," Nancy protested. "I make them with love." Then she eyed El Buscador with a pity for the naïve. "My place has been burned and we've got to work out of this food truck. This morning the tires were shot out. And you're worrying about quality control?"

El Buscador nodded with resignation. "I guess you're right."

"Of course, I'm right," said Nancy. "We should be back in a couple of hours."

JoJo threw in. "Watch out for stray bullets."

As Nancy and JoJo strolled in their Sunday best toward the bank, El Buscador yelled out to them, "I always do."

El Buscador blew out a sigh of relief, a sigh he'd made when his parents first left him home alone for the night almost fifty years ago. He pulled out of his athletic bag a five-pound block of high-grade mozzarella and big cans of San Marzano tomatoes. He dumped Nancy's big pot of tomato sauce outside and started again, simmering garlic in extra virgin olive oil.

During all those years of being on the run, from giving exclusive underground tours, El Buscador had this bizarre, secret dream of running a restaurant. He figured these few hours at Una Nonna's would be the one opportunity to get that dream out of his system. He asked Mavis to come along, since he thought he might as well try out marriage for the afternoon too – even though his cooking partner had no idea that she was so engaged.

Mavis shredded the cheese and talked Tolland with him. "How long are you going to make me sit on this story?"

"A couple of more days. Just waiting for a few more shoes to drop. Meantime, let's make some pies."

Yes, the sauce could have used much more time to deepen and mellow, but El Buscador had his new pies out to the customers an hour in. To his chagrin, the first two patrons didn't notice the difference.

The third did. And she started texting. More customers than usual arrived. Given the fire, the food truck, and the GoFundMe campaign, Una Nonna's was already on many residents' radar. They'd been secretly waiting twenty years for a better product to arrive.

Which explained the flash mob.

El Buscador confessed to Mavis, "I'm no good at throwing dough. Could you be in charge of that?"

Instead of answering, "Thanks for the warning," Mavis rolled her eyes, took out a metal tin, and started pounding into a dough as if it were El Buscador's head. Thank goodness it was a nice day. The customers who lined up outside the truck swapped stories about their first Una Nonna's pie. Apparently, getting a pizza from Una Nonna's was a common form of parental punishment and served as an ongoing threat to make children behave: "If you don't clean your room, you'll know what you'll be having Friday night."

But El Buscador noticed several customers arrived at the Food Truck only to turn away. The crowds were the reason for their departure. He could tell they were looking for something else from the food truck, something that was not a pie, something that only JoJo and Nancy could provide. He had observed this behavior before, the side glances of sketchy characters who had entered Una Nonna's without pizza on their minds. Now, from his new perspective behind the counter, he was starting to put a few pieces together. All this time he'd been so focused on the horrible quality of Una

Nonna's pie that he failed to see what else was going on here. Even now, he could not ponder the implications, since he had pizza to get out of the oven.

As each pizza made its way to a smiling customer, the whispers were that these pies weren't half bad. Hey, it's not like they were on par with Totonno's or Spumoni Gardens, not even close, but they were better than any they've had here before, inspiring many residents to hang around the burnt-out property and have a picnic. El Buscador knew if Tolland got wind of what was happening, he'd have a stroke, which was the idea.

But Tolland wasn't the only one who would disapprove. When Nancy and JoJo returned, they had the look of angry parents who'd gone away, only to discover their child had thrown a wild party. Rather than yell at El Buscador, Nancy asked him a simple question: "What the hell are you doing here?"

"I thought I'd employ a few quality control measures."

"You live under a rock and you're going to employ quality control measures on my business?" Nancy asked a reasonable question.

"Well, I thought some careful apportioning of ingredients and an upgrade in their class would go a long way toward consistency of the product." El Buscador delivered this argument with a sheepish hesitancy, what sounded to Mavis as the essence of guilt.

"Product? Product? This is not a product. This is a pizza." Nancy looked at JoJo and asked, "What do you think about all of this?"

JoJo shrugged his shoulders. "I think I'll take a swim in the canal."

As El Buscador and Mavis left, night put a dimmer on the sky's light and the picnickers watched JoJo do laps. Mavis nodded to El Buscador, "Where do we go now? Are you going to make me work with you at McDonalds, so we can assemble a fancy Big Mac and piss off the owners?"

El Buscador laughed. "Nah. I think I'm better off doing what I'm good at."

"You're good at something?"

El Buscador tried look hurt. "I have a secret place I want to show you."

"Oh, so you're back in the tour guide business. Do I have to pay you?"

"You already paid me in labor."

As she followed him onto Smith Street heading north, Mavis noted, "If that's the case, then I'd say you owe me money."

El Buscador smiled. "Let's just say I am permanently in your debt."

As they pressed onward with the monstrous erector set of the G-train running above them, Mavis asked, "So are you going to tell me where we're going?"

"You presume I know."

They crossed the numbered streets, counting down, Tolland's massive construction site to the right finally giving way to the high-end housing project and the Whole Foods that signaled the gentrification of Gowanus. They pressed forward at a steady, nearly rushed pace. Grabbing El Buscador's arm, Mavis said, "I'm certain you know where we're going because this is the first time you've walked in a straight line for months."

They crossed Union and five minutes later Bergen and five minutes beyond that they hit Atlantic where El Buscador looked left, then right. To the left was the hidden path by Court Street that required their opening a manhole cover on busy Atlantic Avenue and clambering down a rope ladder. To the right was the entrance he burrowed by Hoyt in the basement of a boarded-up storefront. The one to the left was the work of Bob Diamond, an explorer El Buscador admired more than anyone in the entire city – the man who better earned the title of El Buscador, but he wasn't going to get it, since the Tour Guide would hold onto his name no matter what crisis consumed him.

He had no choice but to go to the right. As he picked the lock on the green, metal basement doors, Mavis muttered. "Oh, so it's going to be one of those."

El Buscador handed Mavis a flashlight from his backpack as they descended stair after stair until they reached an opening of broken paneling, busted walls studs, and crumbled bricks. They ducked through two crevices to where a soft wind blew. When they could lift their heads again, they entered into an arched opening that was two stories high. Here El Buscador pronounced, "Welcome to the oldest subway tunnel in the world."

"Is that one of your lines you use on vulnerable middle-aged women?"

"Besides today, no. In case you're curious," El Buscador had his doubts, "it was built in 1844."

Walking this way and that, Mavis shot the flashlight in all directions. "This isn't as nice as your old digs." El Buscador winced at the mention of the abandoned city hall subway station, with its arched, abbey-like tiles, its skylights, and its charming carvings. "In fact, this is just a big old tunnel."

"That it is." El Buscador smiled. "A bunch of Brits had Irish workers dig it. One contractor told the men they'd have to work on Sundays and miss church. They shot the contractor. He's buried behind one of these walls."

"Lovely."

"Come along. I have something to show you."

"I'm not interested in seeing any dead bodies."

Without waiting for Mavis to follow, El Buscador pronounced, his words reverberating off the old tunnel walls, "This body you'll want to see."

In five minutes, they stopped at what looked like the end of the tunnel. That's where El Buscador followed the edge of a busted track to a pile of debris. He climbed up on it and started pushing away bricks, dirt, and hunks of concrete. The chimney appeared first on the locomotive and then the dark metal of its nose. Mavis watched El Buscador, now a cloud of dust and debris, as he excavated right down to the buffers.

"Did you discover that train right before my eyes?"

"No, I found it yesterday and covered it back up. I wanted you to see it the way I first did. You know I can be a bit of a drama queen."

"You don't have to tell me."

"It's a steam locomotive. They'd outlawed these things in the tunnel, which ended up shutting down the tunnel with it."

"Are you going to put all that crap back on the locomotive?"

"No, now I'm going to keep excavating it. It'll be my new hobby."

"That's good to hear. Because if El Buscador was going to become a pizza man, I might just have to drown in a pot of sauce."

El Buscador feigned woundedness. "I'm so sorry to hear that. I thought we could open a place together."

"You'd spend your time better if you used that twisted brain of yours to figure out how to shut down Tolland's business instead of opening your own."

"Even mighty steam locomotives, given the right circumstances, can be stopped dead in their tracks. There's a big Nor'easter coming in two days; it's supposed to drop three inches. You'll have your story then. I'm asking the Graffiti Sisters to wait until the rains come too. I know I have no right to ask you, especially for someone's whose business is to scoop everybody else, and I know lately I don't seem like I know what I'm doing, but I think I've got a handle on this."

Even though she hadn't been drinking, Mavis wasn't sure she was thinking straight. "Alright, I'll wait. I'm supposed to be off tomorrow anyway."

They left the tunnel and headed back up the stairs. El Buscador stalled until they returned to Atlantic Avenue and the open air before he posed the next question. "Since you're off tomorrow, could you help out Pratt?" He pretended he didn't see the fury in Mavis's eyes. "Everything needs to be done before the rains."

"There are no limits to your gall, are there?"

"Not one goddamn scruple."

"I'm not digging. You want digging? Do it your damn self."

"No, no. No digging. Just planting. Pratt digs. You plant."

"You still got some nerve."

"Yeah, well, I'm gonna need that nerve to make it through the next couple of days."

CHAPTER 25
THE BAT CAVE

Before the operations reached their final phase, El Buscador checked in with Edmund J. Coppa who was kind enough to delay his daily appointment at the Pint O'Plenty. El Buscador took Coppa to his new digs in the basement of the old Coignet Concrete Stone Company. Coppa was duly impressed with the elegantly carved columns, balustrades, and pilasters that adorned what was once a showroom for the company, but now merely El Buscador's sleeping quarters.

"This is almost as nice as the city hall station."

"Yeah, let's hope it's better constructed than the Tolland District." El Buscador grabbed Coppa by the wrist to make sure he had his full attention. "You certain the concrete will go if the rains come?"

"Ah, if the rains come, that concrete won't make it. It didn't properly cure. My crew is bad, but I was checking out Stevenson's team and they're worse. The stuff's already crumbling and it's right above a sewer pipe. The stupid bastards put a backhoe on top of it. A little rain and the whole thing goes tumbling down."

"Are you sure?"

Coppa grinned. "If it holds, I'll make sure it won't."

"Eddie, my good friend, you will do no such thing. Let me let you in on a little secret. The only reason you haven't been caught in your sordid life is that nobody has taken the trouble to catch you."

"Is that what's happened to you?" asked Coppa.

"Exactly," said El Buscador, "although, I have a feeling that's about to end."

"Well, isn't that typical El Buscador bullshit," said Coppa. "You've been telling me for years you are about to be imprisoned, beaten, killed. And yet here you are, frigging Chicken Little."

"Yeah, yeah, I know. I'm more of an alarmist than I've ever cared to admit to myself. But let me make one thing clear: do not touch the concrete. If it crumbles, great. If not, I'll deal with the fallout. If you mess with the concrete, not only will you be caught because they will check for sabotage, but you'll elevate Tolland rather than destroy him."

"Got it," said Coppa. Then he added, assuring himself as much as El Buscador. "Believe me, the concrete can't hold. It hasn't cured. I'm surprised it hasn't broken yet. With that rain, it's got no choice."

Coppa departed and El Buscador stood in the shadows of Whole Foods' solar-powered carport, waiting for a limousine to arrive. The VIPs were a half-hour late for their appointed midnight meeting but that was better than not showing up at all. Cynthia Newland stepped out of the limo first, followed by Matt Aruba, who instructed his two bodyguards to stay in the car. It would not be good for Matt Aruba to go off on a secret adventure with the legendary El Buscador and decide to have protection in tow.

"Are you ready?" asked El Buscador.

"Why the hell not?" answered Cynthia.

Aruba followed and smiled. It wasn't much a journey. The notorious Gowanus Bat Cave was across the street and a football field down the canal from Whole Foods. In its earlier days, it housed drugs dealers and assorted ne'er-do-wells. Now with the moldy mattresses and the unpleasant soaked rags removed to make way for a looming art collective, the Bat Cave would become the site for business transactions no less seamy but exponentially more lucrative than any that had gone down there in the past. Waiting at the entrance for them was Luna Graffiti, the most creative and volatile of the sister architects.

After El Buscador broke them in with his Bogota Quad pick, they were greeted by wild, richly colored walls of graffiti. The center floor sign that served as a welcome mat read, "What Fresh Hell Is This." The absence of a question mark at the end of the message always got to El Buscador. He would speak the words, puzzling out just which inflection he should use in the pronunciation. Thank goodness for the clean-up work by the art collective, since this cavernous building which once was the old power station for the Brooklyn Power Transit Authority had been a smelly shamble. With the renovations, he was able to set up folding chairs around a screw-together table before they arrived. From his backpack, he took out two bottles of chilled Alsatian Riesling, aged Manchego cheese, creamy Camembert, some freshly sliced pancetta, fig jelly, and membrillo. As he corkscrewed open the Rieslings, Luna passed out glasses and plates, sticking knives in the hunks of cheese.

Before they got down to business, El Buscador gave them the full act. He pointed to various bubbled graffiti words on the wall and shot out lurid anecdotes about the artists – many of them spectacularly apocryphal. His tale of the bright blue words "You Go Girl," framed by a face with three layers of sun glasses, featured the former heiress Rachel Zagelbaum, who gave up everything to find her vein-thatched beau down in Honduras (hence the sunglasses) only so the star-crossed couple could return together to the Bat Cave, spending their last three months on earth strung out on heroin. Some of the art demanded an explanation ("That 'HEART' in all caps filled in with newspaper print describes the murder of a girl who had her heart impaled by a runaway trailer hitch"). Meanwhile, the symbolic meanings that could be fathomed from the numerous squids and mustaches drawn on the walls sent El Buscador bounding from the realms of Egyptian hieroglyphs to the rituals of Olmecs.

Moving on to the Batman exhibition, he explained that the figure speaking to Batman may or may not be Robin. Whatever the case, the speaker definitely had a man-bun and was ready to confess: "Look! My friends & I painted a mur—"

But from his reply, Batman would have none of it, "Stop letting in crackheads."

El Buscador described how the residents of the Bat Cave had policed themselves for years until the floods and hardened elements came in and the bodies piled up. Then El Buscador pivoted. "But we are not here to talk about the past of Gowanus; we are here to forge the future."

"Isn't that Tolland's Gowanus?" asked Luna.

"I thought it was yours for a while there. You Graffiti Sisters have some of the best plans I've seen in years."

"We've heard your praise loud and clear," said Luna.

"We did too," said Aruba, "so much so that we were afraid you had gone legit."

El Buscador grinned, "Just legit enough to find my way into this hole."

Cynthia wanted to get down to business. "I've been telling Matt to buy up shares Crystal Enterprises." The financing company behind the Tolland

Project, Crystal Enterprises surprisingly did not have Tolland as a majority shareholder – a little nugget that Mavis dug up. With his 35 percent interest, Tolland has been able to hold sway over the entire operation.

"Are you willing between the two of you to buy up enough to get a majority?"

Aruba nodded confidently. "We're almost there. But if you're saying that some sort of catastrophe is going to happen, how is this a good investment for me?"

"Because what's going to happen will drop the shares for a few days. And it will put you in prime position to take over the project."

Luna could hold off no longer. "Wait, wait. Why should the Graffiti Sisters turn their backs on Tolland since he's given us the chance of a lifetime?"

El Buscador smiled. "I think it's time to call in my associate."

Both Cynthia and Aruba turned their heads, fearful that associate might have a gun.

"Mavis," he yelled.

Mavis appeared from below a catwalk. "Goddamn. It's about time. You sure love your theatrics, don't you?"

El Buscador shrugged. "Sometimes they're necessary. Cynthia, Matt, Luna, this is Mavis Wellington, editor of *The Herald.*"

"We're familiar," said Aruba.

"She has some blueprints to show all of you. First, Luna, has Tolland asked you to come out to the site yet?"

"No, he said the crews were just doing some preliminary excavating and clearing. We were supposed to begin next month."

"Ah, I was wondering why I didn't hear any howls from you. Mavis can you show her the pictures first?"

Luna could immediately see problems. "Where's the forty-foot setback from the canal for the buildings? And those aren't footings for bridges."

"Every day, I've been at the construction site. Each day, the crews make clearer that they are not following one bit of your plan. Mavis, can you show them the real blueprints?" Mavis scowled a bit. She wanted to say, if you keep treating me like Vanna Goddamn White, I'm going to toss you into the canal. "Mavis's investigative work has been incredible." Nice recovery, Mavis thought.

As she passed Luna the blueprints, Mavis said, "You may recognize the authors of the work, since they're some of Tolland's oldest friends."

"Lud, Gib, and Nirob," Luna read. "Son-of-a-bitch. I'll kill him with my bare hands. How can he get away with this?"

"You remember the original Atlantic Yards Plans and the Barclays Center. The architect was Frank Gehry and if his plans were realized, the place would've been a titanium wonderland. But all of a sudden, when they had to go through with the project, after the community and boards approved it thinking they had added a magnificent Gehry jewel to downtown Brooklyn, the developer said he was short on funds. They got stuck with a choice to take either a mediocre version of the original project – in other words, no Gehry and structures that looked like every other damn commercial facility and arena that the greedy and uninspired have erected for years..." El Buscador pulled back here, since Newland and Aruba might have been counted among the greedy and uninspired. "... Or have a broken mess of a construction that just sat there. The community saw the bad version of Atlantic Yards and Barclays as their only choice. And believe me, the people of Gowanus are used to rotten choices, so they'll definitely go for the Lud, Gib, and Nirob plan."

"Ah, the old bait and switch," said Aruba,

"You got it, brother."

"Where do we come in?" asked Cynthia.

"Right after the flood."

"What flood?"

"You'll see," said El Buscador. "I'd stay back in Manhattan for the next few days. Anyway, can you understand the ramifications if you took over Tolland's project and built what he couldn't? Could you see what would happen if you built what the Graffiti Sisters have designed? You would be the Queen and King of New York."

Newland and Aruba clearly liked that phrase. Cynthia added, "And we humiliate Tolland too, perhaps even destroy him. You forgot to mention that."

"Must've slipped my mind."

They continued to talk, but soon Mavis and El Buscador knew the conversation was beyond them, that the Graffiti Sisters would be negotiating with the two who would soon be the majority owners of Crystal Enterprises.

CHAPTER 26
OF PITS AND TRENCHES

On this warm spring night, the rat pit stunk like nobody business: more sweaty patrons and the air conditioner not yet up and running. The main talk was in anticipation of Chester, a white pointer with blotchy, brown splotches more commonly found on cows. He'd been thrown into the midst of the zinc-lined walls last week and sent a charge into the crowd. While Chester broke no speed records, he made up in ferociousness what he lacked in efficiency. Chester tended to make certain that a rat was dead before he moved on, which meant an inordinate amount of chomping and shaking. The smelly crowd would laugh and jeer as the pointer furiously wriggled what looked like bloody blue chew toys. Chester fumed with a hatred that must have been deeply embedded in the genetics and history of his breed.

Pratt had heard less about the Tolland District than usual, except now the talk was the project could well rise over 40 stories. As Aristo explained, "Once you hit over ten floors, nobody makes a big deal about how high you go." But El Buscador seemed to already have heard the news. The big talk tonight was about the Gwaken. Cartwright, who tended to know these things, had indicated that Tolland either had captured the creature or was about to. Pratt had been around the rat pit long enough to know he couldn't ask questions like how anyone could be on the verge of capturing the Gwaken. The hunt couldn't be planned; it had to be spur of the moment. Instead, he shut up and waited for Chester to finish – something about his speckled head thrashing and growling that made Pratt suppress many winces.

When Chester had finally mutilated his last blue rat, Pratt observed the carnage, rodent bodies matted with blood strewn about, clumps of fur hovering in the thick air. Pratt lingered until Cartwright placed his next bet – this one on how long it would take Señor Socks, a sharp-eyed beagle, to get kill his first ten blues. Then he asked, "How's Tolland getting the Gwaken?"

Taking a swig of his warming, flattening beer, Cartwright said, "Oh, he's a great hunter, that man. Somebody said it was with a fishing pole and a net, but everybody knows that Tolland is lethal with a spear."

"Yeah, he's quite famous for that," Pratt said, trying to avoid asking him more questions. The workers who come to the pit to blow off steam get suspicious when asked more than one question.

"He's killed buffalo and lions with that spear. Garvey even said he felled a rhino on a safari. Knowing Tolland, I tend to believe it."

During his long days over the past week digging a trench through the alley, Pratt had not seen the Gwaken. Neither had Pygmalion. He would have to ask El Buscador if he's spotted him, since that freak covered the canal from end to end during most days of his weird, restless existence. Pratt slipped out earlier from the rat pit than usual. His physical exertions were much more exhausting than his previous life of pumping out investigative articles and barbed columns.

The next morning he arrived at the alley with its hodgepodge collection of iron catwalks and fire escapes hovering above to give the space an industrial tightness that occasionally cramped his efforts. Mavis stood at the Nevins Street entrance, arms folded, flats and pots of flowers lined up, ready for planting along the trench's edges. Day lilies and peonies and phloxes and pansies and lilacs made Pratt sniff voluntarily for the first time since last week, when Mavis previously appeared with her floral roadshow. Mavis looked tired. "You've been out partying in the clubs without me?" asked Pratt.

"No, just your idiot friend. Everything's nocturnal with him. Just because he's a vampire doesn't mean I am."

"You could use some sleep."

"I'll get to sleep after the rains come," said Mavis.

"Tell me about it," said Pratt. "El Buscador has a lot riding on this rain. If it doesn't pour, I have a feeling all his plans will go to shit."

"It'll rain. I bet El Buscador is off in the corner doing a Druid dance."

Pratt grinned. "I don't know. I see him more of an Iroquois, lots of feathers and shells, maybe a hint of turquoise."

Mavis laughed at the image of the trench-coated El Buscador in the garb of a high priest or shaman. "Enough of this nonsense," she said. "Since when have we had so little to talk about that we have resorted to conversations about the weather?"

"Don't worry, next we'll talk about the Mets."

"No, we won't."

They were silent for a good hour. While Mavis dug holes, mixed peat moss with the dirt, and dropped in the plants, Pratt tamped down the clay in the trench, stamping the pole forcefully, its heavy metal square boot leveling the channel and creating a water barrier. He'd spent the last three days putting six inches of clay back into the four feet he'd cleared from Nevins to the canal. Where the hell El Buscador got all the clay from, he wouldn't say – in one of his goddamn mysterious moods. Anyway, even though a mound of clay remained, Pratt had enough of tamping. If he was going to lay gravel and sand above it, he'd better get a move on.

As she grumbled about El Buscador, Mavis felt blessed that she had her hands in the dirt and was brightening this funky, shadowy alley. She constantly teetered at the precipice of the clay trench. She could smell the rain, but she and Pratt were determined to finish a rare feat in this city of skyscrapers: they would let something in instead of build something over.

As they continued to toil, Pratt asked, "Hey, have you seen the Gwaken lately?"

"No, he must be hiding or something. How about you?"

"Not for a while. You think something happened to him?"

"I sure hope not," said Mavis. "But you've got to admit, anything that swims in the canal can't be long for this world."

They made familiar jokes of contamination and toxicity. Pratt naively proffered, "Maybe part of El Buscador's plan is for the rains to wash away the pollutants."

Mavis burst out in laughter, hearty, cleansing guffaws. "This is El Buscador we're talking about."

Pratt chuckled too. "Yeah, that means it's going to get worse."

"I'd think Noah."

Mavis and Pratt spoke of all things: politics, broken families, the new restaurant on Reade Street ... until Pygmalion arrived and Pratt's attentions were diverted. Each day the relationship between the two had become increasingly flirtatious. For the first time since he quit *The Herald*, Pratt had returned to his verbose ways, making painfully clear to Pygmalion that he was more than some common laborer.

He pointed to her massive dirt sculpture of the Gwaken and said, "Now a prodigious monument to what has failed to be seen rises from this loamy ash."

"Loamy ash," repeated Pygmalion, not bothering to put down her carving tools to answer, forever cutting into the dirt, with a dedication to detail that bordered on the rococo. "You pompous jerk."

He admired her work. "Now that's a snout that could guide the past into the future. And those barbels tongue the injustices of all that has stained these lavender waters and rendered loss without conscience, suffering without consequence."

"Shut up," said Pygmalion, embarrassed and marginally titillated, her arresting green eyes sparkling.

Pratt abandoned his verbal gymnastics to keep her off balance. "All right, let's see what Mavis thinks."

"No," Pygmalion objected.

But Pratt was off to the channel with his wheelbarrow's worth of sand. When he returned, Mavis was with him and took a long slow walk around the Gwaken. She said, "It's very good." She continued to walk about and think.

Pygmalion could tell Mavis spotted a problem. "What," she said, no questioning in her tone; instead, a trace of dread. Pygmalion got a good dose of those penetrating eyes that Pratt had come to know all too well, the ones cast upon so many of his articles, the ones that sent Mavis's fingers flying, forever slashing, tightening, and sharpening.

"The scales. They look like more traditional fish scales. The Gwaken is a sturgeon. That means the scales are more like armor; more prehistoric."

"That's it?" asked Pratt. He looked at Pygmalion. "Boy, you got off easy."

"She's good," said Mavis, walking back to her flowers.

"What's that mean, that I'm not?" said Pratt.

Mavis enjoyed not answering. She put her last pot in the earth.

Pygmalion got right to work on thickening up those scales. Pratt shoveled another wheelbarrow full of sand and rolled over to Mavis.

"Your girlfriend's got quite a creature there," said Mavis. Pratt waited for the other shoe to drop. "But let me ask you something? What's going to happen to that thing when the rains come?"

Pratt shrugged his shoulders.

CHAPTER 27
THE FLOOD

The rains started early that morning, but the heaviest didn't hit until the afternoon. All day long Edmund J. Coppa feared he was wrong. The flooding of the canal and the surrounding streets were no surprise. Miserable, noxious ... E Coli for the masses. For years, the EPA had been cleaning up the Superfund site, shoring up bulkheads and seawalls, removing centuries of noxious sludge. The residents got the feeling the project would never end. For years, the city had been installing more drains and sewers, a slow, painstaking effort to tame nature's inflows. The residents got the feeling the project would never end. And just to remind them of the bad old days, the heavy rains would come. The residents trudged through the floods and heard the promises that someday these flash cesspools would swirl down some magical drain.

Eddie met El Buscador up on the rooftop of Whole Foods. They bought beers and peered west, looking out on the cranes. Eddie kept apologizing, something he did often when he was drinking beer, and he kept asking El Buscador what he would do now. Whatever happened in the rain, Mavis would be running her stories on the architectural blueprints and on the transgressions of zoning regulations in *The Herald* tonight. She had jeopardized her scoop for too long. The battle would begin even if all of the troops hadn't arrived at the front.

Eddie was staring down at his beer and El Buscador was buying another round when they heard the crash and the sinking of a backhoe. Water and sewage bubbled and shot up through the swamp with all the intensity of a gusher in an oil field. Eddie smiled like he'd been the one who'd struck it rich. He didn't like disappointing his old friend.

As he studied the turbid ebb and flow of the roiling waters, El Buscador calculated. Just how far would the damage stretch? He took out binoculars. The floods had long passed Smith Street and flowed beneath the overpass for the G train. It would flood St. Mary's Playground and soak the little hobbit doors of Dennet Place. My God, the waters would crash in waves onto the foundations of St. Mary Star of the Sea and invade the neat and lovely streets of Carroll Gardens. Westward, the floods would cross below the BQE and swamp Red Hook, but the deluges were also coming back toward him through the numbered streets.

El Buscador chose wisely in picking the artificially high ground of the Whole Foods roof. He wondered if management would shut the market soon since the Third Street Bridge below him was under water as were the Carroll and Union Street bridges further inland. Ah Gowanus, the place that stored the crap of the city now housed the sodden crap of the city. In theory, and under the spell of Noah, floods should be this great cleansing, purifying moment. But in urban reality, floods were saturated ambassadors of mold and disease. El Buscador felt a twinge of guilt since he might've prevented a bad flood from being worse.

But he knew the only hope for Gowanus was that the industrial wastelands be ripped right down to the pillars. After their share of total excavations, the factories and domiciles around the canal had long learned the lesson that sheetrock and carpeting had no home in Gowanus – nothing that absorbed could be installed. Tomorrow, bleach would come, and the next day, and the day after that. All the muck and mire would be cleansed ... until the next time.

Yet with this rupturing of the sewer line, the workers and residents of Gowanus, who had seen everything, had encountered something entirely new. In the most repulsive terms, they had been confronted with what Tolland would be delivering to this community: how he would take the sludge and misery and aggrandize it. Amazingly, Tolland had seized with extreme prejudice the very worst of Gowanus and compounded the stains on its misbegotten soul.

After the flood, El Buscador knew *The Herald*, the Governor, and a few choice voices would make abundantly clear that the Graffiti Sisters with their forward-thinking design offered a way out. And all who were knee-deep in this mess must come to understand that with Tolland around, there would never be a chance to follow the proper path.

Mavis had made sure the inspectors would be down here on this very day to examine the combined sewer systems so central to Gowanus's contamination from the start. With Edmund J. Coppa on hand, they would get an earful about the paltry portions of cement used to pour the concrete above the sewer lines and how the construction violated zoning codes in both placement and delivery.

El Buscador signaled Eddie to finish his beer. "I think you're on, my friend."

Taking a mighty slug and slamming the mug on the bar, Eddie waved, turned left, and headed down the stairs in search of building inspectors.

El Buscador trained his binoculars on Una Nonna's in the distance. Long used to the rains in Gowanus, Nancy drove the truck up on a concrete plinth. So as not to be stranded on an island of dough and sauce, JoJo made a footpath out of the cinderblocks. It may have well been the least charming footpath ever constructed, but the people of Gowanus would be able to get their goddamn pizza.

Through his binoculars, El Buscador spied a hardy patron who stepped gingerly on the blocks, a lightness and urgency in his nimbleness that struck an observer as an ossuary caretaker skipping across rows of skulls. He must have ordered in advance because within two minutes he was back out, teetering and tottering, box in hand, negotiating cinderblocks and floodwaters. At the end of the line waited another customer, patiently allowing for the pie and patron to pass since JoJo had only fashioned a one-way path. Two others joined the cinderblock conga line. In Gowanus, catastrophes, floods – one part act of God, two parts acts of septic neglect – were damn good for business, and nobody knew that better than the proprietors of that tragedy on wheels, Una and the Nonnas. Yet, from the zeal of the patrons willing to run this gauntlet, El Buscador found his suspicions building that perhaps something else was in those pizza boxes. An investigation of just what that product was happened to be low on the priority list today.

El Buscador turned his binoculars inland to Pratt and the trench he dug between Nevins and the canal. Pratt painstakingly followed his awakening stream, saddened to see the very top layer of sand he tamped down wash away. He was thankful the clay and the gravel and the other three inches of sand stayed in place. Seeing this preview, Pratt was beginning to understand what El Buscador was after. The actual stream would be another matter, but not a bad trial run. While the stream had been El Buscador's vision, he understood that Pratt (he of the sore back, the blistered hands, and the violated wheelbarrow) had more invested in the channel. The deluge abated and, with it, Pratt's stream. Soon the channel was such a mere trickle that Pratt looked up and prayed for rain.

Instead, he was delivered Tanvi.

Since he'd left *The Herald*, Pratt had avoided her, knowing he couldn't date her, given her dogged severities. Her deadline clarity did not fire desires within him, desires so mired in hazy postponement.

And yet now she stood in this soggy, virulent hellhole, goulashes the only thing separating her from trench foot. Appropriately, he hid in his own trench and eavesdropped. She was speaking to a teacher who worked in a middle school around the block. From what Pratt could divine from his sorry vantage point, she was young, black, female, with a big head of hair. He caught her name – Toni.

"What brings you out on this dark and stormy afternoon?" asked Tanvi.

"I thought I'd check out the oysters," Toni answered.

"Wow," said Tanvi. Pratt imagined her opening her arms to signal the flood damage. "Why now? Couldn't you wait until tomorrow?"

"I could, but I thought it would be better to see how the oysters deal with the discharge today, and I'll check again tomorrow."

Tanvi pointed to Toni's sodden clipboard, pen marks smeared everywhere. "Can you read that?"

Toni laughed. "Enough." Then she pointed to her head. "Most of it's up here. I'll transfer the notes when I get home. I'm almost done. This is the twentieth line I pulled, been making my way to the head of the canal."

"Yeah?" said Tanvi. Pratt knew that Tanvi's memory and concentration were so impressive that she never took a note. In a little while, she'd find a dry place and talk-to-text the whole article. After complimenting Toni on her dedication, Tanvi asked, "So what are the preliminary results? Lots of dead oysters?"

"Surprisingly few," said Toni. "There may be many more to come in the next couple of days or weeks as the toxicity courses through the mollusks, but I don't think so."

"Why not?" asked Tanvi. "I'd think most of them would be wiped out."

Gazing down at her clipboard, Toni said, "If what I've found in the other heavy rains bears out, then the oysters presently in the canal are much hardier than the earlier batches. Like the rest of us, they seemed to have adapted to Gowanus, although this rain appears to be more violated than any I've seen since I worked here."

"How can you tell?" asked Tanvi.

"You work here long enough," said Toni, a bit of world-weariness in her young voice, "you start scratching your skin when it gets bad."

Tanvi shrugged her shoulders. "Maybe you should've put on a Hazmat suit?"

Toni scowled. "Hazmat suits are for uptowners. There are no frightened turtles here in Gowanus."

Hearing the jangling of chains and the rattling of cages, Pratt popped his head out of the trench to get a better view. Toni had pulled the oysters from the canal bed, counting them and giving them a careful study. Tanvi leaned her head in, "What are you looking for?"

"Oh, just dead ones and seedlings," Toni said. Then she pointed, "See that. That's a dead one. The good news we got some seedlings."

Tanvi leaned back, "Ew, what's that?" Even from his distance, Pratt could see a small creature flopping in the mud.

"Oh, that's what I call the oyster posse. Ever since I've been pulling up oysters, we get more of these little fish. They're always covered in mud. They must like it down there."

While Tanvi continued to question Toni, Pratt noticed that the light had changed in the sky. It was soft and smoky. As he gazed into the horizon, he was treated with a magnificent double rainbow. It formed a halo above Tanvi's dogged earnestness. He wanted to climb out of the trench that very instant and take her into his arms. Pratt liked to think the rainbow had cursed him with temporary insanity and that his love for Tanvi would vanish with the setting sun, but truth is, the lurching affection had been building a long time. After those five intense years at *The Herald* where she had been his work wife, here she was in Gowanus, a woman strong enough for this tainted world.

Before he could rise and explain himself, maybe even profess himself, Tanvi had bid her farewell to Toni. Pratt had been too deeply immersed in the reverie of romantic contemplation to notice where she had gone. Oh, he knew he would find Tanvi ... just not today.

As he plotted his future seductions (perhaps he'd take her to an oyster bar), he heard clanging next to the building above him. Turning to his right, he spied Pygmalion tossing grappling hooks onto the roof pediments. Her dark, willowy arms set off by a sleeveless orange flannel, she wore a harness. After making sure the hooks were secured to the building, she steadily winched her way up, spray cans tied to every fabric on her body.

First, Pygmalion hopped from one part of the brick-face to another, touching the walls, checking for the dampness. Fortunately, the building's overhang was large enough that it kept the brick relatively dry even in such a deluge. Next, she brandished a gray spray can, shaking the cylinder back and forth intensely, the ball-bearings scrabbling about its innards, rattles and knocks echoing across the canal.

From what El Buscador had told him, Pygmalion had only plied her graffiti after midnight when most authorities were asleep and those awake would be inclined to engage in other business. Pratt looked below the building where she had exhausted the past month sculpting a mighty Gwaken from the dirt he had carted out of the trench. Alas, despite the tarp over her sculpture, the heavy rains and subsequent flood had not been kind to her creation ... what remained looked like a fossil of the work she had created.

Perhaps, as the rainbow began to fade, Pygmalion thought that the deluge would occupy the authorities, or even better, they might figure everyone could use instant art in this instant disaster. She bounced on her ropes while she sprayed in undulating motions to form the outline of a creature no one had seen in weeks now. She was free to paint what she'd always created in Gowanus, beasts of mythology that emerged from the fetid imagination of these lavender waters. After she completed the outline of the Gwaken, she took a blue spray can, drew a wavy line six feet up from the building floor, and wrote "High Water Mark" next to the date and the hour.

For the second time today, Pratt needed the shovel to steady his knees. Skinny, wiry, and loopy, that Pygmalion was some woman. With slashes of her lithe arms, she built up taupe streaks for the Gwaken's dinosaur-like scales; then attaching tiny extension tubes to her sprayers, she striped the caudal fin to finish off the back end and followed by lining the dorsal fin with wavy streaks. After fleshing out the bottom fins, she wristed quick flicks with the tubed sprayer to make the barbels below the snout. Pratt thought she might've been done then because the Gwaken looked damn good. Rising like some boggy phoenix not from ash, but from a pile of muck, it was bound to draw the attention of the entire neighborhood.

Yet as she hopped from maw to tail, she grabbed more spray cans, cans of fabulous yellows and reds and greens, day-glos that belied the murky residue of the neighborhood. With each stroke, Pratt feared Pygmalion would ruin her mystical monument. Yet, she persisted layer upon layer until he finally saw that despite its mottled depths, her Gwaken surged with a tropical urgency. He struggled to put his finger on it. Pygmalion was careful not to sentimentalize the beast, not to make it too pretty or too vibrant. With the darker outlines of the scales and fins, the electric colors were burdened with a greasiness that spoke of dance clubs the morning after. Her Gwaken glided through the canal illuminated to its very gills by a toxic rainbow, a creature that sent a message to all hungry leviathans of its inner poison.

Pratt sighed. How the hell could he fall in love with two different women on the same day? God, what's in the water here? He thought of Pygmalion's hands and Tanvi's mouth. He thought everything wrong with Gowanus became right simply by their engaged presence.

Pratt rose from his trench and called out to Pygmalion, giving a yell and a wave, which she returned. "May I escort you to Pig Beach?" he asked. Pig Beach was a barbecue joint overlooking the canal. It had an elevated deck, so Pratt figured the floodwaters would be below the floorboards.

"What?" Pygmalion asked. She took a moment to register. "Oh, no," she said giggling. "Look at me."

Pratt gave her a once over. "Oh, you mean the crimson stain on your shirt, the mustard mark on your pants, and the spray splatter all over your fingers."

"Yeah that. And my hair."

"I don't know if you'd heard, but we've had an epic deluge here ... a biblical flood. I think under normal circumstances you'd be fine going to Pig Beach. It's friggin' Pig Beach. But today, you'll look like the princess of the ball there."

"You've got a point."

"So, shall I rescue you from your castle high in the sky?"

Pygmalion balked. "I don't need any rescuing." Pratt lifted his hands to indicate no offense meant. She smiled. "But I could use some ribs."

•　　•　　•　　•　　•

From his rooftop vantage point, El Buscador gazed wistfully upon the romantic couple, enraptured in inconvenient voyeurism. He thought of Mavis below, giving the inspectors more than they needed. He thought of Jeanne across the river, ready, willing, and able to tumble out of her wheelchair. But he knew he had to see another woman for whom his passions were strictly entrepreneurial. Now was not the time for lovey dovey. It was the time to meet with Cynthia Newland and seal the deal.

CHAPTER 28
THE NIGHT TRAIN

Eight hours earlier, Tolland had been out on one of his noctambulisms, Ingrid following him as if her job depended on it. Eschewing the park this time, he headed south and far west until he wandered into Hudson Yards, the hulking development that would soon be humbled by his own in Gowanus. He tried to ascend the honeycombed staircases known as the Vessel, but alas, it was closed for the evening, as was the High Line. Foiled, he roamed the park plazas south of 36th Street between 10th and 11th Avenue until he hit the subway station and took the escalators deep underground.

Tolland had never been on a subway before. Clearly, his subconscious wanted to take a ride. Ingrid scowled as she had to send him through on her MetroCard swipe and had to swipe again to follow him onto the 7 Line. Part of her wanted to lose him. It would serve him right to land at the end of the line in Flushing, wandering around its Chinatown, searching for Peking Duck but only finding Moo Shu Pork. Boarding the train, Tolland sat next to a sleeping homeless man sprawled out, yo-yoing on the 7 from Queens to Manhattan from Manhattan to Queens, rocked to sleep by the clattering and thrumbing through the chthonic darkness into the broken bodega light of the outer borough.

Ingrid found a seat across from Tolland. She hoped he would hop off at Times Square or 5th Avenue or even Grand Central, but no, Tolland was going across the East River to his land of origin. Well, sort of. The 7 Line would not get him near his birthplace; only a limo could take him there. Staring at sign after sign at stop after stop, Tolland did not rise until a dozen stations into Queens. Of all the choices, he selected the stop right in the heart of the barrio at 82nd Street in Jackson Heights. No fewer than five subway lines rose above the raucous Roosevelt Avenue where the noises from the constant passing trains competed with the blaring reggaeton music reverberating from the cars and the clubs.

Tolland marched down the stairs of the elevated subway and stayed below the clatter of the tracks on the avenue where small women sold pupusas and international calling kiosks did a brisk business. He tried to cut the line to get into a club and was fast on his way to being beaten up by someone who used to be way in front of him ... that was until Ingrid stepped in. Even then, the clubgoer wouldn't let go of his arm until Ingrid gave him her phone number. As she walked away with Tolland, the clubgoer blew kisses at her and pointed to his phone in what the ungenerous might describe as lecherous intent. Now she was dragging Tolland's arm, pulling him out view of the clubgoer before he dialed her number and discovered it happened to be one digit off.

After the day's rain, the Roosevelt Avenue throng was especially wooly tonight, laughter and car beeps dancing with incessant passing subway trains. Ingrid had hoped the din would awaken Tolland from his zombie-like state. Yet he continued to press deeper into the barrio, settling in at a rotisserie place called Pollos Mario. There he ordered half a chicken while Ingrid grabbed a coffee and a churro. Thankfully, the service was fast at this turn-and-burn restaurant, but Tolland had some plate in front of him: besides the chicken, he was served rice and beans, salad, tostones, even an arepa. Nibbling her churro, Ingrid waited while Tolland methodically moved his way through each quadrant of his plate. Twenty minutes later only half the arepa remained; in the end, he stared at the biscuit not knowing what to make of the pasty, mushy disc.

He tried to leave without paying. Ingrid had to foot the bill. Then she got him back up the steps to the 7 train; again she needed two swipes of the Metrocard. She calculated how much money she was spending tonight, money she knew she would never get back from Tolland. The ride to Midtown seemed even longer than the one there. By the time she got him back to the penthouse, the sun was rising. Mercifully, he fell asleep for a few hours.

•　　•　　•　　•　　•

He woke up in the morning with a headache. Ingrid benignly neglected to carry in *The Herald* with the bacon, eggs, and biscuits. He noted that the *Times* and the *Journal* had taken their shots at him, but he had a feeling *The Herald* would be much worse. His suspicions were confirmed when Ingrid delivered the paper with the sports back page facing up. He flipped *The Herald* over to the front cover, which screamed, **Tolland's Folly** in a 200-point type headline. The subhead read, *Mogul's Shoddy Construction Leads to Disaster in Gowanus.* Opening to page three, he was greeted by an article from the figure who had replaced El Buscador as his main nemesis, Tanvi Khotari. He'd spoken to his Russian friends about scaring her a bit, even roughing her up, but he still had enough of the gentleman in him to think it was the wrong way to treat a lady. Reading her article, he decided she was no lady. Repeating line after line, Tolland tasted a heavy splattering of bile in his breakfast.

Gowanus Assaulted
By Tanvi Khothari

A broken sewer pipe in the proposed Tolland District in Gowanus has unleashed a gusher of accusations against embattled real estate mogul Timothy Terrance Tolland. The allegations have been further validated by a slew of construction and zoning violations issued by the city on the site.

"Tolland has broken the rules and workers have come forward to claim he used substandard concrete that led to the sewer pipe break," said city councilwoman Shirley Kendrick. "Plus, the footprint he's been building on looks nothing like the beautiful architectural rendering he's been floating to the council over the past six months."

The article only became more brutal from there. As he finished his breakfast, he knew he'd have to take control of the situation.

• • • • •

Timothy Terrance Tolland had been speaking at the press conference for a half hour, pointing to a multitude of architectural renderings that were a far cry from the playful, industrial/residential wonderland designed by the Graffiti Sisters. As if to counteract the architectural deficiencies, these revised renderings featured a canal of sparkling Caribbean blue waters. Like a magician, Tolland waved his hands across the stippled drawings. "True to the area's colorful past, I am committed to guaranteeing that you will now have a beautiful blue Gowanus, one that will attract visitors from miles away."

In the renderings, the color strongly resembled that of a flume ride at a theme park. Much of the audience murmured approval of the blue canal. Given Tolland's history with rats, they knew that if Tolland had one skill, it was how to apply dye. Sensing his momentum building, he offered disarming modesty sprinkled with hope.

"As you can see, the infrastructure is not nearly in place for the original plans I have presented. However, I am not giving up on Gowanus. I have shown you a new way forward. One that is sturdy and invests in jobs and housing in the community. One that will transform Gowanus into Brooklyn's greatest neighborhood."

Sitting right up front, Tanvi wanted to interrupt his speech right now to ask how does he expect to turn Gowanus into Brooklyn's greatest neighborhood when his updated plans mimicked the drabbest developments in the entire city, plans of height without elevation, plans of waterfront without access, plans of sky without sunlight. But she had been to enough Tolland pressers to know how this one would go. He would talk for an hour and then he would not take questions.

"We New Yorkers often get caught up in the glitz of this place, but I think it's important to remember that what makes this city tick are rock-solid jobs with rock-solid workers who make rock-solid buildings." Tanvi wanted so badly to yell out, *You mean the type that crumble the minute you put a little weight on them, you mean the type that bust sewer pipes?* Instead she listened to Tolland ramble on. "That's what I'm offering you. I am offering the people of New York a district that will make Gowanus into something that will no longer be the butt end of jokes, but the shining face of this great metropolis."

Despite the lofty phrasing, Tanvi could not erase the bottom-basement architectural rendering by Lud, Gib, and Nirob from her vision. No matter how blue Tolland made the Gowanus, she was certain that those in the audience, those following the news alerts on their phones, even those watching New York 1, would sigh with the collective deflation felt down in the bones of their toes. Tanvi had been composing her article in her mind; she would have to do something clever with Tolland's blue Gowanus sales pitch, maybe play with dyeing and dying. Mavis had instructed her that she wanted the story on the web immediately, since the editor decided to wait to post her scathing editorial until the article screamed out on the top of every loaded page and news blasts hit every phone in the tri-state area. Yes, the desperate would be willing to give Tolland's new plan a shot. But *The Herald's* editorial would describe the bait and switch in uncluttered terms. The flood of sewage would only be the beginning ...

As he did at the opening of the press conference, Tolland at the close returned three times to the podium. On each occasion, he merely stood and looked out at the press corps for roughly two seconds, turned tail, and strode out. This latest eccentricity garnered a few chuckles, but nothing like the hilarity and adulation of Tolland in his heyday, when he served the homeless snacks from a coffin, urinated with vigorous gusto in the grand atria of Midtown, and populated the streets and subways with the ubiquitous, iconic blue rats. Tolland's rich madman act had gotten old, oppressively old. Everyone in the room except Tolland could sense that his power waned, a deterioration commensurate with his fading aura. Indeed, except in the Madison Street pit, the blue rat had become an endangered species (even in the pit, the keepers would occasionally have to scrounge a few prosaic brown rats and give them such a fast spray of indigo that the paint stained the mouths of Yorkies and the paws of Labradors that exterminated them).

As Tolland made his concluding remarks, Matt Aruba and Cynthia Newland were meeting with Governor Rosenthal and Mayor Condon to make sure the freshly named Arubaland District Project in Gowanus – a district that embraced and promised full financing of every whimsical, wondrous detail of the Graffiti Sisters design – would be fast-tracked. After yesterday's flood disaster, the heavy fines levied against Crystal Properties for construction and zoning violations, and the bait and switch revelation in *The Herald*, enough stakeholders bailed for Aruba and Newland to acquire majority control. Since those shares were snapped up by such bland entities as the Paperweight Company and the Mass Corporation, Tolland had no idea that Crystal Enterprises had been untimely ripped from him. Quite soon he would be disabused of his vision of what he would be doing next with his life.

Tolland would not take the news well. Ingrid believed her job had been difficult before. She had no idea how much worse it could get.

CHAPTER 29
A BRAVE NEW PIZZERIA

Cynthia Newland had been treated to a secret and deliciously illegal tour of the Coignet Stone Company Building, yet she was in no mood to be gracious. "You are running out of favors, El Buscador."

El Buscador tipped his fedora. "When are you going to learn, Miss Newland, that every time I ask you to do me a favor, what I am actually offering you is another gift?" They moved onto Third Street past Whole Foods to the north side of the canal.

Cynthia laughed. "Some gift. Now I've got to convince Mamma Greaseball and Papa Garlic Knot into signing onto something they should kiss my ass even to get a sniff at."

El Buscador explained the situation again: how Tolland burned their place down and shot out the tires of their food truck, how they turned down millions to sell the property. "You've got to admit," he said, "they have grounds to be suspicious." They wended their way along the bend of the canal toward Smith Street.

Like Tolland, Cynthia was not used to accommodating two-bit mediocre types, especially pizzeria owners specializing in soggy, forlorn pies. Yet so far, El Buscador's acumen when it came to the Gowanus District could not be denied; the shadowy figure had never been so right in the daylight in his entire life. Still, she couldn't help saying, "I'm certain I'm throwing my money away with this little scheme of yours." Cynthia had forked over a considerable fee – even with the discount El Buscador negotiated – to design the architectural plans for the pizzeria.

El Buscador was reassuring. "I guarantee that if you get Nancy and JoJo to put up that structure, it will increase the value of the Gowanus District because it will now be seamlessly integrated into the vision of your project."

"You guarantee?" Cynthia, who could be a bit of a drama queen herself, shared a huff. "You guarantee? By the time the pizzeria's built, you'll be down some hole looking for bodies. I feel like I've made a deal with a vampire." El Buscador opened his eyes wide, bared his incisors, and vogued his best Dracula. He waited, since he knew Cynthia needed to get it all out. "The bottom line is I am doing all this for a pizzeria I don't even own."

El Buscador held up a finger, requesting to get in a word. "It's worth remembering, Cynthia my dear, that you don't have to own everything."

She smirked. "Not everything. Just what I want."

They arrived at the APizza the Hun food truck. After the flood, with the cinder blocks cutting a brutish path, the food truck looked gloomier and more unsavory than ever. El Buscador elegantly flourished his hands like a game show model introducing a new product. "Do you really want to own this?"

"No," she said, rifling through her pocketbook until she found the architectural rendering by the Graffiti Sisters. She shoved the plans in his face. "But I really want to own this."

With a measured calmness in his tone, El Buscador reiterated, "I'm sorry you can't own this property. You never can." Cynthia arched her left eyebrow, struck by his naiveté. El Buscador pressed on. "You can do what the rest of us do – look at it and appreciate it. You can even take satisfaction in knowing that you were instrumentally responsible in building the most funkily capricious pizzeria in all of New York."

Cynthia rolled her eyes. "You truly are a lame boob, aren't you?" El Buscador could have continued to cajole and persuade; he didn't bother because he sensed Cynthia would shroud all of her covetous qualms once they stepped into the food truck.

He was right and a darn good thing he was because Nancy and JoJo could not understand why they should build such a "freak house" (yes, that's what Nancy called it) instead of reconstructing the old place, brick by brick. "Una Nonna's was fine the way it was," said JoJo.

"You bet it was," chimed in Nancy.

Cynthia kept speaking about the future; Nancy kept speaking about the past. Cynthia talked mosaic tabletops; Nancy talked Formica booths. Cynthia laid exotic tiles; Nancy rolled sturdy linoleum. Cynthia saw farm to table; Nancy saw can to box. The more Nancy and JoJo rejected Cynthia's vision and the architectural plans that gave it habitation, the more Cynthia tried another tack. During the entire animated discussion, JoJo kept pumping out pies as Cynthia tried not to look horrified at the sagging discs emerging from the oven. To be fair, the customers refrained from too many signs of outward dissatisfaction.

Deeply moved by Cynthia's spirited arguments, especially after hearing her misgivings on the walk over, El Buscador realized that Nancy and JoJo could not be reasoned with. He had to step in. "Nancy and JoJo, I know I have no right to ask you, but I'm asking, no I'm begging, could you build the pizzeria according to these architectural plans?"

Nancy took out a wooden spoon and started smacking El Buscador on the head with it. These were no love taps either. She meant business. The happiest she'd been all day, Cynthia held back her laughter. Covering his valued brain, El Buscador lifted his arms and let them take the blows. "You son of a bitch! I knew you were going to ask me that." She slammed down the spoon hard on his shielding forearm, breaking it in two. "Now look what you've done!" She adjusted the stub of the spoon still in her hand and started jabbing it at his chest. If El Buscador were indeed a vampire, he was in danger of losing his life, especially with all the garlic about the place.

"Hey! Hey!" said El Buscador, "That's enough!"

Nancy found another spoon and started in again. "I'll tell you when it's enough." After getting in a few more whacks, she dropped the spoon. She hadn't had a workout like that in months. She looked around the food truck which to her was now home, a home that El Buscador got for her and JoJo when she had none. "Will it cost us more money?" she asked.

An hour ago, Cynthia would have said *damn right it's going to cost you more. You are getting top-of-the-line instead of piece-of-crap.* But after seeing what a couple of thickheads she was dealing with, she assured them. "You will not have to spend a cent more." Cythia figured a few hundred thousand was worth the aggravation and if it turned out to be more, it'd be too late for Nancy and JoJo to balk, and they'd have to fork over the rest. El Buscador deftly managed to consummate the agreement between Cynthia and Nancy without their sharing a celebratory pizza, to Cynthia's infinite relief. As they tiptoed across the cinderblock pathway back to Smith Street, he knew he'd need her good will for what he'd be asking her next.

"By the way," he said, even though they were not currently engaged in conversation, each of them letting the absurdity of the concluded negotiations sink in, "I could really use those sewer pipes you said you might be able to get your hands on."

Cynthia smiled at him. She was finding El Buscador increasingly attractive, not so much that she'd like to date him or anything – Matt Aruba clearly was the right man for the moment – but she was considering making him fall for her. "You're surprisingly needy, you know that? You've gotten much more than you deserve. What are you going into the construction business? I've got enough competition."

El Buscador pulled his Fedora down slightly on his forehead, an effect that left his slightly handsome face in shadow, an effect that made him more mysterious, almost alluring. "I think it's a good idea that you don't know what I'm doing."

"Yeah?" she challenged. "So why should I help you?"

El Buscador walked with a purpose. "I could use a drink. How about you? I'm buying."

"Why not?" she said, succumbing to the will of the evening. "But don't think I'm giving you those sewer pipes."

After they settled in at the bar at Lavender Lake (Cynthia ordered a sangria, El Buscador said make it two), they toasted to their successes. "I'm working on one more," he said.

"Are you doing something illegal again?"

"Perhaps."

Cynthia frowned. "I can't afford to have my name associated with this, especially not at this phase in the Gowanus District."

"I promise you by my word as a gentleman: if I get caught with those sewer pipes, I will tell the authorities that I stole them from you or whoever is your supplier."

Cynthia nodded. She could tell that El Buscador was indeed a gentleman. "Keep talking."

"I also promise that whatever I will do with those sewer pipes will serve you and your district quite well."

"What *are* you doing?"

"As I've indicated," El Buscador took a sip of the sangria and dropped his voice, "I can't tell you for your own protection."

"Haven't you had enough intrigue?" Cynthia asked. "My God, you're worse than Thackeray."

Mildly miffed that he'd been hearing that comparison a lot lately, El Buscador answered, "Not yet. Can I get the sewer pipes?"

"I guess I can figure out something."

"Wonderful. Could you make sure that nothing is bigger than six-foot length? I'll be in some tight spots and cutting will be a nuisance."

"Of course you will. Are you sure you won't tell me?"

"I'm sure. But on the bright side, you will certainly know what I've been doing once I'm done."

Cynthia exhaled. "Alright. Be that way. But buy me another drink, will you?"

El Buscador had his arm up for the bartender. "Two more please."

"You are getting the much better end of the deal," she said.

El Buscador smiled, "Just remember the deal could be so much worse for you."

Her thin eyebrows arched skeptically, Cynthia asked, "How so?"

El Buscador smirked. "I could have ordered us a pizza."

●　　　●　　　●　　　　　　●

If El Buscador had been an old timer in Gowanus, he would have thought nothing of the floating debris as he took a seat on the canal-side bench that terminates at DeGraw Street. He would've looked back down at his Una Nonna's pie and grimly proceeded to the task at hand. But he had not yet been completely inured to the wonders that surfaced from the unthinkable depth of Gowanus. He could not ignore the long gently curved body of the prehistoric fish that rose before his eyes.

Although he had been expecting to see a dead Gwaken from the moment its dorsal fin first left a current in its indelible wake a month ago, his body trembled with a maudlin numbness upon encountering the actual corpse. El Buscador swelled with discomfiting privilege that the Gwaken died for his eyes, and he immediately began to consider how to assure the corpse would remain for his eyes only. Yes, a part of him was inclined to lift the fallen sturgeon and to show her to all of Brooklyn. He knew he wouldn't because he hated the ending to this story. Too definitive. The tales El Buscador revealed to his clients and to his friends, even the ones whispered about him, had been riddled with mystery.

For El Buscador, days without mystery were unbearable. For this mystery to work, he could not tell Mavis or Pratt – they would be too tempted to reveal the truth. Someday, he might tell Jeanne, since she would have no interest in the Gwaken. But tonight, or this morning (hell, it was 4:32 a.m. after all), he would perpetuate the myth all by his lonesome.

He broke into the flushing station and grabbed two long poles with gaff hooks on their ends – he didn't even want to think about what the station workers used them for – and returned to the floating carcass. He considered crossing the two poles to hoist out the eight-foot corpse, but he wasn't sure he had the strength to pull it off. Plus, for such an operation, someone was bound to see him commit the body snatch; the heavy trucks were already rumbling about Gowanus, awakening anyone aware of sound.

El Buscador stepped to the edge of the canal with his long poles, guiding the dead Gwaken as close to him as possible. The carcass rolled until the soft, white, fleshy belly was exposed. At that moment, the Gwaken delivered one more gift: eggs spilled from the swelled opening of her uterus just below the pelvic fins, eggs more darkly lavender than the water itself, eggs that plunged into the murky depths – the possibility of a larva thriving as improbable as a sturgeon finding her way here to spawn in the first place. If one egg did survive, that would mean returns for generations to this home in the canal. He kept turning her with the gaffs, watching the eggs spill steadily like chickpeas boiling out of a pot. And when no more broke free, El Buscador continued to roll the corpse, just to make certain.

Then he guided the two gaffs so that they led her unwaveringly downward below the surface. Perhaps the eggs still in her belly would find shelter in the depths. At first, he felt resistance, like the Gwaken was rejecting another dunk into the Gowanus, as if to say, she'd had enough of that. With persistence, however, El Buscador continued to sink the fish. When he felt the Gwaken hit the sludgy canal bottom, he pressed deeper, until the corpse was a foot or two embedded in the black mayonnaise of coal tar and sewage.

As he removed the poles and stepped back, El Buscador half expected the Gwaken to rise from the depths, sooty, yet triumphant – a perverse resurrection in keeping with the neighborhood. When no such miracle transpired, El Buscador sat back on the bench. He fiddled with the pizza box while he wept. He only started to have these crying fits in the past year (before that he had last cried when he was twelve). From the first incident forward, he wondered if the tears were part of a deteriorating mental condition like dementia or signaled something worse.

As morning rose over Gowanus, El Buscador tried to get a grip. El Buscador tended not to believe in bad omens, but a dead Gwaken was not something that could be easily dismissed.

At Una Nonna's and in the back alleys, he would spread rumors of sightings of the Gwaken lurking under bridges. If the Gwaken liked bridges, then the people of Gowanus might like bridges too. He'd also spread word that the Gwaken often hid in the nearby streams and springs, the purity of those waters strengthened the old creature for her return to the canal.

Yes, the Gwaken would never swim through these currents again, but the community would hear of the many secret places where she lingered, plus a big harbor loomed out there beyond Red Hook and, beyond that, an even bigger ocean. The legend would grow. El Buscador would make certain of it.

He would further spread tales of the eggs she left in the canal, weaving an epic of her rendezvous with a majestic, old twelve-foot male out in the East River. The explosive results of this union were the strongest, most resilient spawn possible. Each of the thousand eggs offered another story. For once, hope sounded so much like truth that El Buscador's memory would permit no doubts.

As he put away the gaffs, he noticed an egg stuck to the longer of the two poles. He returned to the canal and shook the egg free ... just in case.

CHAPTER 30
TALES OF GWAKEN

When Pratt wasn't chasing down Tanvi or Pygmalion, he tracked the legendary Gwaken, peering into the murky depths of the canal, gathering rumors at the shore, gabbing in the barber shop, yakking on the street corners, picking up short snippets and tall tales. Since he left *The Herald*, where he had written every day for a decade, words had only trickled from his tongue, no longer tumbling from his fingers. But here in Gowanus, ready to impress a couple of girls, he would compose a piece worthy of the *New Yorker*.

The fewer the sightings of the Gwaken, the more stories he heard. So much for the adage out of sight, out of mind. Gowanus did not follow conventional wisdom. He heard the one about the butcher who threw ten pounds of sausage into the canal for the Gwaken to feast on. When asked how did he know the creature ate the links, the butcher answered, "Do you see any sausages floating in the canal? What do you think happened to them?" Ever the thorough reporter, Pratt brought a pound of sweet Italian links and dropped them in the canal. They sank like piglets with cinderblocks on their feet.

An older Hispanic woman named Izzy swore the Gwaken rose each day at morning's first light. For two weeks Pratt kept a dawn vigil. He must have been at the wrong spot on the canal. Two Korean schoolboys said one day the Gwaken sunned itself on a broken cement slab.

A Haitian man inappropriately named Shorty told Pratt that the Gwaken liked to use sewage waste as camouflage. "If you see shit on the surface, you know what's lurking right below." Pratt wanted to say, well

Shorty, if that's the case, then the Gwaken has always been here in Gowanus and certainly does get around.

The most intriguing story came from the father of a Bangladeshi girl on Nevins Street. Pratt met Shrey in his apartment and got the story firsthand. His daughter Afrah had been diagnosed with leukemia and was set to begin chemo treatment in a few weeks. With Afrah on his lap, Shrey stared deeply into Pratt's eyes with the intensity of a believer. "Afrah and I were just walking around the canal, you know, to get some fresh air. The canal always seems to lift our spirits. And then we saw it." Shrey turned to his daughter perched on his right knee, her little legs swaying, "Isn't that right?"

Afrah smiled, one front top tooth and two below missing. "It was magic."

"Magic," said Shrey. "That's right honey. All of a sudden we saw ripples in the water, like the Gwaken generated its own current. And then it rose and you could see it on the surface. It had been going in another direction when it must have seen Afrah because it turned and came toward her."

"That's crazy," said Pratt.

"Not crazy," said Shrey. "The Gwaken knew. It stayed near Afrah making small circles."

"Why would it do that?" asked Pratt.

"At first, I didn't understand," answered Shrey, "but then I also knew. He was making those circles to pull the poison from Afrah. I saw her shake and shudder with my own eyes. Afrah almost fell. I had to hold her up. But the Gwaken was making a whirlpool and I could tell right then that the poison was being drawn from her body and was being pulled toward the sucking vortex. I could see her poison being drawn away into the abyss."

Shrey cried for a few minutes and Afrah wiped away his tears. The sentimental, feel-good nature of the story wasn't usually Pratt's thing; the women were clearly getting to him. Pratt waited, giving Shrey time to gather himself. To emphasize the certainty of what had transpired that day in the canal, Shrey poked Pratt with his right index finger and whispered, "I just knew." Shrey looked at his daughter. "You too, Afrah, you knew it too, didn't you honey?"

Afrah big eyes opened to the size of coffee saucers as she nodded, "I did. I knew Daddy."

Shrey turned his attention back to Pratt. "Before we started the chemo treatment, I got her retested, even though my doctor told me the previous results left no doubt. But when the new results came in, my doctor was now the one with doubts." Shrey grew increasingly animated, pointing his finger at Pratt. "The doctor ordered yet another round of tests, and what did he find? The same as the retest! Afrah had no malignancies!"

Once Shrey seemed calm enough to listen again, Pratt asked, "Do you think the Gwaken absorbed the poison within him?"

"What?" asked Shrey, confused enough to answer Pratt's question with his own. "Why?"

"Well, you know ... the Gwaken absorbs contamination every day."

"That 1 cannot speak about," said Shrey. "1 will not speak about what 1 do not know. What 1 do know is that Afrah had the cancer before her encounter with the Gwaken and after she had none."

Ever the thorough interviewer, Pratt kept asking questions for the following hour, yielding very little, but receiving confirmation of all he'd already heard. Later that evening, he shared his cluster of stories with Pygmalion. She had returned to her dirt sculpture of the Gwaken, gamely trying to bring strength and solidity to the mud. She had added sand and straw to stabilize it. "Now all 1 need is sun," she said.

"Ah, you are like Pharaoh's bricklayers of old. My God, you are like Moses. May the great God Yahweh provide the light and heat to bake your Gwaken."

"I've heard lime may help too. If this falls apart again in the next storm, I'll try that next."

Pratt inspected the rehabilitated sculpture. He noticed that the nature of sturgeon's countenance had changed. The eyes and barbels had looked old and wizened in the previous version. Now the Gwaken had a quality that approached angelic in its searing ethical gravity. He smiled mischievously at Pygmalion. "Wow, the last time I'd seen a visage like that was in a cathedral. 1 think it was a fresco of St. Francis. If 1 didn't know better, you have just bestowed unto Gowanus its first saint."

"Which saint is the Gwaken?" asked Pygmalion.

"I'm not sure," said Pratt.

"Which saint tended to the lepers?"

"1 think it was Saint Damien," assured Pratt.

"1 was thinking of a woman," said Pygmalion.

"The Gwaken is a woman?"

"Of course she is," said Pygmalion, snickering. "I can't believe you didn't know that."

"How would I know that?" asked Pratt. "I haven't had a chance to lift its skirt."

"Knowing you, that means you just haven't had the spare time to sweet-talk her."

"Well, she's been playing hard to get," said Pratt.

Pygmalion could tell that Pratt was stalling. "Do you have a female saint for me?"

Pratt's thoughts ranged to other possibilities, until he conjured the name St. Marianne of Hawaii, who cared for the lepers. He tried to hide how pleased he was with himself.

"How'd you know that?" Pygmalion asked, somewhat weak in the knees.

"Oh, she was just canonized a few years ago," he said, doing his best to sound offhandedly modest.

"So you always follow saints' lives?" she said, wishing she had a cigarette hanging off the edge of her lip, wisps of smoke clouding her misty, green eyes. Ah, she'd like to be a femme fatale.

"Only when none of the sinners will let me follow them," said Pratt.

"Mmm," said Pygmalion. "I know a sinner who'd leave you a trail."

"Do you now?"

As Pratt found the conversation pivoting in the proper direction, Tanvi arrived at the sculpture: she, the patron saint of inconvenient timing.

Tanvi eyed him without any idea that she had interrupted a courting ritual. "Good. I was hoping to find you here."

"What's the matter?" asked Pratt.

"Nothing," said Tanvi. "It's just that I know you've been working on that Gwaken piece and a press conference has been set at Crooklyn Effects. That's a special effects company. They promise stunning revelations about the Gwaken. I'm covering it for *The Herald*. I didn't want you to miss out."

Tanvi had been excited about the prospect of Pratt writing again. He had been more inward and much less charmingly rakish lately without a laptop in his case. Jeez, the way El Buscador had him occupied with a shovel and a wheelbarrow, he was more apt to grunt than to wax poetic. She sensed the ways the story tugged at him. Even as this pretty, intense artist tugged at his belt, the story would pull him to the 9th Street offices to hear just what piece of the puzzle Crooklyn Effects had to offer.

Pratt looked at Pygmalion pleadingly, longingly. "Will you make sure the trail stays warm for me?"

"It's warm until darkness," said Pygmalion. "Then gaze up at the walls around us. You'll find me there."

God, Pratt gulped. Pygmalion was better at this game than he was. Hell, it was looking like even Tanvi was better at it than he was. Best not to think too much. Just throw the former a kiss and follow the other to the press conference.

●　　　●　　　●　　　●　　　●

Pratt understood when they arrived at Crooklyn Effects that he was apparently the only one in Gowanus who hadn't heard about this media event, judging from the crowd. As with most of these gatherings, the whispers in the awaiting audience already unveiled the big announcement: that the Gwaken was actually a state-of-the-art piece of robotics developed at Crooklyn Effects. After a few minutes of murmuring, a young woman who introduced herself as Olivia Mandary rolled out a cart covered by a sheet. Two technicians in blue uniforms flanked her as she stepped up to the podium.

"You are probably wondering why we asked you to be here today, just like you're wondering why you haven't seen the Gwaken lately," said Olivia. "You haven't seen the Gwaken because she's with us. She's needed some repairs. We thought about returning her to the canal, but the water had done her so much damage that we are not sure she can return."

Mandary waited for the murmurs in the audience to dissipate and continued. "Many of you will be disappointed that she is a robot of our design and not a fabulous, living sea creature that found its way to Gowanus. Many of you thought of the Gwaken as magical. I ask you now to understand that if anything is magical, it's Crooklyn Effects." With a flourish, she lifted the sheet and unveiled the robotic Gwaken. The crowd issued forth the appropriate number of gasps and murmurs. Tanvi and Pratt pushed forward to get a better look.

Tanvi raised her hand and Olivia called on her. "Of all creatures you could make, why a sturgeon? Why not something more creative, more mythological?"

Olivia smiled, indicating that she hoped she would get such a question. "We here at Crooklyn Effects strive for accuracy and detail above anything else. We have run many iterations of the Atlantic sturgeon in our design phases, following its motions and respiratory functions to mimic the most nuanced movements of the fish. We first thought about making a small whale but with Sludgie appearing a few years back, we wanted something fresh. We considered using a shark, but we thought it would scare people. As an alternative, a sturgeon is big and strange, but unthreatening. We decided it was the perfect fish for Gowanus."

Tanvi followed up. "But from what I've seen of the Gwaken, the photos and the YouTube footage, this robot doesn't look that much like it."

Olivia laughed. "As you know, you can't trust everything on the internet. I can tell you, the first day we put our robotic sturgeon in the water, we started getting Gwaken sightings."

Tanvi yelled out, "What evidence do we have when you put your robot in the water?" But Olivia had moved onto the next questioner who asked about details of how the robot was designed to look so realistic.

On a screen above, Olivia showed images of the robot Gwaken being guided into the Gowanus by the two technicians holding ropes below its soft white underbelly. As Pratt and Tanvi studied the robot, each of them had come to the same conclusion: the Effects designer had done a good job to make the sturgeon look real, but not a perfect job. So much so, that both suspected the ensuing footage of the robot fish moving through the water was actually footage of the real fish. Ironically, for Tanvi, the claims made by Crooklyn Effects that the Gwaken was just their robot convinced her that the creature in the Gowanus was indeed a living, breathing fish.

Sure, she'd been skeptical about the Gwaken. It seemed like the residents were desperate for a mascot and were willing to suspend disbelief to find one, that most of the population was stoned out on GG and could summon up the Gwaken as readily as a bag of Doritos. And certainly the developers would be all for ginning up interest in the neighborhood and keeping Twitter and the tabloids abuzz with the latest sightings. Yet Mavis and Pratt believed; there was very little those two believed in besides a good cocktail and a side of ribs. Plus, this press conference smelled of a publicity grab. It was mighty convenient that the robot was damaged. She could be more open to Olivia's claims if they dropped their synthetic Gwaken in the canal right now, and she could watch it swim around, gliding with the elegant inevitability that she had seen in Mavis's pictures and videos.

After so many years of working side-by-side with Tanvi, Pratt read her thoughts pretty well, and he was amused by the serpentine route she'd taken to have faith in the Gwaken's existence. He knew with all the certainty of Pygmalion painting pictures of the Gwaken tonight that Tanvi would compose a column worthy of the beast. And he knew what that meant for him – out of luck, Bub. He'd been beaten out by a creature that may not exist beyond the artistry of two women whom he may not get a chance to love.

Tonight, while Pygmalion sprayed graceful lines and Tanvi composed them, he'd walk the canal until it met up with his trench. He'd sleep in there like a soldier from World War 1, peering out at the barbed wire on the gates and rooftops, looking for enemies when all he could see were friends. Late that evening, as he drifted off to sleep, Pratt thought of how strange it was that he and Tanvi could only believe in something that they could no longer find.

CHAPTER 31
GROPING FOR DAYLIGHT

El Buscador knew he could never convince Pratt that his protégé's role in daylighting the old creek was the easy part. He could not tell Pratt that he'd rather have spent the month digging that trench by hand and then laying the clay and the sand. All he had to do to get *that* project going was convincing the art collective to agree. El Buscador explained to the board that the proposal would feature an environmental sculpture and since the trench would provide the dirt for Pygmalion's mighty earth Gwaken, the board found his request credible.

The two factories next to the collective were the problem. The one nearest to the trench and therefore the canal was manageable. Although he knew he would not get the landlord's permission to make renovations to his basement ("You want to do what now?"), the building had been unoccupied for several years and as long as he broke in under the cover of night, he could make it work. Still, he'd have to lug in his share of tools from Lowes and Home Depot, and the work required a good deal of noise.

Unbeknownst to most, all about the Gowanus Creek flowed a web of small streams and tiny tributaries. For years, every builder in the area found ways of diverting the moving water away from the surface. Now El Buscador wanted to raise those waters back up. His night work had been quite thankless, since he essentially had to build an aqueduct in the basement, yet he could not shift the drainpipes until he diverted the water in the neighboring building.

And in the neighboring building was where the greatest challenges emerged. That facility had a huge placard that read, The Brooklyn Sign Company. Appropriate for Gowanus, the sign was completely inaccurate.

The current tenant sold magnets. That tenant's business hours left him only Sundays to work on his renovations in the basement, long, long Sundays to catch up on everything necessary to align the running stream water, currently cutting through the concrete floor, with the aqueduct next door. He had cordoned off his work area with construction tape and cones to give it an official air. He hoped the tenants didn't come down here, or if they did, that they didn't talk to the landlord about what they saw – hey, it's not any of their business. The problem was building a support structure strong enough to hold the weight of the water, water that seemed heavier by the moment. That meant cinderblocks, lots and lots of cinderblocks. He spent more time on Sundays smuggling them into the basement than anything else. He was tempted to ask Coppa or Pratt for a hand but knew that this lonely office belonged solely to him.

As he trudged down the stairs, two cinderblocks at a time, he wondered about heart attacks. Except for a few wounds coming from battles with man and beast, he hadn't been to a doctor in twenty years. He wondered what the cops would think if they found him dead down in this obscure basement, a cinderblock against his chest, his cold eyes staring at a half-built channel, currently collecting no water and apparently heading nowhere. And yet he trudged on, sensing the urgency of what he was doing. A year from now – hell, maybe months – he would not be able to pull off what he was trying to do. But at this moment, before the big infrastructure and building projects commenced, nobody bothered to secure these old factory buildings in Gowanus. It might have been the last bastion in the city without heavy security cameras. Since the buildings would be either torn down or gutted, the landlords didn't have to worry about protecting much.

He wondered why the hell he wanted to daylight this creek so badly. Ever since he'd spoken to the Gowanus Conservancy people about their plans, he'd caught the bug. He knew his approach was the wrong way to go about bringing the creek back to the surface. The Conservancy had a thoughtful lowlands plan for the Gowanus that, if enacted, would be a credit to everything good in New York. But progress in Gowanus moved at a glacial pace. They'd been talking about cleaning the canal for a hundred years, and even with the EPA work and the storage tanks and the tunnels being constructed, when would it be done? A decade, if everything worked out perfectly. In Gowanus, nothing worked out perfectly.

His Sundays were sixteen hours days of cinderblocks and sewer pipes, courtesy of Cynthia, in the basement of the old Brooklyn Sign Company Building. Once he had the base properly elevated, he had to run and adjust the pipes with couplings and valves and connectors, making sure he had just enough of a decline to keep the water flowing. Water flowing: that was the unknown, wasn't it? He'd have one shot to divert the stream that had only flowed underground for a hundred years, a hundred years hidden from the public eye, coursing in the basements of these factory buildings.

El Buscador toiled late into the night. From what his bleary eyes could see, everything was in place. All he needed to do was turn the massive valve and he could rechannel the entire hidden stream. With any luck, next Sunday morning he could let the stream flow.

•   •   •   •   •   •

If El Buscador followed his stream into the canal and then into the East River, he would have encountered one Timothy Terrance Tolland, who was out on what he called a fishing boat, but what the more nautically versed would describe as a yacht. Tolland tried not to stew about losing the Tolland District to his archenemies, Newland and Aruba. No matter how hard he sought to exorcise his recollections, he couldn't help but remember the many wonderful times he bedded down with Cynthia. That made him feel even weaker. Whenever he was depressed and he needed something to do, he hunted. Sure, he'd hunt for buildings and real estate opportunities. That would help. But what really put a charge into him was to stalk big game prey: lions and elephants and rhinos. Now he took it upon himself to hunt the most elusive prey of them all – the Gwaken. Anchoring in the East River at Red Hook, he dropped into a kayak laden with nets, spears and poles, plus line strong enough to pull in a Great White. Dressed in a safari outfit, Tolland drew a great deal of attention as he paddled from the mouth of the canal inland. He looked and searched every current and eddy.

Like El Buscador, he too put in a sixteen-hour day. In that time of tedious scouring and line dropping and trawling, he contemplated just how he lost the Tolland District. He had put everything in place for success. Gowanus was tailor-made for the type of bait and switch plan that he'd designed, and he thought in the end the residents would be grateful. What could give the community more instant credibility than to have the Tolland name attached to it?

He stared into the dirty water and tried to ignore the myriad smells that wafted unpleasantly with every breeze. The question that kept coming back to him was how did they know? How did those two dopes at Una Nonna's know enough to get a food truck the very next day right after their building had been torched? How did the building inspectors and the city regulators know to arrive at the construction sites at the very moments the backhoe collapsed and the water main broke? And most importantly, how would Cynthia Newland and Matt Aruba know that they had the opportunity to steal the Tolland District right from under his nose. He first thought that *The Herald* might have been to blame. They certainly were a nuisance before. But they always had help. More than help, they always had an ace in the hole.

Then for all the murkiness of this hunt for the Gwaken, one thing became clear on this sixteen-hour paddle through Gowanus: El Buscador had been the cause of this greatest of humiliations. Indeed, Tolland had suffered setbacks before, but they'd been in Manhattan as he constructed majestic skyscrapers. If he failed, it was because he was like Prometheus. To make those monumental buildings in Manhattan was like stealing fire from the gods. But now, he failed in Brooklyn, and even worse, specifically in Gowanus. Clearly, this moment was the lowest of his high-flying life.

Who had been there the whole time in Gowanus, puffing up the value of the Tolland District, saying all of the right things? El Buscador. Who had been living there, skulking about like the vermin that he is, sticking his dirty nose into the construction sites? El Buscador. Who'd been eating that god-awful pizza at Una Nonna's (that alone should have killed him)? El Buscador. Who was intimately aware of the architectural plans of the Graffiti Sisters, but also knew of his long relationship with his architects of record, Lud, Gib, and Nirob? And who had broken into his architects' offices before? Goddamn El Buscador. And finally, who would know his history so well and study his finances so well and be able to creep around quietly to make arrangements with Aruba and Newland to pull off a hostile takeover of Crystal Enterprises? Fucking El Buscador.

Tolland had thought he had scared El Buscador into an honest life, at least temporarily. He had thought that El Buscador was the type of zealot who once he had moved onto a new cause, embraced it with a loyalty worthy of the knights of old. How wrong Tolland was. El Buscador was a scoundrel and he'd soon be a dead scoundrel.

Tolland was as certain of El Buscador's death as he was a catching the Gwaken. The only question was which would he chase down first?

CHAPTER 32
ON THE MOVE

Until now, El Buscador hadn't sensed that someone was constantly watching him. Oh sure, Maksim would occasionally use his fedora for target practice, but that was to be expected. In fact, ever since he'd made peace with Tolland and became a public relations shill for his Gowanus District, he had felt almost secure. That changed this morning when he had climbed onto the dead-end streets near the headwaters next to Bond. Though the big man looking at his phone tried his best to appear like he wasn't trailing El Buscador, the fact that the two had also crossed paths at DeGraw and Sackett confirmed that the contract on his life had been renewed.

El Buscador shook his trail in Whole Foods, with some slick moves, using the employee staircase to give him the slip. Gliding over to Union Street, he picked up the R train, crossing the East River into downtown Manhattan. Knowing he might not be able to see Jeanne again, he hopped out at Cortland Street, then moved eastward to Nassau and onto the back alley to her basement apartment. All the while, he took a few random turns to make sure no one trailed him. Picking up the Amazon package at the doorstep, he knocked on Jeanne's door as a courtesy even while popping the lock with his key.

"Oh, look who shows up at my door," said Jeanne. "If it isn't the old power broker himself." Jeanne elicited from El Buscador the appropriate frown, since *The Power Broker* was the title of a renowned biography about Robert Moses – the historical master builder he hated almost as much as Tolland. She called him by his Christian name. "Luke, my dear, could you grab the Grand Marnier and two glasses from the shelf over there." He nodded and turned to the cabinet. Despite his attempts to hide his skittishness, Jeanne could tell that her old lover was on edge. "Luke, my dear, what's the matter?"

"I'm afraid I won't be seeing you for a spell."

"They're after you again?" asked Jeanne.

Luke gave her a grim nod. "I believe so." He poured three fingers of the Grand Marnier, neat, and put it in Jeanne's gnarled fingers.

Jeanne was tempted to lecture him about his self-destructive tendencies, about his monomaniacal obsessions with Tolland, and about his overdeveloped sense of neighborhood fealty. But what could be gained by calling him a stupid fathead? Instead, she gazed at him wistfully. "Then you should probably take me to bed."

He rolled her wheelchair to her bedroom and propped her onto the mattress, collapsing down with her, the two chuckling. Lying on their backs, they rested next to each other until Jeanne turned on her side and Luke spooned, the left arm caressing her hair, the right strapped tight around her waist, hips locked as if they were meant to be together.

Both of them wanted to seduce the other, kissing and touching and rubbing. Neither could figure out how that didn't happen. Instead, they both fell asleep. When they awoke at one in the morning, Jeanne whispered in his ear. "Luke, my love, you should go."

"What?" asked El Buscador, a little disoriented. "Why?"

"Because if you stay the night, I'm sure someone will be waiting for you tomorrow morning. They've staked out this place before."

"But I wanted to spend the night with you," Luke said, a rare tone of gentle sweetness entering his voice.

"I know honey," Jeanne said. "I did too. But I'll be miserable with you being here, knowing that you could be shot when you stepped out the door. You need to go now before they show up. You know once the tracker reports back, they're going to send out an army to the usual spots if Tolland really wants you dead, especially since you survived the last time and then you made him even madder at you."

Luke smiled, "Yeah, well ..."

Jeanne rolled her eyes. "You are a dumb bastard, aren't you? Now get the hell out of here while you can."

"I'll be back," he assured her.

"I doubt it," she said.

Swirling the syrupy lees of the Grand Marnier glass, Luke toasted, "Here's to you being wrong."

"To me," said Jeanne. They clinked their snifters and finished off the Grand Marnier.

Luke washed the two glasses in the sink. He shut the door, climbed the steps, and returned to his identity as El Buscador. As he moved across Nassau, then east to the water and the rat traps below the FDR Drive, he hid in the shadows by the pillars holding up the highway, making sure he didn't spot anyone suspicious. He knew that Pratt tended to check his traps after midnight. He just wasn't sure how late. On the nights when he frequented the rat pit, he would often go to the bar afterward with some of his buddies. Pratt found those gatherings even more informative than the scuttlebutt shared in those lag times between the unleashing of the dogs at the pit.

Staggering with drink, Pratt finally checked his cages at two in the morning. El Buscador scared the hell out of him when he tapped Pratt on the shoulder.

Pratt yelled, "What the hell is wrong with you?"

"Sorry, I was trying to be quiet," said El Buscador.

"Well, when you make someone cry out, that tends to undermine your noble objective," said Pratt.

El Buscador conceded, "You've got a point there."

As Pratt checked his cages, he asked, "So what brings you here at this godawful time of night?"

"I was followed. I believe Tolland has put a price on my head again."

"That's funny. I heard more about him tonight than I have in months."

"Yeah?" asked El Buscador, trying to mask his excitement. News about Tolland always put a charge in him.

Pratt moved rats from the cage to a burlap sack. Only two of the six critters were blue. "Seems like the old boy is not done with Gowanus."

"Really?" El Buscador followed Pratt to the next trap. "He's not trying to get back the District because there's no way Cynthia will let him get his hands of her shares or Aruba's shares."

Lifting his empty trap, Pratt grumbled, then explained, "No, he brought an old factory building. He's wants to turn it into a hotel. Knowing Tolland, he'll put another fifty floors above the existing building."

El Buscador let the idea of an old factory building roll through his mind. Over the past month, he'd broken into a dozen of them. It'd be just his luck if Tolland bought one along the underground creek. Whatever the case, the fact that Tolland's making more moves in Gowanus confirmed how El Buscador would have to act next. "Who are the architects for the project?" he asked.

"Oh, he's back with Lud, Gib, and Nirob," said Pratt. "He learned his lesson after the fiasco with the Graffiti Sisters. He's trying to get the project fast-tracked just like what Newland and Aruba received with the District. His managers at the rat pit think he's become a sympathetic figure since he had the District ripped right out from under him. He's still the biggest mogul in New York and people are sad to see him down. They think the city council might help prop him back up."

El Buscador ran his hands through his hair. "You've got to be shitting me. Leave it to New Yorkers to have sympathy for the devil."

Pratt smiled, "I'm tempted to start singing, but I figure you're having a bad enough evening."

"You're right about that," said El Buscador. "Tell me how am I going to stop this guy if the first time his goons spot me, I get shot in the head?"

"That is quite a problem you've got there." Pratt reset the rat trap and looked up at El Buscador. "You want me to give you the other news, or have you had enough for tonight?"

"You might as well give it to me," El Buscador, adding a huff of resignation. "It can't get any worse."

Pratt arched his eyebrows. "I wouldn't be so certain about that?"

"Yeah?" El Buscador waited with morbid curiosity.

"Tolland's hunting the Gwaken."

"That's not news," El Buscador scowled. "He made a big show of it. Nobody could miss it."

"True, true," said Pratt, "but did you know that he's actually caught the Gwaken?"

"That's a load of crap," said El Buscador, half with anger, half with confusion. "There's no way he caught the Gwaken."

"Well, the boys at the rat pit and others at O'Shaughnessy's are cock sure of it," Pratt said. "They say Tolland's even got video of it."

"I'm sure the video looks an awful lot like the one that came from Crooklyn Effects," said El Buscador, trying to convince both Pratt and himself. "Christ."

Neither said much for the next five minutes. El Buscador had much to absorb. When Pratt was done with emptying his final trap, El Buscador said to him. "Given the way everything is deteriorating, I think we better move up our plans," said El Buscador.

"To when?" asked Pratt

"Tomorrow."

Pratt whistled, "Tomorrow? I don't think we'll be ready."

"We'll have to be," said El Buscador. "I wanted to do a test-run tomorrow and then let her loose next week, but I get the funny feeling I won't be around next week."

Pratt nodded in agreement. "Yeah, I think it's time for you to go into hiding. In fact, I think you better let this go and get out now."

"No, I've put in too much work not to see it through."

Pratt refrained from yelling. El Buscador thinks *he* put in too much work. He wasn't humping wheelbarrow after wheelbarrow full of dirt to dig out the stream bed. Pratt ignored the comment since he knew his old friend's life was in jeopardy and he might not be thinking too clearly right now. Instead, he asked, "What would you like me to do?"

El Buscador appreciated the cooperation. "Could you give the trench a once over, make sure there is no debris in it?"

"Good idea," said Pratt. "There's are always some random paper and bottles that have blown into the ditch. And there's always some asshole who treats it like a garbage dump."

"Great. Can you be done by nine?"

"Nine?" Pratt objected. "When do you want me to sleep and when are you going to sleep?"

El Buscador grabbed his arm and caught his eye. "You can sleep when I'm gone. Just give me tomorrow."

Pratt nodded, strangely wanting to hug El Buscador, and said, "Alright."

Pratt tried to say more, but El Buscador tipped his fedora and disappeared into the night.

Quite the morning awaited him.

CHAPTER 33
TOLLAND'S CATCH

Ingrid had thought long and hard about asking Tolland for a raise, and finally at the moment of truth she had to summon all of her courage to proceed. The real estate mogul invited her onto his settee, sitting a bit too close for happiness, but far enough away to prevent her from pursuing legal action. She spoke about her additional time required to trail him in his sleepwalking adventures and the ancillary responsibilities piled onto her – relatively small requests like running across town to buy a new paddle for his kayak and tweeting every time he lifted a finger, but collectively very time consuming. She spoke of how much she appreciated all the great man had done for her, but the forty thousand dollar salary required many unanticipated expenses (she handed him receipts as evidence), and despite the fact that she had room and board, her job offered her neither the time for acting lessons nor the opportunity to save sufficient money for the chance to stop working long enough to pursue her acting career.

Disarmed by Tolland's gentleness, Ingrid listened to expressions of appreciation and his offer to raise her salary to fifty thousand dollars. She knew it would be rude to ask him to put the new conditions in writing, and yet she feared … He spoke of how much he needed her and how good he would be for her career. "Come with me today to capture the Gwaken," he coaxed. "You will be the star of the film."

After Tolland's second stint paddling the canoe in the canal yesterday, an associate came by with a sturgeon. The first one was too small. When he returned with the second, it lacked personality. The third one was ugly in the wrong way. The fourth one was barely satisfactory, but Tolland needed to get the matter settled, so he took that one. Then he soaked the sturgeon in Gowanus Canal water all night to help give it an authentic hue. By the time Tolland had spoken to Ingrid, the sturgeon that would be the once and future Gwaken was already loaded onto his yacht. Her boss suggested that Ingrid should wear the same bikini that he bought for her when she was called on to serve clients last summer during a pleasure cruise.

"You will be filming the entire capture of the Gwaken, and I will have a separate film crew filming you filming me."

Ingrid tried her best to refrain from incredulity. "Why would anyone look at the film of me filming you?"

"To guarantee the footage is authentic, that you had actually filmed the event live," said Tolland. "Plus, you're in a bikini, who wouldn't want to get an eyeful of that? You'll be an internet sensation: the gorgeous camerawoman."

Even though Ingrid tried to dismiss the notion, she couldn't help but see stories about her garnering as much attention as the Gwaken. It wouldn't hurt to dream. Within an hour, they were on the water. Given the chill in the air, Ingrid wore a cover-up until the filming began. A diver hired by Tolland cradled the sturgeon, dropping into the water near the rocks at Red Hook, a stone's throw away from the mouth of the Gowanus. With the enormous, long-abandoned grain elevator casting shadows on the East River shore, Tolland beamed with pride over the setting he selected. Given his limited imagination, Tolland relished seeing the big building. He hoped one day at that very site to knock down the monstrous relic and replace it with something even bigger, something blessed with the Tolland name.

He and his crew were so focused on the drama they would manufacture in front of them that they did not see Melville in his sailboat furtively gliding up behind. Even as Tolland's men had trailed El Buscador, El Buscador had asked Melville to trail Tolland the moment he launched the yacht.

The diver had two pronged sticks attached to the belly of the sturgeon to jiggle and propel the dead fish into something that resembled motion. By that time Tolland's fishing line was down and Ingrid's camera started to record. "I'm so sad about how sick the Gwaken looks," said Tolland. "I've been trying to help him all day. He's a fighter, I'll tell you. I'm surprised he swam out of the canal. I get the sense he wants one last swim in the larger waters around the big city before he goes. Isn't that the story of all of those who live in Gowanus? They're tough as nails and will take a bite out of the big apple with their dying breaths."

Ingrid leaned over to get a better shot of Tolland and the Gwaken. In turn, the professional cameraman leaned in to get a better shot of Ingrid leaning over. Tolland and the Gwaken played out their drama in the background. All the while, neither cameraman nor beast noticed Melville behind them filming the entire show, from the dead fish being tossed in the water to Tolland's reality-television-style monologue.

The diver did a respectable job of thrashing the dorsal fin even as the front of the fish moved ahead with an inexorable stiffness.

With his fishing line hooked into the maw of the Gwaken, Tolland shifted his pole into his left hand and wiggled a large net with his right. "I don't think he has much left, but all day long I've been getting the sense that before he passes, the Gwaken wants me to catch him," said Tolland. As the big net surrounded his tail and steadily engulfed the scaly midsection, Tolland became increasingly emotional. "I'm afraid we're watching this magnificent creature in its death throes. Just one look at the Gwaken tells you he's as old the Gowanus itself. It's as if he is giving us all permission to move onward and upward as the people of this community always have."

With the help of a few gaffs from anonymous arms, the Gwaken was lifted into the boat. The moment it came over the edge, Tolland held it in a gentle embrace, like what he had in his arms was anything but a cold fish. Even the most discerning observer could not tell in Ingrid's unexpectedly competent framing whether the Gwaken was dead or alive.

After a good thirty seconds of hugging and sobbing, Tolland gave the viewer the answer. "Farewell, our noble friend." Then, to be true to his current public idiosyncrasy, he returned to his embrace three times.

Instantly a shroud appeared and the Gwaken was taken from the deck. A tearful Tolland announced, "My apologies, but I need some time with my friend."

As per Tolland's instruction, Ingrid let the camera roll another thirty seconds from the deck to the sea, to the sea to the deck before she cut the filming. Melville too realized the show was over. He'd get the footage to Mavis, but he knew his record would be the one discredited. Even though he provided what any logical viewer would see as irrefutable evidence that a fraud had been perpetrated, few would be inclined to question what Tolland had so sincerely delivered.

When Ingrid arrived in the captain's quarters, Tolland was yelling on the phone to Lud. "I don't care what they say, we've got to have that observation deck. That's the key to everything."

Since Ingrid had trailed Tolland on his sleepwalking adventures, she had started to ask him many more personal questions. She figured she had a right, given her new role; plus, she thought if she recorded their conversations on her phone and took careful notes, she might get a nice tell-all book out of it – non-disclosure agreement be damned (her lawyers would come up with a loophole). Ever since he bought the Brooklyn Furniture Factory building on the Gowanus, Tolland had a spring in his step. The flurry of phone calls he made over the past twenty-four hours, even when he paddled in his kayak, hinted that he'd already submitted architectural plans for a major luxury hotel on the canal and that sympathetic city councils were inclined to move the plans along expeditiously. Still with Tolland, Ingrid was always curious about the details. "Why is the observation deck so important?"

Tolland smiled at Ingrid, always happy to answer the questions of a beautiful woman. "Because that observation deck will not only look out on the canal, but onto the Gowanus District."

Ingrid was a little surprised that Tolland would want for him or his customers to gaze onto the site of his greatest humiliation. "But why would you want to look at that?"

"Why? Why? What do you think the people will see when they look from my observation deck onto the District?"

Ingrid would have to tread carefully here. "I don't know. Maybe they will sadly think of what might have been."

"No," said Tolland, grinning, so happy he could enlighten her. "They will think of me. Those crooks Newland and Aruba may have put the final window-dressing on the project. But everyone knows the District is mine. From the commanding view of my observation deck, my guests will know without question that the canal and everything around it comes from me. Gowanus will be identified as much with me as Rockefeller Center is identified with Rockefeller."

Ingrid wanted to say that while Rockefeller Center was named after the robber baron, Gowanus was named after ... what the hell was Gowanus anyway? Sounded Iroquois. Looking out as the yacht sailed triumphantly toward the Battery, the one iconic skyline of Manhattan where Tolland had yet to make his mark, Ingrid couldn't think of how to continue the conversation. She changed directions. "So what are you going to do with the Gwaken?"

"Funny, you're the first person to ask," said Tolland. "Everyone else seems afraid to find out."

Ingrid puffed a little with pride. Tolland had a way of making her feel smart and brave. "Are you going to let the public see it?"

"Of course I will. I was so confident I'd capture the Gwaken that I had a new large display case installed in the lobby of the Tollandia for it. My guests kept thinking it was for the rhino I brought down last year. But I think the Gwaken is an even bigger game to catch, don't you?"

Answering Tolland had dramatically improved Ingrid's acting skills, since instead of saying to her boss, *you do recall that you didn't really capture the Gwaken right, that what you did was not much different from going to the fishmonger and picking out the catch of the day?*, she answered, "I do, definitely."

"Yeah, I agree," he said, as if it were her idea. "Wait till you see it. It will float there suspended in formaldehyde. The Gwaken will look every bit as alive as when I first tracked it."

Just so as not to come off as suspiciously sycophantic, Ingrid asked, "Do you think you'll ever want the Gwaken to end up in Gowanus?"

Tolland slapped his knee. Boy was he excited now. "That's the beauty of it. I'm going to make perfectly clear that the Gwaken will be on display in the lobby of the Tolland Gowanus the minute it opens, and that hotel will not open without an observation deck hanging over the canal. That should get the bean counters moving!"

After spending most of the morning trying to avoid what was transpiring before her, Ingrid could no longer ignore how intently Tolland studied her figure even as part of his mind appeared to be focused on soaring platforms and floating fish. When he signaled her to get him a gin and tonic, she knew he only asked to receive a rear view of what he'd been devouring from all other available angles. When she returned with his drink, she had on her cover-up, for her temporary comfort and his interminable chagrin. "Do you require anything else?" she asked.

"No," he said, nodding with approval. "You've done fine work. Why don't you reward yourself with a swim?"

"In the East River?" Ingrid asked involuntarily, her guard down.

"Sorry," said Tolland, still surprised that he continued to say stupid things around pretty girls. "Compared to the Gowanus, it's quite clean, but I wouldn't swim in it either. Well, then you're free to sunbathe."

I bet I am, Ingrid thought. "Thank you," she said, "but I think I'm going to look at the Gwaken. It's not everyday someone captures a legend."

Even as she walked out with her cover-up, Tolland remembered what she looked like minutes earlier. He sipped his gin and tonic and told himself, "She really digs me." He decided he might give Ingrid her own suite in Gowanus when the hotel is up. That should keep her interested. As he picked up his copy of *Angels and Demons*, he looked back across the river to Brooklyn. Skyscrapers were rising everywhere there. He'd come a little late into the game. No matter. The Tolland Gowanus would be his first signature building in the borough. Others would quickly follow. He knew he'd would soon be called the King of Brooklyn and he liked the sound of that.

CHAPTER 34
THE STREAM

They had chased El Buscador down to the cobblestoned dead ends near the canal's head, followed him over the fencing, even braving the barbed wire, broke into reinforced metal doors that looked like trouble, found the back way out (since if there was one thing they had learned about El Buscador was that he never entered if he didn't know a rear exit). They weaved through the gauntlet of heavy machinery that clogged up the parking lots at the headwaters next to the pump station and chased him to the other side of the canal. Hoping to lose their scent, El Buscador left Gowanus altogether, eventually finding his way to the warren of undergrounds by Atlantic Terminal. They thought he'd hopped onto the Long Island Railroad, but instead he jumped on the subway back toward the Union Street station on the R.

El Buscador knew the deception would only buy him a few minutes. Strategically, he could pick no place worse to go than to the basement of the old sign factory. Breaking his own rule, he would be trapping himself in a room where the only exit would be blocked by their guns. So be it. This Sunday morning was his only chance to daylight the creek that Pratt, Mavis, and he had labored so hard to raise to the surface. As he shot out of the subway and ran down Union to Nevins Street, El Buscador told himself to move with ruthless efficiency. If he were precise, he might transfer the flow before the bullets started flying.

Once in the basement, he assessed the situation, disheartened that he didn't put all his tools in place. Instead, he had to grab the massive pipe wrench from across the room before locking it onto the valve that began the transfer of the creek flow. Because the water crossed Nevins Street, the city used three pipes to carry what would collectively be the stream. El Buscador chose this very spot, since here the pipes were almost at street level. Only in the basement of the old sign building did the water cascade into the troughs that flowed freely in the adjoining basement of the furniture factory. Now, as he moved the aqueduct to align with the pipes, El Buscador noticed the swivel was not really true to its name, so he resorted to a lot of jackassing that did neither his back nor the unpleasantly heavy cinderblock stand any favors. He pushed the platform with such a fury to inch it closer to the pipe that it wobbled and threatened to topple.

When he thought the aqueduct trough was finally in line with the diverted pipes, he shifted the valves fully and watched some of the water indeed flow into channel. But about half splashed and poured over the sides, splattering onto the basement floor. To prevent much of the spilling pipe water from bouncing off the distant trough surface and landing below, he needed to tighten the ledge gap between the pipes and the aqueduct channel. So he stacked cinderblock after cinderblock in the basement's corner. Naturally, if he stacked the last cinderblock, the trough edge would now be too high and overshoot the pipes.

So much creek water landed on the basement floor that his shoes were sopped and the tide was rising to his ankles. He wished he had a hood over the pipes and the trough, a hood that could guide most of the water into the channel. He didn't have a hood. He wished he had sponges that would absorb the cascade and then allow the water to flow more gently into the channel. He didn't have sponges. He wished he had more time to rebuild the aqueduct. He didn't have more time. In fact, he started to hear distant footsteps finding their way to the basement. Little wonder given the awful racket he was making.

El Buscador had locked the reinforced door, but that might gain him another thirty seconds at best, given the size and guns of his pursuers. Furious, he picked up a cinderblock and smashed it against the wall. Now, the footsteps really picked up. The cinderblock broke into thirds and he propped one against the tower he'd built on the ledge. It was about a quarter inch too high. In a frenzy, he scraped the cinderblock against the wall, little pebbles of concrete rolling off, gray dust rising. Tolland's men were at the door. After the first two charges against the steel were unsuccessful, they fired at the lock, blasting away the entire housing with more bullets than were necessary.

Clearly, El Buscador had no more time for scraping the cinderblock. He turned and shoved the chunk between the top of the cinderblock tower and the aqueduct edge. It didn't quite fit, but El Buscador made it fit.

Immediately, the water whooshed in the channel with the intensity of a mountain stream at springtime thaw. El Buscador was so damn happy he hardly noticed that Tolland's men had stopped shooting at the door and had started shooting at him.

He recognized the guns and the faces from that shadowy visit to his home in the abandoned city hall station two months ago – God, was it only two months? He was glad that Maksim did not take the lead; otherwise, his Makorov would have already delivered El Buscador to his final resting place. He looked around the basement and realized there was no place to hide. So he ran low, right next to the aqueduct, hoping the cinderblock platform would give him some cover. Then the idea came to him because it was the only one possible, so, as he kept running, he suddenly leapt up high and landed right in the channel of the aqueduct. He sure hoped he built the platform sturdy enough to hold him. Within seconds, he was riding with the current, across the entire factory basement, the ledges of the channel offering cover. Tolland's men tried to gain a clean shot by pressing close and getting above the aqueduct, but by the time they arrived, El Buscador had glided behind the wall leading into the basement of the abandoned furniture factory.

At this juncture, El Buscador started to enjoy the ride, since he had more confidence in the quality of the aqueduct in this section: he had spent twice as much time building and preparing this leg than the one next door. Yes, he was concerned that one of Tolland's men might well jump into the aqueduct and join him. At least, in that case, the assassin's gun wouldn't work. His best advantage was that only El Buscador knew where he'd end up. It takes a very scared man to leap into a trench that may land him in a sewer, and none of Tolland's men looked that scared. Whatever his pursuers decided, he braced himself and tried to lift his head for air because once outside he'd need to swim and run as fast as his old body could muster.

Even in this moment, El Buscador knew he was involved in one of the stranger, more exhilarating experiences of his life. That alone made the entire daylighting of the stream worthwhile. Who knew that he'd also be daylighting himself? If he wanted to get all metaphysical about it, El Buscador could well have been shooting through a cosmic birth canal. Practically speaking, he just wanted to go where the bullets couldn't get him.

Much more had been delivered, the shockingly clean cool water baptizing him, washing away at least ten percent of his sins.

•　　　•　　　•　　　•　　　•

Meanwhile, Mavis was staring down at the channel Pratt had dug and she had edged with flowers. El Buscador had instructed both Pratt and her to make sure they had arrived there a half hour ago. Now she heard the rushing water in the distance. Pratt was still tamping down the clay and sand along the stream bed edges when Mavis called out to him, "You might want to get out of that ditch now." Pratt heard the whooshing too, the initial trickles wetting his sneakers, so he tossed the tamper up and hopped out. Soon the clear water was six inches high, then a foot, then two. Before it was three, a body joined the stream, gliding along like a thrill seeker on a water park ride. The body was moving too fast for Pratt to jump in to catch him. Hell, before they knew it, the body was heading straight into the canal.

Pratt looked to Mavis and asked, "Is that who I think it is?"

Mavis sighed. "Who else would it be?"

The body splashed into the Gowanus. Pratt asked, "Is he dead?"

Squinting her eyes, Mavis pointed, "He's swimming, so maybe not."

Mavis and Pratt yelled out to him, but El Buscador wasn't listening. He only lifted his head to breathe, but his arms were coursing elegantly through the water like he was a lifeguard. He was on the other side in no time, climbing up railroad ties, onto the embankment like a soaked rat. Mavis and Pratt kept calling out, but El Buscador was up and running. Within seconds, they could no longer see him.

"He's one slippery man, isn't he," said Pratt, a hint of admiration in his voice.

"Unless you know how to catch him," said Mavis.

Pratt grinned. "It sounds like you might be considering that."

Mavis eyed the channel and the canal where El Buscador once was. "If he's lucky," she said, "if he's lucky."

CHAPTER 35
AT THE TOLLANDIA AND THE PINT O'PLENTY

The previous night Nathaniel Pratt celebrated the daylighting of the long-hidden creek and the completion of the monumental dirt Gwaken with an enchanted evening. Casting away her paintbrush, her spray can, and her carving knife, Pygmalion resculpted Pratt with her bare hands and whispered verses in his ear. The seduction was so complete that by early morning the sensual fulfillment rendered him utterly in love and unspeakably afraid.

As if to say farewell to all of that, Pratt left his wheelbarrow in Gowanus and return to the other side of the river. More than ever, he'd needed to be in the rat pit. If El Buscador were out of commission, then Tanvi and Mavis would require his services.

He stopped by to tell Jeanne that El Buscador was at the very best in hiding or at worst dead – Jeanne didn't like when he minced words. She kissed him on the forehead and said, "It figures." She didn't have much to add after that.

But when he left, she yelled out. "Let me know if you need any help." Jeanne pointed to her computer, the source of some of the best dirt unburied about Tolland. She nodded, and added, "Ever."

He knew of a video she might want to help go viral, but that was for tomorrow. Today, let her settle in about the loss and let him return to his traps.

Sixty blocks up and five avenues over Tanvi was at Tolland's latest unveiling. A lovely Hispanic woman who could have easily been a game show product model pulled back the purple curtain to thunderous applause.

Initially, Tanvi was slightly impressed by the monumentality of the sturgeon seemingly floating in a glass box. The fish's wizened barbels and prehistoric scales made it appear to be a magnificent relic. Then she remembered where she had seen the setting. Typical of Tolland, he stole the idea from the artist Damien Hirst, who put a glass case around a shark floating in formaldehyde.

In a better mood than at any time in a year, ever since El Buscador and *The Herald* destroyed his dream of building a massive T skyscraper on Canal Street that would have completed a quartet of towers, monuments forever branding the mogul's legacy onto Manhattan, Tolland was willing to take questions from the press at the event.

Tanvi couldn't resist: "Are you saddened by losing the Gowanus District to your rivals Newland and Aruba?"

"Saddened?" said Tolland. "No, not at all. How could I be? Everyone knows that they are making the District with my plan. Even my enemies know that." The crowd laughed. "From no greater authority than the legendary El Buscador has my breathtaking and stunningly original vision for Gowanus been explained to potential investors and residents of the District. Newland and Aruba can build the District all they want. They can name it whatever they'd like – Arubaland or Scubaland or Tubaland – but everyone knows the District is the brainchild of Timothy Terrance Tolland."

Tanvi followed up. "With all due respect sir, we are aware of your original proposal of the project, but didn't the Graffiti Sisters come up with the groundbreaking design? And didn't you try to abandon that design in favor of a much lower cost alternative provided by your architects of record – Lud, Gib, and Nirob?"

Tolland laughed, turning to the rest of the audience, smiling, "How ridiculous are these questions? Everybody knows I design my own buildings. Do you think that I've been so successful because of the architects? I've been so successful because of me. Any fool can see that. And the stuff about an alternative plan are all lies that Newland and Aruba spread to get control of Crystal Enterprises. Well, I hope they're happy because they pilfered a little piece of my glory. They've snatched a thread of my coattails. It's O.K., I've got long coattails and I'm strong. As you can see, they don't slow me down too much."

Tanvi yelled out, "But you're recorded at a press conference pitching the alternative plan."

"Listen to her, will you," said Tolland, smiling, shaking his head. "I try to be nice on this historic occasion where I put on display for the people of New York the greatest creature to ever land on our shores, and all she wants to do is spew lies. I'm done with you. Who else has a question?"

A local Channel 7 news reporter asked Tolland how he managed to capture the Gwaken. Tolland answered with false modesty and had some members of his crew explain his heroics. The pretty woman occasionally opened her arms to show the size and ferocity of the beast, nodding in agreement.

A disheartened Tanvi composed the story in her head until she heard a familiar voice call out behind her. "How do you explain the video from a nearby sailor of you setting up this whole Gwaken capture, planting what is clearly a sturgeon bought from a fish market and getting one of your divers to hoist it up in the East River to make it look like it was alive and that you actually caught it?"

Tolland stared out at the questioner. "Ms. Wellington? It's nice to see you here Mavis. It's so strange to see *The Herald* editor out covering this story. I guess it's true what the *Post* says, I must be the most essential source of news in all of New York City. Anyway, I'm surprised you brought up that video since everybody knows it's a fake."

Mavis persisted, "We have found no evidence of it being a fake. In fact, given the videos released by both of your camerapeople, including the one with the woman in the bikini," here Tolland grinned while Mavis frowned, "this version has even greater authenticity since it captures not only what happened with the sturgeon but how the film crews perpetrated the ruse."

Tolland pointed in what could be interpreted as a threatening way. "You better get your facts straight at *The Herald* because you're telling us a pack of lies, you know it and I know it."

Tanvi would have followed up. Mavis knew better. Her reply was simply, "Uh, huh. If that's all you've got, O.K." Her answer conveyed that his attack was not worthy of further explanation. Mavis understood that most would believe Tolland's account because they wanted to believe the story, and after all, the Gwaken looked quite majestic in that glass case.

Mavis elbowed Tanvi, indicating she was leaving. Her arched eyebrows and sliding neck intimated she'd like her reporter to follow. As she slipped out of the Peacock Room catching one last glance of the majestic prehistoric floating Gwaken, Tanvi wished she hadn't been barred from asking further questions since she would have loved to have found out if Tolland knew who Damien Hirst was. She grabbed Mavis's arm. "Back to the office, chief?"

"No, I think we should meet someone," said Mavis.

Tanvi crinkled her nose. "Oh God, not Thackeray."

Mavis laughed. "No, but it might be someone worse."

"Why? Why?" asked Tanvi.

"You heard him," said Mavis, pointing back to the Peacock Room. "You want that prick to win?"

"No ..." said Tanvi, tentatively.

"Then I think it's time we go to the Pint O'Plenty."

"Jesus," said Tanvi. "If anyone pinches my ass, I'm gone."

"Deal," said Mavis. "Unless of course it's Coppa. Then I promise to break his fingers and we keep talking."

They hopped downtown on the subway and were opening the front door of the Pint O'Plenty in no time. Tanvi was happy to see that Edmund J. Coppa was not alone. Pratt must've been thinking along the same lines as Mavis. Pratt ushered them into what was generously dubbed the Pint O'Plenty Biergarten, which consisted of two dirty white resin tables, each with four filthy white chairs. Pratt grabbed a wad of bar napkins and did his best to clean off the chairs at the table as far away from the rest of the patrons as possible. Coppa came out with two glasses of white wine for the ladies. "They don't sell much of this," he told Mavis and Tanvi, "but the bartender says it might be drinkable."

Mavis frowned. "My, what an unimpeachable endorsement."

After Coppa returned with mugs of beer for the men, Pratt got right down to business. "So has anybody heard from El Buscador?"

"You mean since we saw him tearing ass out of the canal?" asked Mavis. "I haven't seen him."

Pratt sighed. "I'm afraid he might be dead."

After trying the wine and wincing a bit, Tanvi asked, "Wouldn't we have heard if Tolland's men got him?"

"Not necessarily," said Pratt. "The Russians have been known to store a body for quite a while. I wouldn't be surprised if they tied cinderblocks to his shoes and dropped him in the Gowanus." Pratt took in the numb looks of those at the table. "El Buscador wouldn't be the first body dropped in the canal, and I'm sure Tolland would see a certain poetry to such a disposal of his corpse."

Tanvi tossed in dyspeptically, "Maybe Tolland will put him in a glass case and float him in formaldehyde, display him in the lobby next to the Gwaken."

Coppa took a slug of his beer. "It's a sad table when I'm the least ghoulish of the lot."

Mavis knew that at least three people in the biergarten had something approaching love for El Buscador. "I'll search for him tomorrow," she said. Looking at Coppa, she added, "They talk like this because we have trouble believing he's dead."

Coppa laughed.

"What's so funny?" asked Tanvi.

Coppa answered, "That for as long as I've known him El Buscador has been trying to convince people he wasn't alive. He wouldn't be happy with us sitting around the table having trouble believing he is dead."

Tanvi asked, "Then what are we doing here if not burying El Buscador?"

Mavis answered, "Planning our next line of attack on Tolland."

Pratt looked up from his beer. "Isn't that what you guys will be doing at *The Herald* in the investigative team meeting?"

Avoiding drinking from her wine glass, Mavis nodded. "That's what we used to do when El Buscador was around doing a lot of our dirty work."

Coppa and Pratt nodded. They'd been arm-in-arm with El Buscador in that dirty work.

Noting their expressions, Mavis continued, "So you understand. The question is can we keep going without El Buscador? At the very least with a price on his head, he'll be out of commission for a while. And Tolland's moving forward, so there's no time to lose."

With a hint of curiosity in his voice, Pratt asked, "Besides the Gowanus hotel with that nightmare of an observation deck, what else has he got planned?"

"Tolland's advancing on projects all over Brooklyn," said Mavis.

Coppa laughed. "How much damage can he do there? It's Brooklyn."

Mavis stared him down. "You'd be surprised. It's Tolland, after all. The man has a gift for ruining neighborhoods." She took out her phone and showed him a pin she dropped at a property in Crown Heights. "Let's take this 40-story box he's building on Franklin Avenue. A horticulturist at the Brooklyn Botanical Garden tells me that the shadows cast by it will kill half the exotic and rare plants in their collection."

Tanvi whistled, "You're right. It is a gift."

Mavis raised her eyebrows. "You think that's bad." She pulled a map from her bag and spread it out on the slightly cleaner resin table. "Take a look at this."

Pratt laughed. "A map? Don't you have a laptop? My God, the old man is rubbing off on you."

Mavis waved him off. "Some things can't be seen as well on a little screen." Taking out a pen, she started putting down dots in the neighborhood in and around Gowanus. "Here's one proposed Tolland building next to the Barclays Center from Venandi Inc. *Venandi* is Latin for hunter." Everyone around the table nodded, since they all knew that Tolland was quite the nimrod. "And here's another westward on Atlantic from Jagermeister Realty – *Jagermeister* is German for master hunter."

She plotted more two points, one to the south and east, the other to the south and west. "Here are other Tolland properties." Then she plotted the location of the Tolland hotel in Gowanus. From there, Mavis zigged and zagged, connecting the lines. She waited for all to see.

"He's making a frigging pentagram with his buildings," said Tanvi.

"Pretty goddamn weird," said Pratt. "He's summoning either God or Satan with such a design."

"Are you kidding," said Mavis. "The only thing he's summoning is more attention to himself. That and dark shadows over a Brooklyn neighborhood."

"Jesus," said Coppa.

Everyone stayed quiet for a few minutes. Mavis returned the map to her pocketbook. "So what I'm asking is," said Mavis, "are you still with me? Are you still willing to give the commitment I've come to expect?"

Coppa grinned. "You mean ruin-your-life type of commitment."

Mavis pointed to him. "Exactly."

Coppa lifted his mug and said, "Only if you toast to it."

Mavis looked at the most unpleasant glass of wine she had seen a long time. It was mighty dark and dingy for a white. "Really?"

Coppa raised his eyebrows. "And here you are talking about commitment."

Grumbling, Mavis lifted her glass, "Here's to our renewed assault on Tolland. May we descend upon him with the low animal cunning of El Buscador."

After they toasted, Mavis made a point of getting out of the Pint O'Plenty as fast as humanly possible.

CHAPTER 36
THE COMMERCE OF ISLANDS

Mavis woke up a few hours early, more than annoyed. After a week, El Buscador had finally contacted her by US mail with no return address, no salutation, and no signature. And it wasn't exactly a love note. *"Can you get me out of here? Bat Cave, Sunday, 5:37 a.m."*

You'd think he could've at least sent an earlier message, "Not dead." She'd like to believe he had been hiding in some hole all this time and only surfaced to pen the letter. Yet she suspected he was out all week, wandering around Gowanus talking to knuckleheads like those two goombahs at the pizzeria. And now once again he wanted her to get him out of a jam. He asked could she get him "out of here?" To where? To the Cayman Islands or Bora Bora? She was certain El Buscador hadn't worn a bathing suit in this century. She wished she could delete his note like the thousands of Emails she deleted each day. She couldn't burn it because the furtive bastard loved all that cloak and dagger shit. And she wouldn't dare add it to her baggies of stupid-ass notes from him that she had collected. She should just send it to Tolland. That would fix him. No, she couldn't. Instead, she cut the note out in a heart shape and pressed her painted lips against the words. She slapped it up on her editing board like another piece of today's rotten news.

Yet, she had power over him.

He'd asked simply to get out of Gowanus. In his proclivity toward ambiguity that genuinely approached biblical proportions, he did not specify where he wanted to go. Knowing where she would take him, she smiled.

•   •   •   •   •

Mavis was not wrong about El Buscador's visits to Nancy and JoJo. She would never understand that he could not leave until he figured out just what else the two of them were selling. JoJo further confused matters by presenting El Buscador with yet another product. In the wee hours of the morning (the only time when his visitor's life might not be in danger), JoJo led El Buscador to a little temporary shed behind the food truck. The rancid stench hit El Buscador before he could see its cause. He stepped back, choked a little, and hunched over to hold back the retching. "Whatever you want to show me in there, could you take it into the fresh air?" he asked JoJo.

JoJo looked about clandestinely. "Just as long as nobody sees it."

El Buscador laughed. "As long as someone or something doesn't crawl out of the canal, I think we'll be safe."

JoJo slapped him on the shoulder. "That's just it. I have something from the canal." Without explaining further, JoJo stepped into the shed. He pulled out a big piece of plywood with the skeleton of a large fish glued to it. The mounting on the plywood was botched, with the bones skewed and turned under the milky glue (did he really use Elmer's?). Running about eight feet long, the skeleton was at least the right size.

El Buscador understood that JoJo brought him here to examine the skeleton as a test run. He was glad JoJo was at least that calculating. "What do you have there?"

"What do you think it is?" asked JoJo. Without giving El Buscador the chance to answer, JoJo added, "This is the Gwaken."

Uh huh, El Buscador said to himself. "How'd you come by it?"

"I was on my daily swim last week and I came across this giant dead fish," JoJo said. "Half the flesh was already off the thing. I took it out of the canal. It looked horrible, so I decided I'd take the rest of the meat off its bones. I soaked it in water on a very slow simmer, then degreased it in acetone until the bones came clean."

"That's amazing," said El Buscador. "I think you have something special here. I think all of Gowanus and New York will want to see it." JoJo smiled from ear to ear. El Buscador grabbed his shoulders to make sure he was listening attentively. "You have a story everyone will want to hear. You are the most likely person to discover the Gwaken, not some cold-brew sipping kayaker and definitely not Tolland, not the man who burnt down your restaurant and shot out the tires on your food truck."

"I'm glad you understand," said JoJo.

El Buscador nodded. "Yes, I understand how important it is for you to make sure that Tolland doesn't own the story of the Gwaken with all his other false constructions."

JoJo's smile gained a subversive appreciation. He knew showing El Buscador the bones was the right decision. Instinctively, JoJo understood that El Buscador was the perfect man to guide him toward creating a better hoax than Tolland's. "I'd appreciate any advice you could give me," he said with the respectful tone of someone who has had conversations with mafia dons.

"Now the best part of your story is the fact that you swim the canal every day," said El Buscador. "The media will be down here recording your laps. Tolland can't compete with that. You are not only a local, but you are as much a part of that canal as the Gwaken." At this point, El Buscador squeezed JoJo's shoulders a little harder. "The one thing is I think you should have your skeleton remounted. The current one is off. It's been put together so poorly that it looks like you have the bones of a tuna, not a sturgeon. You need to make sure the mount is for a sturgeon."

"A sturgeon," said JoJo. He repeated, "A sturgeon, got it."

El Buscador would say it one more time since the right species of fish was the key. "The size is about right, but make sure it's a sturgeon. And since remounting the bones is a job that requires some expertize, I will find a guy for you. You are going to have to pay for that expertize, but that expert will be very effective and very, very quiet."

As El Buscador offered more suggestions, JoJo asked few questions, but they were good ones. He clearly understood hoaxes better than pizzas. They circled around the subject of whether the mount should have flesh on its bones. So much depended on the quality of the sturgeon JoJo could procure. Since JoJo had a couple of friends in the fish business, he was confident he'd not only get the species right this time but acquire the whole sturgeon.

Knowing he would not be around to see this matter through, El Buscador explained the next steps. "Once the Gwaken is mounted and all the world can see it is the true beast of Gowanus, then have Nancy call the press. Dressed in your swim trunks, you show them the Gwaken mount.

Then you jump in the water and point to the exact place in the canal where you found the body. Then make sure you do a few laps for the cameras. That'll put a bug up Tolland's ass and Nancy will be selling a few more pies to boot."

JoJo had the good sense to not ask El Buscador where he was going. JoJo also knew wherever El Buscador was going, he wouldn't want to go with him. Returning to the food truck to give Nancy a farewell hug and kiss, El Buscador spotted her slipping packages into the four corners of a pizza box, a cold, soggy pie filling its center. As he squeezed Nancy, he knew his head was finally uncluttered enough to understand what the hell had been going on all this time at Una Nonna's. He now realized how the residents of Gowanus so readily had their hands on Ganja Ganache.

And like that, everything about the Una Nonna operation made sense. Of course, they had to sell miserable pizza because they couldn't handle operating a very busy drug trade and a lively kitchen too. Only, the desperately hungry would come in to eat. And that explained the limited menu and the high prices. El Buscador had always thought someone had to be out of his mind to eat here (he did not reflect on why he was such a frequent customer), and now he understood why. The front had to function, but not too successfully because high traffic would present more peering eyes, more possibilities of getting caught. The twenty-four-hour availability helped in not only making the front seem viable – El Buscador had been convinced the tremendous accessibility had made the business successful – but it gave all of the real customers the ever-present chance to catch a nice buzz before or after work. The volume of sales for Ganja Ganache would be steady day and night, with a few pain-in-the-ass pizza orderers sprinkled in to varnish the operation with authenticity.

The insertion of the Ganja Ganache bars in the pie boxes also explained why Nancy never kept the pies hot ... can't have the chocolate melting. And no wonder JoJo was constantly sleeping when he was at food truck. He was always coming back from the road to Massachusetts or Vermont or God-knows-where to score the GG. It'd be just like JoJo and Nancy to get the product themselves so as not to pay a middleman. Plus, now he understood what was finally in the huge athletic bag that Nancy clutched so furiously on the night of the fire. He had initially thought that the bag contained their clothes or mementoes (oh, how naïve), and even at his most suspicious he figured she kept their life savings in the bag. But now he knew it probably held ten thousand in GG product. That also explained why Nancy needed to reopen so desperately the next day. Again, he innocently thought she simply wanted to get the business up and running because pizza-making was her life. But if drug-dealing was her life … He even began to wonder if JoJo could comfortably take his daily ablutions in the canal only because he'd been properly medicated with a couple of bars of Ganja Ganache. Finally, it explained why the woman in the yellow hoodie stole the first Una Nonna's pie he had ever bought and why she left it on the hood of the El Camino when she found no GG in the box.

Now, he had to decide if he'd talk to JoJo and Nancy about just what type of business they were running. After his incredible gullibility in not seeing the drug operation all along, he decided to find his quiet bench on DeKalb and sip whisky until he could determine what would be the smart course of action. He wasn't through half the flask before understanding that he would not be telling Nancy and JoJo a damn thing. Yes, he could see the whole operation being exposed, especially when the fancy renovation was completed. No wonder they gave Cynthia and him such a hard time agreeing to what seemed to be a dream offer. How can a good drug business function in such a high-profile establishment? He wondered if JoJo and Nancy were already scheming to end up at another quiet site. They'd cash out the place high, acting like they'd never want to leave, but willing to go if they were blown away.

Oh, he'd shut his mouth alright. He wasn't happy that he had dealers as his friends, but he had some solace that they were not his enemies. They hated Tolland, and they really did owe El Buscador loyalty.

•　　•　　•　　•　　•

Mavis checked more than a half dozen times to make sure she hadn't been followed. She popped the lock and entered through the back door of the Bat Cave just like El Buscador had taught her.

She stood in the center of the cave, graffiti on every side of her, and said in the loudest whisper possible. "About now would be a really good time to come out." When she heard no footsteps, she threw in, "unless you'd like to stay here forever."

The answer reverberated through the rafters. "God no."

Still, the stealthy El Buscador managed to sneak up on Mavis, tapping her on her shoulder, giving her a startle. "Jesus, you creepy bastard," she said.

El Buscador grinned. "And I thought you loved me."

"Loved you?" Mavis poked his chest. "I'm on a stray dog rescue mission here. Anyway, I don't even recognize you without the whole forties detective getup."

"Even without the outfit, I'm still the same mysterious, charming figure from the days of yore."

"Uh, huh," answered Mavis, knowing this might not be the first or last time she'd heard such a line of bullshit. "I'm going to leave before somebody starts shooting at me. Unlike you, I don't have to live dangerously. You coming or not?"

"Let me just pack my stuff," said El Buscador.

"Your stuff?"

El Buscador tapped his backpack. "Just kidding. I'm ready."

"Well, you better have a year's supply of underwear in there," said Mavis.

"Even better, I've got cash in there, often valuable when bartering for both boxers and briefs."

"Why don't you just wave the money around?" asked Mavis. As she led him out of the Bat Cave, she added, "How is it possible you're not dead yet?"

"Thinking about you keeps me living," he said, draining the glibness from his voice.

"Well aren't you the romantic little turd." They were in the back lot of the Bat Cave.

El Buscador pointed to the subcompact Toyota Tercel, a model that must've been twenty-five years old. "Is that your ride?"

"I had to borrow it again from my sister," said Mavis. "The last time was also to save your ass."

"You are truly a wonderful woman," said El Buscador, emotion filling his voice, his eyes moist; the whole response unintentional and slightly embarrassing.

"I know," said Mavis. "I'm a goddamn saint. Now get in the backseat and keep down until we get out of Brooklyn." Mavis put on the radio and they listened to the local stations. After a few songs, the weather forecast, and a house fire report in Woodside, news of the daylighting of the stream in

Gowanus was given man-on-the-street coverage, with residents coming from near and far to watch the water flow. One nameless onlooker said, "It's like a whole new part of the city opened up. It's pretty cool."

Mavis made a tittering sound. "You happy now, you happy? All that, putting your life on the line, for what? A two-minute news item that will be forgotten tomorrow and for some guy swilling a PBR to say," here she adjusted her voice to lower both in octave and IQ, "*It's pretty cool.*" Then added, "I hope you're happy."

A voice rose from the depths of the backseat, "As happy as I'll ever be."

For much of their tortured journey out of Brooklyn (there is no easy way to ride out of Brooklyn), Mavis peppered El Buscador with questions about his escape through the daylighted stream. "Didn't you think you'd get stuck in those makeshift aqueducts you slapped together?"

"I was hopeful," he said. "I hadn't been eating much lately. The trip was quite refreshing. I think it was the cleanest water I've ever bathed in."

Mavis suppressed a chuckle. "I'm sure when it dumped you in that canal, you felt quite differently."

El Buscador lifted his head so Mavis could catch his eye roll. "They keep saying they're cleaning up the canal. I can't say I experienced much evidence of it. I might as well have been swimming through a sewer."

Mavis nodded. "I must say that I don't think I've seen anyone swim faster in my life than you in that canal."

El Buscador laughed heartily. "I had to sneak into the gym in the middle of the night and shower three times to feel somewhat clean. You should see the skin lesions it left me with."

"I'll pass," said Mavis.

"I thought I was much tougher. I used to be much tougher. Every day JoJo walks out of Una Nonna's and takes a dip in the canal. He looks perfectly normal, even if I can't say the same about his pies. The Gwaken swam around in that mephitic sludge for weeks. Yeah, I'm sure in the end, he sunk into the abyss, but he was in there for weeks. I lasted seconds."

Mavis looked in the rearview, catching El Buscador's eye. "Let me ask you something? Why do you do this to yourself?"

"What?" asked El Buscador, confused. "Do what?"

"You know, all of these machinations with Tolland," said Mavis. "You already beat him by ripping the Gowanus District right out of his hands. Don't you ever know when enough is enough?"

"Enough is never enough with Tolland. You know that, especially since he bought the furniture factory and is putting up the hotel." He popped his head into the front seat. "Can you tell me what you heard? I've been kind of out of commission for the last few days."

"Yeah?" said Mavis, "the Bat Cave is not exactly CNN central, is it?" Mavis told him how quickly Tolland was moving with the new construction and his unveiling of the Gwaken.

El Buscador interrupted. "Did Melville get the footage? I was hoping he'd be able to track Tolland's yacht."

"He did," said Mavis. "But don't expect much from it. There's been lots of reporting that Melville's footage is bogus."

"But it's not," said El Buscador.

"We both know that doesn't matter," she said. Finally skipping through the endless lights on Eastern Parkway like a hippopotamus over hurdles, the Tercel crossed onto the Jackie Robinson, riding above many a gravesite. Now was as good of a time as any for Mavis to break more bad news to El Buscador.

The long drive allowed her to relate the following: After seven days of unauthorized euphoria in Gowanus, the daylighted stream that had given the canal a much-needed boost of fresh water would be sealed off. Pump station authorities would route the flow back to the pipes and troughs that had served the community for a hundred years. With the stream running through his new property, Tolland will have two choices: he could divert the stream below his lobby, basically the option he had always taken (giving Mother Nature a beat down at every opportunity had been his life code), or he could run it right through the lobby.

Whichever the case, El Buscador would not be happy. If the stream were diverted by Tolland, it was likely to never see the light of day again; if he let the stream run through the lobby, he would be given all types of accolades for his ingenuity and environmentalism. That success, in turn, would give him more power to once again inflict greater damage on his fair city. El Buscador cursed. How the hell does it work out that every time he takes down Tolland, the real estate mogul ends up increasing his celebrity?

"Son of a bitch," said El Buscador.

Mavis laughed. "You are a miserable bastard. It's pretty funny that by opening up the stream you gave Tolland a whole new possibility. Plus, you gave his men just another chance to shoot at you."

El Buscador tended not to explain his actions, since he rarely had a receptive audience, but for Mavis, his rescuer, he'd make an exception. "If you think about it, there was nothing else for me to do." He sadly acknowledged that with Tolland's oversized hotel straining the already maxed out sewer lines, the canal would probably never be cleansed. Indeed, it might well be filthier than ever. El Buscador caught his breath. Ah, what's the use? "Where are you taking me?"

"Long Island."

"Oh, God," said El Buscador.

In a gesture of admonishment, Mavis shook her head back and forth. "You have left me with no choice. The only other option was stay here and die."

"How about Queens?" El Buscador bargained. "I'd even settle for Queens. God, anyplace but Long Island."

Mavis laughed. "Maybe I can get you to Queens in a few months, if you're a good boy."

That night El Buscador slept in the spare bedroom in the Carle Place home of Mavis's sister, Regina, who happened to be a very nice person. As Mavis put it, "Who the hell else would take you in? You're not exactly a prize, you know."

El Buscador had to admit that the bed was incredibly comfortable. Plus, the screeches and chugs of the nearby Long Island Railroad delivered just enough noise pollution to lessen the withdrawal pangs from urban life. That night he dreamed of the Gwaken gliding along hidden streams, but soon his visions of the creature shifted to seeing his own desiccating body swimming from end to end of the Gowanus Canal, under bridge after bridge, swimming with an ease and elegance of a Michael Phelps. When he had awoken, he was pleasantly surprised it wasn't in a cold sweat. His laps along the Gowanus did not make for a nightmare, but a dream.

El Buscador knew that as folklore would have it, Gowanus was named after a Native-American chief, the Canarsie sachem Gouwane. Gouwane's name translated is sleep. Only now that he had left Gowanus could he discover that the word had more resonance than he had heretofore considered. He sat up in bed, thinking, figuring out a way to get back.

●   ●   ●   ●   ●

The next morning he boarded the very first Long Island Railroad train of the day. He liked to work at night, but El Buscador understood his contact would be otherwise employed during the somnambulistic hours. Instead, he would cross her path during her morning run as many admirers wondered whether she was a model or an actress who desired more fresh air than the call-back studios permitted. El Buscador crooked one shoe along the Central Park streetlamp, fedora tilted down, pointing to a labyrinthine path designed almost two centuries ago. Ingrid knew as she turned to the streetlight, she was actually turning toward the shadows. This morning he would take her to places she could not find, and she would tell him tales he could not know.

ACKNOWLEDGMENTS

Thank you to Ken Darr and Joe Edd Morris for their continued advice and support. Most of the material for *Blue Gowanus* came from walking in and around the Gowanus Canal, along with regular journeys through the streets and undergrounds of New York City. In addition, I read routinely about this endlessly fascinating urban landscape. In my efforts to offer moments of both historical accuracy and verisimilitude, I would like to note my indebtedness to atlasobscura.com, *The New York Times*, and Joseph Alexiou's *Gowanus: Brooklyn's Curious Canal*.

ABOUT THE AUTHOR

Whenever he gets a free moment, Michael Hartnett wanders around New York City...of late along its most toxic canal. He is the author of the precursor to this novel, *The Blue Rat*, plus the novels *Fools in the Magic Kingdom*, *Generation Dementia*, *The Great SAT Swindle*, and *Universal Remote*.

NOTE FROM THE AUTHOR

Word-of-mouth is crucial for any author to succeed. If you enjoyed *Blue Gowanus*, please leave a review online—anywhere you are able. Even if it's just a sentence or two. It would make all the difference and would be very much appreciated.

Thanks!
Michael

Thank you so much for reading one of **Michael Hartnett's** novels.
If you enjoyed the experience, please check out our recommended
title for your next great read!

The Blue Rat by Michael Hartnett

"A fun-on-every-page romp through the city that never sleeps.
Hartnett at his best!"
– Len Boswell, author, *A Grave Misunderstanding*

www.ingramcontent.com/pod-product-compliance
Lightning Source LLC
Chambersburg PA
CBHW011134100726
47898CB00009B/2969